Just Jimmy Again

Richmal Crompton, the creator of *Just William*, was born in 1890. Her first William story was published in 1919, and she went on to write 38 collections of stories about William, many books of short stories, and several novels for adults before her death in 1969.

Much less famous than William but no less charming, her stories about *Jimmy* first appeared in the *Star* newspaper in February 1947, and this collection was first published in book form in 1951. It has been unavailable for decades. *Just Jimmy* and *Just Jimmy Again* introduce this rediscovered classic to a new generation of readers.

SOMEONE DREW THE CURTAINS, REVEALING TO THE STARTLED
GAZE OF THE AUDIENCE A SMALL BOY, TOUSLED AND GRUBBY.

(see page 125)

RICHMAL CROMPTON

Just Jimmy Again

Illustrated by Thomas Henry

MACMILLAN
CHILDREN'S BOOKS

First published 1951
This edition published 2000 by Macmillan Children's Books
a division of Macmillan Publishers Limited
25 Eccleston Place, London SW1W 9NF
Basingstoke and Oxford

Associated companies throughout the world

ISBN 0 333 71233 1

1 3 5 7 9 8 6 4 2

A CIP catalogue record for this book is available from
the British Library.

Typeset by SX Composing DTP, Rayleigh, Essex
Printed and bound in Great Britain by Mackays of Chatham plc, Kent

Contents

Chapter 1

The Prehistoric Monster

"It means no pocket money for weeks," said Roger disgustedly.

"An' a row over it as well," said Bill.

"It seems to seal our doom, all right," said Charles, who was apt to take a dramatic view of things.

"It makes you want to turn into a real criminal just to show them," said Roger.

Roger, Bill and Charles, known as the Three Musketeers, were holding a meeting in the tool-shed in Roger's garden. Earlier in the day they had organised a "curling" competition in the field at the back of the Palmers' house, and a specially strenuous effort on Roger's part had sent a stone through the central pane of the Palmers' greenhouse, demolishing not only the pane of glass but also a fuchsia plant that Mr Palmer had raised from a cutting and on which he had lavished all his love and care and a rich assortment of fertilisers. Mr Palmer, usually a meek apologetic little man, had issued from his gate, purple-faced with rage, and informed the Three Musketeers that he would lay his complaint before their fathers that evening.

"Well, we could turn into outlaws," said Bill thoughtfully.

"And ravage the countryside," said Charles, his expression brightening.

"No, that's no use," said Roger. "That'd only get us into a worse row than ever."

"It's jolly unfair," said Bill. "My father knows a man that's famous for somethin' – I've forgot what, but, anyway, everyone knows his name – an' he broke a cup the las' time he came to see us an' all they did was smile an' say it didn't matter."

"That's what we ought to do," said Roger thoughtfully. "We ought to do something to make us famous."

"To make the world ring with our names," said Charles.

"Yes, something like that. If we were famous, they wouldn't dare make a fuss about a bit of broken glass and a plant that the top came off."

"Well, what'll we do?" said Bill.

"We could – well, we could discover something," said Roger a little vaguely.

"What?" said Bill, who was inclined to be practical. "Everything's been discovered already."

"I bet it hasn't," said Roger. "I bet there's heaps of things not discovered yet."

"Countries an' animals," said Charles. "My father once met a man that'd seen the Loch Ness monster."

"What's that?" said Bill.

"It's a prehistoric monster that comes up out of a lake to breathe once every hundred years. I bet there's heaps of them about if only people knew where to look for them. Well, nat'rally, if they only come up once in a hundred years, not many people see them. I bet if we found one of those it'd make us famous, all right."

"With notches in the Temple of Fame," said Charles.

"Yes. I bet they'd make us Knights of Bath or Mayors of London, same as they do to famous people."

"There aren't any lakes round here," objected Bill. "Not big enough to hold a monster, anyway."

"Well, there's woods," said Roger. "I bet there's prehistoric monsters hiding up in woods, too. I bet no one's ever been over every inch of the woods round here. I bet there's all sorts of monsters hiding up in the thickest part of them an' only comin' out once in a hundred years, an' I bet we find one, too, if we have a good look. An' then Mr Palmer'll feel jolly silly makin' a fuss about a bit of glass an' an ole plant when we've discovered a prehistoric monster."

"An' been made Mayors of Bath," said Charles.

"I expect they're a bit fierce, prehistoric animals," said Bill rather nervously.

"We'll have to go armed, of course," said Roger.

"We'll be going into the jaws of a dilemma all right," said Charles.

"I'll take my new penknife," said Roger. "The big blade's as good as a dagger any day. I could cut its head off."

"You'd have to get jolly near it to do that," said Bill, "an' it'd prob'ly have bit yours off first. I think I'll take my catapult an' a stone, same as David did with Goliath, an' stand right away from it."

"I'd like to strangle it with my bare hands," said Charles, looking down at those not very powerful members, "but I think I'll take my bow an' arrow, 'case it's got a specially strong neck. An arrow's a pretty deadly weapon if it hits a vital spot."

"When shall we start?" said Bill.

"This afternoon," said Roger. "We've got to be famous by the time Mr Palmer comes round to see our fathers tonight."

"An' – I say," said Bill.

"Yes?"

"We're not goin' to have any kids in on this. Don't let Jimmy know anythin' about it. He's only seven an' he'd mess the whole thing up."

"He's prob'ly been listening all the time," said Charles morosely, aware that Jimmy, Roger's younger brother, possessed an uncanny instinct for knowing exactly what was going on, particularly when it was something they wanted to keep secret from him.

"Leave him to me," said Roger.

He strode to the door and flung it open, prepared to discharge the full weight of his eleven-year-old authority on the youthful eavesdropper. There was nothing to be seen, however, but the empty lawn and the upturned garden seat that had been Jimmy's "submarine" earlier in the morning.

"No, he's not there," he reassured them.

Jimmy was not there. He was over at Bobby Peaslake's, discussing the situation with his friend.

"I heard them p-planning it," he was saying. "They're going out to find a prehistoric monster in the wood this afternoon."

"There aren't any prehistoric monsters in the wood," said Bobby.

"Yes, there are," said Jimmy earnestly. "They hide up in the bushes an' c-come out once in a hundred years same as that monster in that lake. It's goin' to be jolly d-dangerous. They're takin' weapons, but it might g-gobble them up before they've time to get 'em out."

"Well, we can't do anything," said Bobby.

"Yes, we can," said Jimmy earnestly. "We can follow them s-secretly an' rescue them."

"We wouldn't be much good against a prehistoric monster," said Bobby doubtfully. "There's a picture of one in my hist'ry book an' it takes up a whole page."

"No, but we could r-run an' get help," said Jimmy. "I'm goin' back now to f-find out their plans."

They went out into the road. Araminta Palmer was making her way along it, hopping from side to side, her red-gold curls bobbing as she hopped, her battered toy monkey, Sinbad, under one arm. She made an attractive picture, but Jimmy and Bobby were not attracted by it. They disliked her for her dominating personality and despised her for her youth.

"Hello, Jibby Banning," she said. "Where are you goig?"

Araminta had had her adenoids removed some months ago, but, despite her parents' agonised entreaties, continued to talk as if they were still there.

"Mind your own b-business," retorted Jimmy.

"Will you cub ad play with be?"

"*No!*" said Jimmy emphatically.

"Why dot?"

"We don't want to play with kids of five."

Araminta considered this.

"I'b big for five," she said at last, "ad I'b clever."

"You're *not* clever," said Jimmy.

"Yes, I ab," said Araminta complacently. "I'b at page six id by Reader ad I cad draw little houses with chibdeys ad smoke cubbig out."

"Well, go away. We don't want you."

"Where are you goig?"

"We're going to the wood and we don't want you," said Bobby.

"You shouldn't have t-told her where we were going," said Jimmy.

"I'll cub ad play id the wood with you if you like," said Araminta with an air of condescension. "I'll play fairy tales with you id the wood."

"No, you won't," said Jimmy, "'cause we d-don't want you."

Araminta tossed her head.

"I dode care," she said. "I dode want you either. I'll play fairy tales with Sidbad id the wood. I'd rather play with Sidbad thad you ady day."

"You're only a s-silly baby," said Jimmy, "an' your father's a m-mean ole tell-tale, gettin' Roger into a row for breakin' a bit of glass."

"I dode care," said Araminta. "It serves hib right."

With that she resumed her erratic progress down the road.

"Good r-riddance!" said Jimmy. "Now let's go an' find out their p-plans."

The Three Musketeers had met under the large oak tree that they always used as their headquarters when playing in the wood. Roger had his penknife, Bill his catapult, while Charles had brought a disused toasting fork with bent and rusty prongs.

"It's the sort of weapon natives use," he explained, "but theirs are a bit longer and they call them assegais. They've got twisted points same as this an' they're the mos' deadly weapon there is. It's jolly strong, too. I bet it'll pierce the heart if I get it in the right place."

The others looked at it a little doubtfully.

"I think your bow an' arrow would have been better," said Roger.

"No, it wouldn't," persisted Charles. "It's the twisted ends that make it deadly, 'cause, once they're in, they can't be got out. Anyway, I only had one arrow an' I shot it into a bread-an'-butter pudding by mistake when I was practising in the kitchen this morning an' my mother's taken it off me for a week an' there wasn't time to make another."

"Oh, well, it doesn't matter," said Roger. "Now let's scatter over the wood an' look in places where prob'ly no one's been for hundreds of years."

"Untrodden by the foot of man," put in Charles.

"Yes, an' we'll meet again here at three o'clock an' report if we've found any monsters."

When they had gone, Jimmy and Bobby arose from their cramped positions behind a small holly bush that was near the oak tree.

"Shall we follow them?" said Bobby.

"No," said Jimmy. "They'd be s-sure to see us if we did an' anyway we couldn't follow all three. No, let's s-scatter, too, an' look for a monster an' come back here at three o'clock s-same as them."

On the first stroke of three Roger appeared, looking tired and disappointed. Bill joined him almost immediately afterwards.

"Well, I've not found one," said Roger. "Have you?"

"No," said Bill. "I bet there aren't any left. I bet they've all died off or got turned into men."

"Turned into men?" said Roger. "How could they?"

"They do," said Bill. "I heard my father talkin' about it once. A man called Darwin started them doin' it."

At this point Charles came running up. His face was flushed, his eyes starting from his head.

"I've found one," he gasped. "It's crouching in that bush by the keeper's hut. It's got the mos' f'rocious face I ever saw an' a great big furry body like a bear's."

Roger gaped at him, then quickly gathered together his forces.

"We've got to catch it," he said. "Come on."

"Do you think it's safe?" said Bill, adding: "I'm going to the pictures tomorrow an' I don't want to do anything rash."

"Come on," repeated Roger. He had assumed his generalissimo manner. "We'll approach the hut from three different points so's to overpower it, an' we'll crawl along like Indians so's to take it by surprise."

Roger leading the way, Charles following, Bill bringing up the rear, the Three Musketeers set out on their adventure.

Jimmy and Bobby emerged once more from their holly bush.

"Gosh!" gasped Jimmy. "They'll never overpower a monster like that. We've g-got to go an' get help for them quick."

The two set off at a run down the woodland path to the road. And on the road they found Mr Palmer, scurrying along in the direction of the village. He looked pale and harassed. Jimmy seized him unceremoniously by the arm.

"Quick!" he panted. "C-come along! This way!"

With unexpected docility Mr Palmer turned to accompany them, and the three hastened down the path to the keeper's hut. And there a strange sight met their eyes. Roger, Charles and Bill, on hands and knees, were approaching a bush that grew by the door and in the shadow of which crouched a curious apparition. Without a moment's hesitation, Mr Palmer went up to the curious apparition, removed a Guy Fawkes mask and a fur rug, and revealed the sleeping form of Araminta. Next to her lay Sinbad, swathed in a red scarf. Araminta sat up and rubbed her eyes.

"I was playig Red Ridig Hood," she said. "I was the wolf an Sidbad was Red Ridig Hood ad I went to sleep by bistake."

"We couldn't think what had happened to you, my darling," said her distracted parent, lifting her to her feet and brushing her down. "We hunted everywhere – your mother's in a terrible state – and I was on my way to the police." He looked round at the five boys. "I can never thank you boys sufficiently for finding her and sending for me so promptly. I – I take back all I said this morning about that wretched plant and—" He dived into his pocket and distributed half-crowns recklessly, then, with a "Come along now, darling," he collected the wolf insignia and led Araminta, still blinking sleepily, from the scene.

Roger, Charles and Bill stared after them, open-mouthed.

"Gosh! It was only Araminta, after all," said Roger.

"Well, it's jus' the same as if it'd been a prehistoric animal," said Charles philosophically. "For us, I mean. It's better really. We're not goin' to get into a row an' we've got half a crown each."

"An' it was much less dangerous," said Bill.

Then they all turned to Jimmy.

"How did you *know* it was Araminta?" they said.

Jimmy thrust his hands into his pockets.

"Oh, I sort of g-get ideas," he said nonchalantly.

Chapter 2

Roman Remains

"Hi! Jimmy!" yelled Bobby, balancing himself precariously on the top rung of his garden gate.

Bobby's house was just opposite Jimmy's, and the two were wont to carry on conversations across the breadth of the road. Peaceful old ladies in the neighbourhood sometimes complained that their afternoon rest was shattered by these long distance calls, but the "whispers" that resulted from the complaints were even more penetrating.

From the back regions of Jimmy's house came the answering owl-call that was the usual signal between them, and soon Jimmy emerged, carrying the bucket and spade that, usually, did not see the light between one summer holiday and the next.

Bobby was so surprised that he lost his balance and fell into the road.

"What have you got those for?" he said, scrambling to his feet and giving his knees a perfunctory brush. "We're not at the seaside. I thought we were goin' to fish in the stream."

"Well, we're not," said Jimmy firmly. "We're goin' to d-dig."

"Dig?" said Bobby. "Where?"

"Where the others are digging. We're goin' to dig for Roman r-remains same as them."

It happened that, in the last year of the war, a small house just outside the village had been destroyed by a rocket and that recently traces of a Roman encampment had been discovered among the ruins. This had been the cause of much local interest, and an Archaeological Society, formed for the purpose, was now starting operations on the site.

"But it's a grown-up thing," said Bobby. "They won't let us join in with it."

"I b-bet they will when they find out we're good diggers," said Jimmy. "I'm a j-jolly good digger. That time I tried to dig down to Australia when I was at the seaside, I n-nearly got there. Well, a real sailor that was watching me said I did, an' he must have known 'cause he'd been there. 'Sides – 'sides Miss Tressider's the secret'ry an' she's diggin' there with them an' – an' – well—"

He didn't finish the sentence, but Bobby understood. Miss Tressider was on the staff of the school that Jimmy and Bobby attended, and was, moreover, both young and pretty; and the two spent a good deal of time and energy trying to impress on her – not always successfully – their intellectual and physical superiority over their fellows.

"Yes," said Bobby. "She called us little idiots las' week for gettin' our sums wrong. She'll think a bit different about us when she sees us diggin' up Roman remains."

"Well, get your bucket and spade an' we'll go along an' s-start," said Jimmy.

Bobby fetched his bucket and spade, and together they hurried down to the site.

The Archaeological Society had marked out the plot into squares, and in each square a member of the Society was busy with spade and trowel. Miss Tressider, a businesslike figure in slacks and a pullover, was working in the first square.

"What do you want, children?" she said, as Jimmy and Bobby approached.

"Please, c-can we dig, too?" said Jimmy.

"No, of course not," said Miss Tressider. "Only members of the Society are allowed to dig."

"C-can we be members, then?" said Jimmy. "I'm a g-good digger. I nearly got down to Australia once."

"An' we're int'rested in Roman things," said Bobby, adding somewhat confusedly: "I got nearly blown up by a Roman candle las' Guy Fawkes day."

"No, we don't want children," said Miss Tressider firmly, "so run away."

Then she turned her attention once more to the work of excavation.

Jimmy and Bobby withdrew and stood watching proceedings disconsolately from a distance.

The Vicar was hard at work in the next square to Miss Tressider's, and beyond him was a young man who, despite the energy with which he flung his long thin body to and fro as he shovelled up spadefuls of soil, still managed, surprisingly, to retain a monocle in his left eye.

"It's ridic'lous to think you can't dig just 'cause you're small," muttered Bobby indignantly.

"Yes," agreed Jimmy. "L-look at worms. They're smaller than us an' they d-dig for miles."

"Let's go away an' stop watching them," said Bobby.

But Jimmy couldn't quite bring himself to do that, and the two were still hanging about when the members of the Society stopped digging and gathered together to eat sandwiches, drink coffee out of thermos flasks and discuss the situation.

"The exasperating part of the whole thing," said the stout, bearded man who was in charge of operations, "is that this is only the outlying part of the encampment. The main part obviously lies in Sir George Bellwater's grounds."

"I know," said Miss Tressider, looking at the imposing chimneys of Sir George's residence, which could be seen through the trees. "But it's hopeless to try to get permission from him to dig there. We all tried and he was most offensive. We even asked him to be President of the Society, but he simply ordered us out of the house."

"He sounds an antisocial bloke," said the young man with the monocle.

"He is," said Miss Tressider.

"His attitude is a disgrace to the neighbourhood," said the bearded man. "He's robbing posterity and hindering the course of knowledge."

"It's certainly very annoying," said the Vicar mildly, removing a clod of earth that had lodged itself in the collar of his open-necked shirt.

It was at this point that Jimmy seized Bobby by the hand and dragged him away.

"Listen," he said. "I've g-got an idea."

"What?" said Bobby.

"Well, they'd have to m-make us members if we got Sir George to let them dig in his garden."

"Gosh!" gasped Bobby. "We couldn't."

"I d-don't see why not," said Jimmy. "We can ask him, anyway. We can tell him he's hindering the c-curse of knowledge, an' all the other things they said. We can sort of p-plead with him."

"But he's the savagest man anywhere round," objected Bobby.

"He may be g-good underneath," said Jimmy earnestly. "S-some people are. Anyway, I'm goin' to try an' you needn't come if you don't want to."

"All right, I'll come," agreed Bobby dispiritedly, "but I'll be s'prised if we get back alive. I nearly made a new will las' night. I wish I had done now."

Bobby made a new will every few weeks. His most treasured "effects" consisted of the large watch that he always wore, though it lacked both works and fingers, a fossilised shell that he had found in a stone on the rockery, an unsavoury collection of seaweed, an elderly and lethargic piebald rat, a broken pipe, a whistle, an old army dixie, a ball of putty and a "chess set", consisting of a castle, half a bishop and two pawns – and these he distributed and redistributed among his friends and relations in his successive wills according to whether they were in or out of favour.

"Well, never mind that now," said Jimmy. "Let's g-go an' see Sir George."

The two made their way along the road to the big iron gates of The Hall, then walked slowly up the avenued drive to the porticoed front door.

Sir George's butler answered their knock. He was a distinguished-looking man with grey hair and a world-weary expression.

"Please, we've come to s-see Sir George," said Jimmy. "We want to ask him to let the Archlyogical Society d-dig in his garden."

"Sir George," said the butler with dignity, "is not at home." Then, abruptly discarding dignity: "So clear off, and be quick about it, you impudent little nippers."

The two cleared off. Halfway down the drive, Jimmy stopped and looked back cautiously. The butler had vanished and the front door was closed.

"I'm not jus' goin' to g-go back," he said. "I want to be a member an' dig."

"Well, you can't," said Bobby. "He wouldn't even listen to you."

But a thoughtful look had come into Jimmy's face.

"Tell you what!" he said.

"What?" said Bobby, a little apprehensively.

"Let's start diggin' here ourselves."

"Gosh!" groaned Bobby. "You do think of awful things."

"No, it's all right," Jimmy reassured him. "He's out, so he won't see us an' I bet if we start n-now an' dig quick we'll have found some remains before they've finished over there an' then they'll *have* to m-make us members. Come on. Let's look for a good place."

Bobby shrugged helplessly and began to accompany his friend on a tour of the grounds.

"We can't dig in the flower-beds," said Jimmy, "'cause someone might see us from the w-windows."

"An' it might spoil the flowers," said Bobby mildly.

"Well, we can't b-bother about a few flowers," said Jimmy. "I bet the Romans didn't when they p-put the remains there. Come on. Let's try the shrubbery. They can't see that from the windows."

But a recent dry spell had hardened the soil so much that Jimmy's spade could make little impression on the shrubbery.

"This isn't any good," he said at last, raising a red but still resolute face from his task. "There mus' be some place that's easier than this. Let's have another l-look round."

They made their way down to a large greenhouse and

wandered round to the back. Jimmy's eyes gleamed excitedly.

"Look!" he said. "Sand! Sand's easy to d-dig in."

"But it's not Roman," said Bobby, eyeing the heap of sand doubtfully.

"How do you know it isn't?" challenged Jimmy. "They landed at the seaside, didn't they? They prob'ly brought it along with them. Sand gets all over you at the seaside. It used to come out of me in h-heaps when I undressed at the seaside las' summer. Anyway, it's soft an' it'll have made the ground underneath it soft, an' I bet we soon get down to r-remains once we start. Come on!"

They dug for some minutes in silence, then Jimmy gave a yell of delight.

"L-l-look!" he said, bending down to pick something up.

"L-L-LOOK!"
SAID JIMMY,
WITH A YELL OF
DELIGHT.

Together they examined a gold signet ring with an animal's head engraved on it.

"It's a w-wolf," said Jimmy excitedly. "Gosh! It mus' have belonged to Romulus an' Remus. They were m-mixed up with a wolf. There's a picture of them in Roger's Latin book. I bet it's the best Roman remain that's ever been f-found. Let's take it to them quick."

They ran as quickly as they could back to the site of the excavations. And there they stopped short in sudden dismay. Sir George stood in the centre of the group of excavators. His face was brick red, his voice upraised in anger.

"The impudence of it!" he shouted. "The gross impudence of it! Sending your insolent messages by a couple of children! Outrageous! I'll go to the police. I'll have the whole thing stopped. If you think I'm going to let myself be intimidated by a crowd of ill-mannered nincompoops . . ."

His voice died away in splutters of inarticulate rage.

"But I don't understand," said Miss Tressider.

"What two children?" said the Vicar.

Sir George had caught sight of Jimmy and Bobby on the outskirts of the group.

"Those two children," he bellowed, pointing at them. Then suddenly he noticed the ring in Jimmy's hand. "What's that?"

"It's a R-roman remain," said Jimmy proudly. "It's a wolf an' it belonged to Romulus an' Remus."

Sir George had snatched it out of his hand.

"It's my signet ring," he said. "Where did you find it?"

"In the s-sand behind your g-greenhouse," said Jimmy.

Sir George began to chuckle.

"Good Lord!" he said. "That was the sand-heap my little grandson used to play in when he stayed with me in the summer. The little beggar was crazy over this ring. He liked the horse's head on it – my crest, you know. He called it his gee-gee and was always wanting to look at it and play with it. He must have pinched it and taken it to his sand-heap. I couldn't think what had become of it. I've been worried to death. It belonged to my great-grandfather, and I wouldn't have lost it for anything. I'm – I'm most grateful to you." He looked round a little sheepishly. "Well, I apologise to you for my outburst and you can all come along to my place and we'll go into this digging business. I see no real objection. We'll consult my head gardener, anyway." He put the ring in his pocket and turned to them again with a twinkle. "You'd better come quickly and stake your claim before I regret it."

"Thank you, Sir George," said the Vicar.

"Don't thank me," said Sir George. "Thank those two young rascals there."

"Please, can we be m-members?" said Jimmy anxiously.

They all laughed.

"Certainly you can," said Miss Tressider.

"We make you honorary members here and now," said the bearded man.

"Come along! Come along! Come along!" said Sir George.

The Archaeological Society set off in a straggling line towards the Hall.

At the end of the procession, heads erect, buckets swinging, spades held proudly against their shoulders, marched the two honorary members.

Chapter 3

The Witch

"Ill-wished, that's what I am," said Aggie, surveying the cake that she had just taken out of the oven.

The cake, like Aggie, wore a sad and crestfallen air. Where it should have stood up bravely to meet the world, it sagged supinely to the bottom of the tin.

"Ill-wished?" said Jimmy, gathering up a few currants that lay on the kitchen table among the flotsam and jetsam of Aggie's cake-making paraphernalia.

"What's 'ill-wished'?" said Bobby, drawing the wooden spoon across the table and sampling a mixture of syrup, flour, orange-peel and eggshell.

Aggie was Bobby's family's maid, and the two had been "helping" her make a cake. Their "help" had, as usual, consisted of eating as many of the ingredients as they could lay their hands on, and they had employed the time while the cake was in the oven by scraping out the bowl, licking the spoon, demolishing what was left of the orange-peel and carrying on a spirited battle, armed with flour-sifter and egg-beater.

"It's havin' a spell put on you by a witch," said Aggie.

"I think it's a jolly g-good spell," said Jimmy, looking longingly at the cake. "I like them l-like that."

"Maybe," said Aggie darkly, "but" – nodding her head

in the direction of the sitting-room – "*she* don't. Nor I don't neither. Ill-wished, that's what I am."

"But there aren't any witches now," said Bobby, taking an experimental mouthful of baking powder. "Gosh! It's awful! I bet that's what's wrong with the cake."

"*Aren't* there witches now!" said Aggie impressively. "Aren't there *just*! I could tell you things that'd make every drop of blood in your veins stand on end."

"Oo, *do*, Aggie!" they pleaded eagerly.

"No. I 'aven't time," said Aggie, bundling spoons, knives, forks, basins, sifter and egg-beater into the mixing bowl. "I've got to wash up these 'ere."

"But just because a cake's sat down in the middle," objected Bobby, "that doesn't mean you're ill-wished. Besides, Mother says the regulator thing on the gas cooker's out of order."

Aggie, who had taken up the mixing bowl, put it down again and leant across the table, her small, pale face tense.

"Reg'lator!" she said. "It's somethin' more than a reg'lator. It's somethin'," her voice sank to a whisper, "not of this world."

"G-g-gosh!" said Jimmy.

"An' it's not only cakes," said Aggie. "It's everythin' that's 'appened to me this las' fortnight. Why've I broke me shoelaces an' laddered me stockings? Why've them new gloves I bought turned out to be too small? What's 'appened to me horseshoe brooch with Aggie on in real silver? Vanished like thin air, it 'as, same as me luck. Why did Bert never come in for a word with me when 'e cleaned out the dustbin las' Friday? Tell me that!"

Bert was the dustman and Aggie's young man.

"Why?" said Jimmy.

"'Cause I'm ill-wished," said Aggie simply, sweeping a small heap of flour from the table on to the floor with an absent-minded gesture. "Ill-wished, that's what I am."

"But there aren't any witches round *here*, anyway," said Bobby.

"Aren't there!" said Aggie, pursing her lips as she took up the mixing bowl and carried it into the scullery. "That's all *you* know!"

They followed her into the scullery, scuffling for the possession of a sugar carton to which a few stray grains of sugar still adhered.

"*Who's* a witch round here, Aggie?"

"G-go on, Aggie. Tell us."

Aggie closed the door and sank her voice to a thin penetrating whisper.

"It's a fortnight ago all this 'ere started to 'appen to me. An' 'oo come to the village a fortnight ago?"

"Who?" said Bobby.

"I know!" said Jimmy excitedly. "Miss B-Bedford."

"That's 'er," said Aggie, emptying her collection of cooking implements from the mixing bowl to the washing-up bowl and dropping into the rubbish bin the handle of a cup that had become detached in the process. "There! That wouldn't never 'ave 'appened to me if I'd not been ill-wished."

"But you don't *know* it was her," said Bobby.

"Don't I!" said Aggie with a hollow laugh.

"Well, is there any way of *p-proving* if a person's a witch?" said Jimmy.

"Yes, there's a way, all right," said Aggie, swirling her dishcloth round among the crockery. "You throw 'em in a pond an', if they float, they're witches. Water don't receive no one what's a witch."

"Gosh!" said Bobby.

"But you can't throw Miss B-Bedford into a pond," said Jimmy.

"No, I don't need to," said Aggie simply. "I *know* she's one, all right. I've *proved* it."

"How? Go on, Aggie! Tell us how."

Aggie draped the dishcloth over the tap and turned to them, sinking her voice again to a penetrating whisper.

"All right. I'll tell you. First time I saw 'er I'd gone out to the pillar-box to post a letter. Dark an' rainin', it was – just the night for a witch – an' I met 'er under the light by the pillar-box, an' she gave me a look that went right through me same as if it'd been a dagger. A proper witch's look, it was. Started ill-wishin' of me right away, she did. The next night I was in the kitchen, a-knittin' of me pink an' marooned jumper at the kitchen-table, when I looked up an' – believe me or not – there she was, with 'er face pressed against the window, a-givin' me another Look. She was gone before you could say Jack Robinson, but she'd been there, all right, an' that very night I tripped over me broken shoelace an' fell flat as a pancake. It was 'er spell startin' to work. If it'd been stronger, I'd have broke me neck. Yes, an' that's not all."

"G-go on, Aggie. What else?"

"You won't 'ardly believe this, but it's true. The nex' night I went round to 'er cottage after dark – takin' me life into me 'ands, as they say – to see what I could see, like, an' I looked through 'er window an' – guess what she was a-doin' of."

"What?"

"She was makin' a little figure. That's what they do, you know. They make little figures an' stick pins into them. An' – sure as eggs is eggs – it was me she was makin' the little figure of, an' that very night I had a pain in me toe where she mus' have been startin' runnin' pins in."

"Gosh!" said Bobby.

"Isn't there anything p-people can do to keep witches off?" said Jimmy anxiously.

Furtively Aggie brought a handful of shrivelled berries from her pocket.

"Rowan-berries," she said. "Me grandmother once told me that rowan-berries break a witch's spell."

"That's mountain ash, isn't it?" said Bobby. "There's a tree in the garden."

"I know," said Aggie. "I picked these off of it yesterday. But it 'asn't done no good. Look at me cake."

"Perhaps they oughtn't to be in your pocket," suggested Bobby.

"Maybe not," said Aggie, frowning thoughtfully. "Me grandmother never told me 'ow to use 'em. But I've got to do somethin' quick. There she is a-stickin' pins into that there little figure of me. She'll start meltin' it next an' then I'll pine away. I've got a sort of pinin' feelin' comin' over me now."

The two gazed at her in silent dismay.

"Tell you what!" said Jimmy suddenly. "Let's try putting the berries at her f-front door. It might sort of k-kill the spell as it comes out."

"Yes, that's a jolly good idea," said Bobby. "Let's go 'n' do it now."

The following afternoon Jimmy and Bobby were again in the kitchen, discussing the situation with Aggie.

"We p-put them there."

"We put them in a heap on her front doorstep."

"LET'S TRY PUTTING THE BERRIES AT HER FRONT DOOR," SAID JIMMY. "IT MIGHT SORT OF K-KILL THE SPELL AS IT COMES OUT."

"An' they'd g-gone this mornin'."

"Gone abs'lutely. Not one of 'em left."

"V-vanished in the night."

"Yes, that shows it worked all right," said Aggie, her green eyes shining with excitement. "If they hadn't of gone it wouldn't have worked. But it's broke the spell. Me old grandmother was right. Me cake rose this mornin' an' I found me horseshoe brooch – caught in me scarf, it was – an' I 'eard from Bert. Took off the round, 'e was, sudden, las' week an' that's why 'e didn't look in same as usual. An'" – she lowered her voice mysteriously – "guess oo's come to tea this afternoon. In the sittin'-room, she is, this very minute."

"Who?"

"'*Er*. Bold as brass she walked in. But I'm not

frightened of 'er no more, 'cause 'er power over me's broke."

In the sitting-room, Miss Bedford – a short, stout, kindly-looking middle-aged woman – was gazing admiringly at a cake with a crisply rounded top that stood on the top rung of the cake-stand.

"I wish I could make cakes like that," she said.

"Aggie made it," said Mrs Peaslake. "She's been so depressed because her cakes haven't been rising lately, but today the man from the gas company came and put the regulator thing right and so all's well again."

"Good!" said Miss Bedford. "By the way, talking of cookery, it was very kind of you to send those mountain ash berries round."

"Mountain ash berries?"

"Well, you know, I was saying the other day at Miss Pettigrew's that I wanted some ash berries to make jelly. They make lovely jelly, of course – delicious with mutton – and, as you were there and there's a tree in your garden, I took for granted that you'd sent them round."

"No, I'm afraid I didn't," said Mrs Peaslake, "though," looking out of the window, "most of the berries seem to have vanished."

"How mysterious!" smiled Miss Bedford. "I made the jelly last night. I'd been working on my little figures all day and it was a relief to do some cooking for a change."

"How are your little figures getting on?"

"Very well indeed. I've had quite a lot of orders from the shops. I've brought my latest to show you. I thought you'd be amused." She took from her handbag a little package wrapped in tissue paper, unwrapped it and put on the table a small figure in glazed pottery. "Look! It's Aggie. Your maid."

"Why, so it is!" said Mrs Peaslake.

"I'm having a little exhibition of my best pieces in Bond Street, and this is one of those I'm going to show."

"Whatever made you want to do Aggie?" said Mrs Peaslake.

"She simply fascinated me, with her pale face and green eyes and red hair. I saw her first one evening when she was going to the post and I took a good look at her, and then, I'm afraid, I came to your kitchen window and had another good look at her, but I don't think she saw me. Then I set to work on her – in that long dark mackintosh cape that she was wearing the first time I saw her. It's rather effective, isn't it?"

"It's most attractive. What are you going to call it?"

"The witch," said Miss Bedford.

Chapter 4

The Missing Museum

"'Course Archie Mould's taken it," said Roger.

"The only museum we've ever had," said Bill.

"A living monument to a by-gone civilisation," said Charles, who had recently attended a lecture on "Ancient Barrows" given by a visiting archaeologist in the Village Hall. He had attended it under the mistaken impression that it was to be a sale of second-hand wheelbarrows, in which he had decided to invest his savings of one and twopence halfpenny, but, after discovering his mistake, he had stayed to hear the lecture and had brought away some useful phrases. The ordinary speech of ordinary people always seemed tame and ineffectual to Charles.

"They were the best things they dug up, too," said Roger.

The archaeological excavations in the village had aroused much interest among the junior inhabitants, and the course of digging had unearthed what had obviously been a refuse dump of fairly recent date. Seeing these discarded by the diggers, the Three Musketeers had seized upon them eagerly.

"They are remains, aren't they?" Roger had asked anxiously.

"I think that's a pretty good description of them," the

director of operations had said with a twinkle, and the Three Musketeers had been satisfied.

It was Charles who suggested the formation of a "museum" and Bill who wrote the labels. "Part of Gulius Seasar's shaving mirrer" . . . "Peece of Gulius Seasar's attashy kase" . . . "End of Gulius Seasar's umbreller" . . . "Gulius Seasar's pen gnib" . . .

"I bet they didn't have things like that in Roman times," objected Roger.

"'Course they did," said Bill. "Well, they shaved, didn't they? They mus' have done 'cause there's a photograph of Julius Caesar in my Latin book an' he hasn't got a beard. An' they mus' have had something to keep off the rain an' to carry their papers to their offices. An' Julius Caesar wrote Latin translation books – an' rotten ones, too – so he mus' have had a pen nib."

"Well, I bet all those things didn't belong to Julius Caesar," said Roger.

"I bet they did," said Bill. "He came over to England, didn't he, an' I bet he brought a lot of stuff with him. Anyway, he's the only Roman I know the name of an' I'm goin' to stick to him."

"It makes a jolly good museum," said Bill judicially.

"The spirit of craftsmanship triumphant over Time," said Charles.

"I bet it's as good as the British Museum, any day," said Roger. "I shouldn't be s'prised if they want to borrow it. We'll charge them a lot of money if they do."

"How much?" said Bill.

"Five shillings?" said Charles with the air of one making a daring suggestion.

"I don't s'pose they'd pay all that," said Roger.

"What about half a crown?" said Bill.

"Y-yes," said Roger, "but," bringing the whole thing down to a realistic basis, "axshully we'd let 'em have it for sixpence if they promised to bring it back."

"Where'll we keep it?" said Bill.

"At our headquarters," said Roger.

The headquarters of the Three Musketeers was the kitchen of a blitzed house at the end of the village, and thither the three conveyed the "museum", neatly packed in a cardboard box.

"We'll have to take care the Mouldies don't find out about it," said Roger.

Archie Mould was the head of the rival gang, known as the Mouldies. Between his gang and Roger's was a hostility that flamed up every now and then into open war. Archie had a certain advantage owing to his craftiness and defiance of the rules of decent warfare, but the Three Musketeers generally made up for this in courage and determination.

"I don't s'pose Archie'd want it," said Bill.

"You never know," said Charles. "They're steeped in villainy. They'd stick at nothin'."

Archie had at first shown a somewhat patronising interest in the excavations and had hung about the site trying to enliven proceedings by various tricks at which he was an adept. He was unpopular with the diggers, but it wasn't till he was discovered in the act of stretching a wire outside the director's hut over which that gentleman would probably have tripped and fallen headlong, that he was finally warned off the site. Since then he had professed contempt for the whole affair, but there was no doubt that he intended to get his own back on somebody and was only biding his time.

"Where'll we put it?" said Bill, as the three stood in the

derelict room, gazing round at the cracked floor, shattered fireplace, and the festoons of mouldy wallpaper that adorned the walls. It was a room that always thrilled the Three Musketeers by its suggestion of mystery and adventure, but it did not contain many hiding places.

"I know!" said Roger. "Let's put it in the fireplace. Right behind all that rubbish. We'll hide it there till Saturday an' then we'll put it all out an' invite people to see it." He placed the box in the fireplace and covered it with the broken tiles and bricks. "There! Archie'll never find it behind all that."

But Archie – or somebody – did. Charles's face was pale with horror when he brought the news to Roger and Bill.

"It's gone," he panted. "There's been foul work on foot."

"Archie Mould!" said Roger and Bill simultaneously.

"Yes, Archie Mould," agreed Charles. "He's always dyed deep in crime."

"Come on," said Roger. "Let's go 'n' find him."

They found Archie Mould in his front garden and taxed him with the theft. Archie denied it with a snigger that was itself proof of guilt.

So on Saturday Roger assembled his gang and addressed them.

"We've got to get our museum back from the Mouldies. I bet they've got it hidden in that ole shed."

Of late the Mouldies had been using as their headquarters an old shed that was part of an abandoned chicken farm in the field behind Archie's house.

"If they have, they're sure to leave someone on guard there," said Bill.

"Never mind," said Roger. "We'll attack them in force an' take it by storm."

"An' make them rue the day," said Charles.

The gang all offered enthusiastic support except Toothy. Toothy looked, as usual, pale and woebegone. His long irregular teeth seemed to droop abjectly behind the gold bar that inadequately enclosed them.

"I can't come," he said. "I've got to go to a party."

"A party?" said Roger incredulously.

"I can't help it," said Toothy dismally. "It's Cissy Goodwin's birthday an' she's havin' a fancy-dress party an' I've got to go to it."

"She's only a kid," said Bill.

"Fancy wanting to go to a kid's party!" said Charles.

"I don't," said Toothy, almost in tears, "but my mother says I've got to. She says that Mrs Goodwin lends her her mincin' machine whenever she wants it, so I've got to go to Cissy's party."

There was a silence, in which they wrestled helplessly with this piece of grown-up logic.

"There's no *sense* in it," said Roger at last. "She—"

At that point a scout came running up to them.

"The Mouldies are collectin' by the shed," he reported. "They must have heard that we're goin' to attack."

"Come on then," said Roger. "We'll reconnoitre the neighbourhood first an' then attack them in strength."

Roger considered no campaign complete without a preliminary reconnoitring of the neighbourhood in which he could use his home-made binoculars and Bill his map of Uganda.

The gang marched off in spirited disarray, and Toothy trailed miserably homeward.

For once Jimmy did not tag along after his elder brother's gang. His position as an honorary member of the Archaeological Society had at first given him much pride and pleasure, but the novelty had gradually worn off and he had begun to find proceedings rather boring. With the theft of Roger's "museum", however, all his interest had revived. And he did not think that the Mouldies had taken it to their headquarters. Their mustering at the place was too obvious. It was, Jimmy considered, merely a ruse to deceive their enemies. Moreover, Georgie Tallow, Archie's trusted lieutenant, had not joined the rest of the gang at the shed that was their headquarters. Jimmy had seen him, lurking in his garden, which was next door to Archie's, a secretive, triumphant smile on his face, and Jimmy had a strong suspicion that the "museum" was actually concealed on Georgie's premises.

He waited till the Three Musketeers and their gang had vanished from sight, then slowly made his way to Georgie Tallow's house. Georgie was still in the garden, and his face still wore the secretive, triumphant smile.

A plan had gradually been forming in Jimmy's mind as he walked along the road. It wasn't, he considered, a very good plan, but it was better than nothing. He stopped at the gate.

"Hello, Georgie," he said.

"Hello," said Georgie, coming down to the gate.

"Someone's stolen Roger's museum," said Jimmy.

"I know," grinned Georgie. "Too bad, isn't it? Wonder who it could have been."

"I'm jolly s-sorry for whoever it was," said Jimmy.

"Why?"

"Well, it's l-like those old tombs in Egypt. People that s-stole things from them were haunted by the g-ghosts of the people the things used to belong to."

"D'you mean ole Julius Caesar's ghost'll be coming to haunt me?" said George with a burst of laughter.

"If you've taken the m-museum, I shouldn't be surprised if it did," said Jimmy earnestly.

Georgie doubled up with mirth.

"Gosh! Ole Julius Caesar's ghost! Gosh! Wouldn't I laugh!"

Jimmy went on down the road, pursued by Georgie's derisive laughter. No, it hadn't been a very good plan. Georgie hadn't been in the least impressed . . . But, as he turned the bend in the road, every other thought was driven from his mind by a strange and arresting figure that was approaching him. It was Toothy going to his fancy-dress party. Toothy's mother was notoriously vague, and it had not occurred to her to make any plans for his costume till about half an hour before the party. Then, distractedly, she had consulted a history book and had been reassured to find a picture of Henry the Third's effigy in Westminster Abbey.

"It just looks like a sheet and a crown," she said. "I can easily fix that up."

So Toothy, draped in a sheet turned sides to middle and patched in so many places that whatever happened to it now could make little difference, wearing a crown hastily fashioned from brown cardboard and insecurely trimmed with bits of gold paper, crept miserably along the lane towards the Goodwin homestead.

"Gosh!" said Jimmy. "What are you s-s'posed to be?"

"I've forgot," said Toothy irritably, "but I'm something out of a hist'ry book. Well," still more irritably, "I *look* historical, don't I?"

"You l-look awful," said Jimmy, shocked into candour.

"Well, shut up about me," snapped Toothy. "She said

it was the best she could do in the time. I expect some of the others will be pretty awful, too."

"She", in Toothy's vocabulary, always meant his mother.

Fascinated by the strange apparition, Jimmy accompanied it to the Goodwin front door. And there they met Cissie — a short but massive child with long rope-like plaits — just coming out of it, wearing a gym tunic and sucking a stick of rock.

"I've come to the party," said Toothy.

"It's not till next Saturday," said Cissie dispassionately. "What on earth have you come today for?"

"Gosh!" said Toothy in horror. "She'd lost the invitation, but she thought it was today."

"Well, it's not," said Cissie. "It's next Saturday. What are you supposed to be, anyway? A ghost?"

"I'm historical," said Toothy with mournful dignity. "Well, what am I going to do?"

"You'd better go home," said Cissie.

"I can't. She's gone out to tea and locked up the house. She's going to call for me here on her way back."

"Well, you can't come in," said Cissie, rolling her tongue round the stick of rock with lingering relish. "Everyone's out but me an' I'm going out to a netball practice and I've got to shut the house up and I'm late already, so goodbye."

She slammed the front door, went down to the gate, turning to say indifferently: "You can stay in the garden if you like", then disappeared from view.

Toothy stood gazing after her.

"I don't know why awful things always happen to me," he said with a burst of anguish. "They don't to other people."

"You can c-come to our house if you like," said Jimmy.

"No, I can't," said Toothy. "She's calling for me here. She wouldn't know where I was. I s'pose I'll have to wait in the garden."

He trailed round to the garden at the back of the house and sat down on a wooden seat.

Jimmy went home to tea. He ate in silence, so lost in his thoughts that he absent-mindedly refused the chocolate biscuit that Mrs Manning offered him and ate some rhubarb and ginger jam without remembering that he didn't like ginger. Gradually another plan was forming in his mind, a plan suggested by Cissie's question "What are you supposed to be, anyway? A ghost?" It seemed even wilder than the other, but he decided to try it.

Slowly, thoughtfully, he rose from the table. Slowly, thoughtfully, he made his way back to the Goodwins' garden. Toothy still drooped on the garden seat – a silent motionless figure, wrapped in crumpled sheeting and sunk in gloom.

"I can't stand it much longer," he said. "People can see me from the road. They've been laughing at me."

"Well, your crown's a bit 'spicuous," said Jimmy. "Let's see if we can c-camouflage you."

Toothy was past caring what anyone did to him. He took no interest in the fact that Jimmy was picking laurel from a bush near the seat and making a sort of wreath with some string he brought out from his pocket. He still took no interest when Jimmy removed the crown and put the improvised wreath on his head in its place. It drooped over his eyes but he made no effort to straighten it. Dusk was falling, a mist was rising and there was a drizzle of rain in the air.

"I'll prob'ly be dead when they find me," he said, "an' p'raps that'll make them sorry."

"L-listen," said Jimmy. "I've got an idea. If you went to Georgie Tallow's he'd give you some tea an' you could stay there till your mother came. It's jus' near here an' you'd see her pass the window."

"Georgie Tallow?" said Toothy. "Do you think he'd let me?"

Georgie, of course, was a member of Archie's gang, but Toothy had long passed the stage of distinguishing friend and foe. He had forgotten everything but cold and damp and misery.

"Yes, I'm sure he would," said Jimmy. "Come on. Let's t-try."

Surrendering himself dismally to whatever else Fate might have in store for him, Toothy allowed himself to be led out of the gate down the road and in at the gate of Georgie's house.

"Go on in," said Jimmy, crouching behind the fence. "He won't w-want me, too."

Toothy opened the gate and began to walk up the path. Georgie saw him from the window. His face stiffened. His mouth dropped open. Though he had treated Jimmy's warning with derision, he had secretly been a little nervous about it ever since. Julius Caesar's ghost . . . The thought sent shivers up and down his spine . . . He had added pipe and spectacles to the pictures of Julius Caesar in his Latin book, but the face had still retained its august dignity. And now, looking out at the darkening garden, through mist and a drizzle of rain, he saw the dread figure approaching. The toga . . . the laurel wreath . . . There was no mistaking it . . . He gave a yell of terror and ran upstairs.

Toothy put his finger on the bell and rang. The door was opened a few inches . . . and at that moment came a deep muffled voice from the dusk behind him. "Give me back my r-remains!" The cardboard box was thrust into Toothy's hands and the door slammed in his face. Then, before he could recover from his astonishment, the Three Musketeers and their gang came marching down the road. Toothy met them at the gate.

"Well, we had a jolly good fight," said Roger, "an' we captured their headquarters, but we've not found the museum." His eyes fell on the box in Toothy's hands. "Gosh! You've got it! Where did you get it from?"

"Georgie gave it me," said Toothy, still blinking with bewilderment.

"But why?" said Roger, opening the box and ascertaining that all the exhibits were still there.

"GIVE ME BACK MY R-REMAINS!" SAID JIMMY IN A DEEP, MUFFLED VOICE.

"I don't know," said Toothy.

"Perhaps he was troubled by the still small voice," suggested Charles.

Roger looked at Jimmy.

"You were there, weren't you, Jim?" he said. "What did happen?"

Jimmy considered.

"Well, yes," he said. "He was t-troubled by a voice, but it was quite a l-large one."

Chapter 5

The Circus-Master

Jimmy swaggered out of the gate into the road. He had been to the circus the day before, and he was not a small boy in a rather grubby shirt and well-worn flannel shorts: he was a ringmaster in a magnificent uniform, cracking a whip and issuing orders to hordes of wild animals, who obeyed his slightest movement. Elephants sat down on tubs at the flicker of his eyebrows. Lions jumped through hoops at the snap of his fingers. Dogs walked on tight-ropes at his nod. Seals threw up balls and caught them again . . . bears stood to attention . . . a monkey drove a little goat-cart round and round the ring . . .

And Jimmy, the circus-master, stood in the middle – fearless, godlike, omnipotent, lord of creation.

He slackened his pace as he passed the gate of the next door house, where Sally lived. Sally had blue eyes, golden curls and an entrancing smile, but from the height of her nine years she looked down with contempt on Jimmy's immaturity. Jimmy had admired her all his life and often felt that, if she could see him as he really was, she would treat him differently.

Suddenly he saw her coming out of the front door. He increased his swagger, cracking his imaginary whip with one hand and passing the other over an imaginary moustache. She opened the gate and came out into the road.

"Hello, Sally," he said with an ingratiating smile.

Her eyes rested on him in dispassionate contempt, and he realised, with the shock that such realisation always brought with it, that she did not see the magnificent figure of his imagination. She only saw a small scruffy boy, bearing on his person the marks of his day's activities. She was obviously tempted to pass him by without recognition, but she had something of importance to communicate, and she couldn't help communicating it even to Jimmy.

"I'm going to have a lovely picnic next Saturday," she said.

"C-can I come to it?" said Jimmy with the directness of youth.

"Of course not," said Sally scornfully. "I'm not having babies like you at my picnic."

"I'm not a b-baby," said Jimmy earnestly. "I'm seven an' three-quarters an' a b-bit an' that's nearly eight an' eight's n-nearly nine."

"You're a baby," said Sally firmly. "You play with babies. You play with babies like Araminta Palmer."

"No, I don't," protested Jimmy. "I d-don't play with Araminta. I don't like her . . . I say, Sally!"

"Yes?"

"If I was someone important would you l-let me come to your picnic?"

"You aren't anyone important."

"No, but if I g-got to be? If I got to be by Sat'day?"

Sally considered.

"Perhaps," she said, "but you couldn't. A baby like you couldn't."

With that she turned and went down the road.

Jimmy walked on slowly and thoughtfully. At the bend

of the road he ran into Bobby Peaslake.

"Hello," said Bobby. "Where are you going?"

"Nowhere," said Jimmy. "Listen, Bobby. I've g-got to be a circus-master by Sat'day."

Bobby stared at him.

"A circus-master?" he gasped. "By Sat'day?"

"Yes," said Jimmy. "It's important. It's s-something to do with Sally."

"Oh, Sally!" said Bobby in disgust.

He had never shared Jimmy's admiration for Sally.

"Listen," began Jimmy again earnestly then stopped.

Araminta Palmer was coming towards them, hopping down the road, her toy monkey under her arm.

"Hello," she said. "Did you go to the circus yesterday?"

"Yes," said Jimmy shortly.

"I didn't," said Araminta complacently. "I had a code id by head so I didn't go. By bother bade sub oradge jelly for be, ad I'd sooder have oradge jelly thad go to a circus."

"Yes, you w-would," said Jimmy in a tone that should have quelled her but didn't.

"I've got an uncle cubbig to tea toborrow," said Araminta, "ad he works id a circus."

Jimmy's expression of disgust changed to one of eager interest.

"Works in a c-circus?" he said. "Where?"

"Id Oxford," said Araminta.

"Gosh!" said Jimmy excitedly. "D'you mean he *really* w-works in a circus?"

"Yes," said Araminta. "Ad get out of by way. I'b tired of talkid to you."

With that, she continued her progress, hopping erratically from one side of the road to the other.

"Now l-listen, Bobby," said Jimmy. "I've got an idea."

"All right," said Bobby resignedly. "What is it?"

At first the idea astounded Bobby so much that he could only gape, but gradually his imagination was inflamed by Jimmy's eloquence.

"You see," said Jimmy, "if we did some good c-circus tricks, he'd give us a job in his circus. Then we'd be circus p-people for the rest of our lives an' we could rise to be the man that stands in the middle an' t-tells the animals what to do."

"Gosh, yes!" said Bobby.

"An' I bet Sally'll ask me to her picnic nex' Sat'day when she knows I'm a p-person in a circus."

Bobby was less interested in this aspect of the affair.

"What'll we have for the tricks?" he said.

"We'll have a d-dog walkin' on a tightrope for one," said Jimmy.

"What dog?"

"Sandy."

Sandy was the mongrel who had attached himself to Jimmy some months ago and had been a member of the Manning household ever since.

"But he can't walk on a tightrope," said Bobby.

"I b-bet he can with a bit of practice," said Jimmy optimistically. "He's jolly clever."

"An' what else?"

"Well, we might have a lion-tamer. I've always wanted to be a lion-tamer."

"What about a lion?" said Bobby.

"Well, there's you," said Jimmy.

Bobby's jaw dropped.

"*Me?*"

"Y-yes," said Jimmy. "You can wear that ole rug that's on your landing. It's made of fur an' a lion's made of fur, so it's the s-same as a lion. I 'spect that's how lion-tamers s-start. I 'spect they start on people in fur rugs an' get on to real lions gradu'ly."

Bobby considered this.

"I don't know that I want to be tamed," he said doubt-fully. "How'd it be if I was the tamer an' you the lion?"

"No," said Jimmy. "It's me that's got to be a c-circus person by Sat'day."

"All right," agreed Bobby, "but," with spirit, "I'm not goin' to be the sort of lion that's tamed easy. Not even for you."

"No, that's all right," said Jimmy. "You needn't be. You can be as f-fierce as you like. He's more likely to give me a lion-tamer's job if he sees I'm good with f-fierce lions."

"All right," said Bobby. "I'm goin' to be a jolly fierce one. How shall we start?"

"We'll start by teachin' Sandy to walk the tightrope," said Jimmy. "Come on. Let's go 'n' get a tightrope an' f-find Sandy."

The rope was procured by the simple method of taking Mrs Manning's clothes line from her clothes-basket, and Sandy was discovered in the back garden, digging for Henry in the heap of leaf mould behind the greenhouse. Henry was Jimmy's tortoise. He had gone into hiberna-tion in the leaf-mould heap last autumn, but Sandy had dug him out at such frequent intervals that Jimmy had finally taken him round to Freddie Pelham's to finish his hibernation in peace . . . and ever since then Sandy had been trying to find out what had happened to him. He was quite willing, however, to abandon the search for Henry in favour of his circus training. He was, in fact, delighted with the idea . . . He snatched the rope from his trainers' hands and ran round the garden with it, pulling gleefully at one end, when Jimmy and Bobby had managed to secure the other. At last the stage was set, the rope tied firmly to two apple trees and the tightrope walker introduced to the imaginary audience. The result was, perhaps, less finished than Jimmy, in his enthusiasm, imagined it to be. With Bobby holding his front paws and Jimmy guiding his back paws, Sandy traversed the rope in a series of leaps and wriggles that, in Jimmy's opinion, added zest and picturesqueness to the performance.

"That's goin' to be all right," he said. "I told you he was j-jolly clever."

"What about our fight?" said Bobby.

"We don't need to practise that," said Jimmy. "Fightin' comes n-nat'ral to people."

Araminta's uncle was having tea with his sister and niece. He was sitting with his back to the window and was only vaguely aware of slight disturbances heard fitfully from the direction of the garden through the spate of his sister's chatter. Mrs Palmer was too much engrossed in her recital of her neighbours' doings and the enormities of her daily help to have attention to spare for anything else. It was Araminta who looked out of the window and said in her deep adenoidal voice:

"Subthig's happenig id the garden."

They turned to the window, and the spate of Mrs Palmer's chatter died away as her eyes met the amazing sight of a small scruffy dog running round the rose trees with a rope in its mouth, and two small scruffy boys, one of whom had a mat attached to his neck, engaged in what seemed a life and death struggle on the lawn.

"It's Jibby ad Bobby," said Araminta.

THEY SAW TWO BOYS IN WHAT SEEMED TO BE A LIFE-AND-
DEATH STRUGGLE ON THE LAWN.

Mrs Palmer advanced upon the intruders through the French windows, her eyes blazing with wrath.

"What," she said sternly, "is the meaning of this?"

The combatants abandoned the combat with obvious reluctance.

"It's a c-circus," panted Jimmy.

And then the light of indignation faded from Mrs Palmer's eyes and a fond all-embracing smile wreathed her face.

"The darlings!" she said. "Oh, the darlings!" She turned to her brother, who had followed her into the garden. "Araminta missed the circus because she had a cold and these dear little fellows are getting up a circus of their own for her, to make up for it."

Jimmy's face was blank with horror.

"No, l-listen—" he began.

But Mrs Palmer had caught sight of Sally and her mother, who were passing the gate.

"Isn't it sweet!" she gushed, going up to them. "My little Araminta missed the circus because of her cold and Jimmy and Bobby here have got up a little circus of their own for her in the garden to make up for it. They're devoted to her. Her little sweethearts, I call them."

Jimmy's face was crimson.

"B-but listen—" he began again and was again interrupted by Mrs Palmer, who was introducing her brother to Sally's brother.

"This is my brother," she said. "He loves getting out into the country for a change. He works in an office in Oxford Circus, and a breath of country air's a real tonic to him."

"L-listen, Sally—" pleaded Jimmy, but Sally gave him a glance of icy contempt, then walked on with her mother.

There was nothing for Jimmy and Bobby to do but go home, pursued by effusive thanks from Mrs Palmer. The odious words "little sweethearts" followed them down the road. Only Sandy seemed satisfied with the afternoon's work. He pranced on ahead, tail aloft, the remains of his rope still hanging out of his mouth.

"It was a bit of a mess-up," said Bobby.

"Yes," agreed Jimmy dolefully.

"It's a place, not a circus."

"Yes," said Jimmy with a sigh. "I don't s'pose I'll ever get to be a circus-m-master now, an' Sally won't ask me to her picnic."

"Well, there's nothing more we can do," said Bobby.

There was a long silence. In the silence Jimmy's air of

depression gradually faded and a zestful light dawned in his eyes.

"Yes, there is," he said.

"What?" said Bobby.

"We can go home an' f-finish the fight."

Chapter 6

The White Hen

Jimmy and Bobby were walking slowly through the village on their way home from school. It was Friday afternoon, and a leisurely holiday atmosphere hung over everything. An evening free of homework . . . no more school till Monday . . .

They stopped at the window of Mr Prosser's second-hand shop, trying to decide what they would buy if they had any money, torn between the rival attractions of a concertina and a punch-ball.

"There aren't any handles on the c-concertina," said Jimmy, who favoured the punch-ball.

"Well, you could make handles," said Bobby, "an' that punch-ball's all flat."

"You could blow it up."

"I bet you couldn't. Not for sixpence halfpenny. I can see a hole in it, too."

"Anyway, you c-couldn't make handles. Half the end's broke away."

"Oh, well, never mind," said Bobby, tiring of the problem. "Let's go an' see if there's any new sorts of sweets in Mr Mince's."

"It's no g-good to us if there are. We've spent our ration."

"Yes, but there's nex' week's. If we have a good look

now, we won't have to decide in a hurry nex' week."

"We never do d-decide in a hurry," Jimmy reminded him. "He always gets m-mad with us."

"I wish we'd got some money," said Bobby. "We could have an ice-cream if we'd got some money."

"Well, we haven't," said Jimmy, "but we can go an' have a l-look at the sweets, anyway."

They went to Mr Mince's shop and flattened their noses against the window.

"Those yellow ones are new since yesterday."

"They l-look jolly good. An' that toffee looks good, too."

"We had some once. It sticks to your teeth an' you can't get it off."

"Well, it w-wears off an' it tastes jolly good while it's wearin' off . . . I say!"

"Yes?"

"If you had five shillings an' there wasn't any sweet r-rations what sweets would you buy?"

The choice took them nearly ten minutes, after which they amused themselves by making patterns with their breath on the window-pane, till Mr Mince – a stout little man with a drooping moustache – came out to stop them and to remove the traces of their pastime with a chamois leather. They watched the operation with interest.

"Have you any ice-c-cream?" said Jimmy.

"Yes," said Mr Mince, looking at him suspiciously.

"Can we have one if we p-pay you nex' week?"

"No!" snapped Mr Mince. "And off with you!"

They went on slowly down the road.

"What'll we do now?" said Bobby.

"Let's go r-round to Miss Pettigrew's an' have a look at Emily," said Jimmy.

Miss Pettigrew's hen-run adjoined the road, separated from it by a hedge, and Emily was a large white hen of dominating personality and tyrannical disposition, in whom Jimmy and Bobby took a deep interest. She spent her time pecking such of her companions as ventured near her and at meal-times was kept so busy driving the others away from the feeding bowl that she must have been hard put to it to find time for a meal herself.

The two wandered down the road to Miss Pettigrew's and stood peering through the hedge. Emily was engaged in chasing a small brown hen round the tree that grew in the middle of the hen-run.

"I bet that brown one hasn't had a thing to eat all day," said Bobby. "Do you remember that time we watched them havin' their dinner an' she didn't let that brown one get a mouthful even?"

"Yes," said Jimmy. "I wish we could give the b-brown one somethin' to eat."

"We haven't got anything."

"N-no, but there's some b-berries in the hedge down the road. I saw 'em this mornin'. Let's get some."

They went down the road to a tall overgrown hedge that bordered a field and collected a handful of berries.

"Berries are f-food, you know," said Jimmy, as they gathered them. "That's what Nature g-grows them for. I bet that brown hen'll be jolly grateful to us."

They returned to Miss Pettigrew's hen-run.

"I'm goin' to th-throw one over the hedge jus' near the brown one," said Jimmy, "so's it'll be sure to get it."

He threw a berry over the hedge just near the brown hen. Emily ran up and got it. He threw another. Emily ran up and got it. He went to the other end of the hen-run, whither the brown hen had now retired, and threw another. Emily ran up and got it. He went back to his first station and threw another. The two hens sprinted across the hen-run for it. Emily got it.

"Let me have a try," said Bobby.

He had a try.

"There!" he said exultantly. "The brown one can't *help* gettin' that."

But Emily got it . . .

In the space of a few minutes Emily had eaten all the berries they had gathered.

"It's no good gettin' any more," said Jimmy. "She jus' eats 'em all. She's a jolly good runner. I'd like to race her an' S-Sandy together . . . Well, let's go home now."

They walked back along the road . . . Jimmy was silent. There was a thoughtful look on his face. At last he said:

"I s-say, Bobby."

"Yes?"

"I hope they weren't p-poison."

"What?"

"The b-berries."

"You said Nature grew them for food."

"Yes, I know, but I've jus' remembered a story I once read where they were p-poison an' the p-person died. Emily ate a jolly lot of them, too."

"Well, we can't do anythin' about it now," said Bobby philosophically. "I 'spect it'll be all right."

"Yes, I 'spect it will," agreed Jimmy. "I 'spect animals have got instincts for c-curing poisons. Same as salmons jumpin' up w-waterfalls."

It was after lunch the next day that Jimmy, passing the door of the dining-room, where his parents were lingering over their coffee, heard his mother say:

"I met Miss Pettigrew in the village this morning. She was terribly upset. She's lost Emily."

"Emily?"

"Yes. That old white hen of hers."

"Lost it? D'you mean it's dead?"

"Yes."

His face paling with horror, Jimmy ran across the road to Bobby's. Bobby was in the garden. He greeted Jimmy exultantly.

"I say, Jimmy! My godmother's been to lunch an' she's given me two-an'-six!"

"They were p-poison," said Jimmy breathlessly, ignoring Bobby's momentous piece of news. "She's d-d-dead."

"Who is?"

"Emily."

"Gosh!" said Bobby, his mouth dropping open in dismay. "Are you sure?"

"Yes. I heard my mother tellin' my father . . . I say, Bobby!"

"Yes?"

"We've got to *do* somethin' about it."

"What can we do?"

"Well, we've killed her hen, so we've got to get her another."

"We can't. We've only got my two-an'-six, an' I bet hens cost more than that."

Jimmy considered.

"We might get a good one second-hand," he said a little doubtfully.

"I don't think you can get second-hand hens," said Bobby.

"We can try, anyway. L-let's go an' ask Mr Prosser."

"I don't s'pose he's got one," said Bobby.

A visit to Mr Prosser's confirmed this opinion. Mr Prosser, who was rather deaf and, out of their confused explanation, only caught the word "hen", offered them a china hen without a tail for fourpence halfpenny and a tea-cosy in the shape of a hen, only slightly moth-eaten, for one and ninepence, then finally lost interest in the situation.

Jimmy and Bobby walked away, depressed and empty-handed.

"You see, you *can't* get hens," said Bobby.

"I've a good mind to s-steal one," said Jimmy.

"We'd be thieves, then."

"That's better than bein' m-murderers. We're m-murderers now."

"Well, we'd still be murderers as well as thieves."

"No, we w-wouldn't," said Jimmy. "Not if we'd p-put one back for the one we'd murdered. We'd only be thieves, then."

Bobby shook his head in a puzzled fashion. The problem was too deep for him.

"We might find a w-wild one," said Jimmy suddenly. "Let's try."

They spent the next half-hour wandering down country lanes in the neighbourhood of the village, looking for a wild hen. There were hens in plenty, but they all obviously belonged to the owners of the properties on which they scratched and squawked.

"Can't think where all the w-wild ones *are*," said Jimmy dispiritedly. "There mus' *be* them. There's wild everything. Anyway—"

He stopped abruptly. They were passing a cottage garden. At the end of the garden was a small enclosed hen-run, inside which a boy of three or four was sitting on his haunches, watching a white hen, slightly flecked with brown, idly pecking at a cabbage stump.

Jimmy approached the hedge.

"Hello," he said.

"Hello," said the boy.

"What's your n-name?"

"Hegbert."

"Are those your hens?"

"No, they're my Daddy's. 'Cept that one." He pointed to a hen that was pecking the cabbage stump. "That one's mine."

Jimmy and Bobby withdrew a few paces to discuss the situation in whispers.

"Let's ask him if he'll s-sell it us for your two-an'-six," suggested Jimmy.

"Let's try two shillings," said Bobby. "She gave it me in a two-shilling piece an' a sixpence, so, if he'll sell it for two shillin's, it leaves us sixpence for an ice-cream."

"All r-right," said Jimmy.

They returned to the hen-run.

"Hello," said Jimmy again.

"Hello," said the boy, without raising his eyes from the speckled hen.

"Will you sell us your hen?" said Jimmy.

"Why?" said Hegbert.

"'Cause we want to buy it."

"Why?" said Hegbert.

"Well," explained Jimmy, "we sort of m-murdered a hen we didn't m-mean to murder, an'—"

But Hegbert had lost interest in the story.

"It's called Hetty," he said, "and once" – proudly – "it had chickens."

"We'll give you two shillings for it," said Bobby.

Hegbert thought deeply for a few moments.

"How much is two shillings?" he said at last.

"It's four sixpences," said Bobby.

"Only four?" said Hegbert. "That's not much."

"It's t-twenty-four pennies," said Jimmy.

Hegbert stared at him, open-mouthed.

"Twenty-four pennies?" he said incredulously. "Twenty-four whole *pennies*?"

"Yes," said Jimmy. "Will you sell it us for that?"

"Oo, yes!" said Hegbert eagerly.

The negotiation appeared to be completed, but it wasn't. Hegbert refused to accept the two-shilling piece that Bobby offered him, and Jimmy and Bobby had to go back to the village to change the two-shilling piece for twenty-four pennies. (Mr Prosser performed his part in this transaction without interest or curiosity. He had long since given up trying to understand small boys.)

Then they returned to the cottage, where Hegbert opened the door of the hen-run for them and took his twenty-four pennies, laying them out in a row on the grass and gazing at them as if spellbound.

"They are real ones, aren't they?" he said a little suspiciously.

"Yes," said Jimmy. "'Course they are."

"An' are there really twenty-four?"

"Yes," said Jimmy. "Can we take the hen?"

"Yes . . . What can I buy with them?"

"Anything you l-like," said Jimmy, who was tiring of the subject. "Come on, Bobby. Let's catch it."

"Can I buy a coal-cart?" said Hegbert, still gazing at his row of pennies.

"I d-don't know," said Jimmy, making a dive at Hetty

and just missing her. "I don't know how much they c-cost . . . There! *Got* it!"

Hetty, an apathetic, spiritless creature, settled down under Jimmy's arm without further protest and, ignoring Hegbert's further questions (he had changed his mind and was toying with the idea of buying a Punch and Judy show), the two made their way to Miss Pettigrew's cottage, concealing Hetty as best they could under Jimmy's coat.

"I 'spect she'll be jolly p-pleased," said Jimmy.

"I dunno," said Bobby doubtfully. "It's not *quite* white."

"No, but she's a bit short-sighted," said Jimmy. "I don't s'pose she'll notice. Anyway, it's a jolly good h-hen."

Fate still seemed to favour their enterprise. Miss Pettigrew's garden was empty, and Jimmy, crawling through the hedge, introduced Hetty to her new quarters. She stood there, looking about her morosely.

"I 'spect she'll soon settle down," said Jimmy a little anxiously. "Look! The brown one wants to be friends . . . No, it doesn't," as the brown hen, deciding to place relations on a more satisfactory basis than they had been in Emily's time, administered a savage peck to the newcomer.

"I 'spect they're only playin'," said Bobby.

"P'raps," said Jimmy. "Well, we can't do anythin' more, so l-let's go home now. It mus' be nearly teatime."

Bobby glanced at his fingerless watch.

"Yes," he said. "Yes, it *is* nearly teatime."

"We'll come back after tea," said Jimmy, "an' m-make sure she's all right an' then we'll g-go to Mr Mince's an' have that ice-cream."

JIMMY INTRODUCED HETTY TO HER NEW QUARTERS.

"Yes," said Bobby, "but we'll have to be quick, 'cause he closes at five."

Once more they walked down the road away from Miss Pettigrew's cottage.

"You know, Bobby . . ." said Jimmy in rather a small voice.

"Yes?"

"I still feel a b-bit of a murderer, do you?"

"Well, yes, I do," admitted Bobby.

Immediately after tea, they returned to Miss Pettigrew's cottage. The garden was no longer deserted. Miss

Pettigrew and a woman in a cloth cap, who held Hegbert by the hand, were standing by the hen-run. The woman's voice was upraised indignantly. There was a look of bewilderment on Miss Pettigrew's prim middle-aged face.

"There's bin 'en-stealin' goin' on in this village for long enough," the woman was saying, "an' now we knows 'oo does it. If that there 'en ain't mine, I'll eat me 'at. I'll eat," raising her voice still higher, "everyone's 'ats."

"But, my good woman," said Miss Pettigrew, "I don't for a minute pretend that it's my hen. I know it isn't, and I haven't the faintest idea how it got into my hen-run."

"Oh, you 'aven't, 'aven't you?" said the woman sarcastically. "Well, it's a funny thing, that's all I can say. It's a funny thing it vanishes out of my 'en-run an' fetches up in yours."

"I quite agree it's a funny thing," said Miss Pettigrew with dignity. "I don't understand it in the least. The whole thing is most extraordinary. One of my own hens was killed by a fox last night. The creature got into the hen-run through some broken wire but fortunately I heard the disturbance in time and only Emily, my white hen, was killed . . . And now this happens."

"Very funny, ain't it?" said the woman. "An' you 'aven't even the pluck to do your own stealin'. Sent a couple of kids pretendin' to buy it off Hegbert 'ere. 'Spect you 'eard that we let 'im call 'Etty 'is own 'en fer a sort of joke, so you sent two boys to kid the poor child into lettin' 'em 'ave 'is 'en. Gave 'im a few coppers to keep 'im quiet an' pinched 'is 'en. S'pose you thought you was clever!"

"But I can't understand," said Miss Pettigrew. "What two boys?"

"You should know," said the woman ominously. "You sent 'em, didn't you?"

"*Them* two boys!" said Hegbert suddenly, pointing to the hedge.

Miss Pettigrew and the woman looked in the direction of his finger.

But Jimmy and Bobby were no longer there.

Their consciences freed of a load of guilt, they had decided to put first things first and were racing down to the village, intent on reaching Mr Mince's shop before it closed.

Chapter 7

The Hold-Up

"It's an insult," said Charles, "that can only be wiped out with blood."

Charles, having been told recently by an aunt that his family was descended from the Irish kings, had made much of the fact, and had rashly boasted of it in the presence of Mr Jackson, a new master of St Adrian's. Mr Jackson's reception of the news had not been encouraging.

"Oh, I know all about those Irish kings," he had said. "They lived in mud huts."

Charles's face had darkened, for the Irish kings of his imagination lived in palaces, surrounded by pages and lackeys and bodyguards and courtiers; but he had contented himself by writing the name "Mr Jackson" on the outside of his Arithmetic exercise book so that it looked like "Mr Jackass" and pretending that he couldn't read the figures that Mr Jackson put on the board.

The affair, however, did not stop at that. Mr Jackson was a man of irascible disposition. He came out of his tempers almost as quickly as he got into them, but during them he employed a varied and colourful vocabulary. He had got into a temper with Charles this morning.

"You nincompoop!" he had shouted. "You lack-wit! You benighted bog-dweller from the Emerald Isles!"

Charles had summoned a meeting of the Three Musketeers immediately after school and was addressing them now in the tool-shed in Roger's garden.

"He's insulted my race," he said, "publicly, in front of the whole form, and I can't go on living with this slur on my name. I've got to wipe it off."

"How will you wipe it off?" said Roger.

"I haven't made up my mind yet," said Charles. "I've thought of challenging him to a duel, but there's the difficulty of weapons. The only weapon I've got at present that works is my bow and arrow and I've never heard of a duel fought with bows an' arrows. Besides, I don't suppose he's got them."

"I don't s'pose he'd fight a duel with you, anyway," said Bill, who was apt to take a realistic view of things.

"He'd be dishonoured for ever if he didn't," said Charles. "There's penknives, of course."

"He took my penknife away yesterday," said Roger gloomily. "Perkins had pinched it and was messin' about with it in Arithmetic and Mr Jackson took it off him and wouldn't give it back to me even when I told him it was mine."

"All right," said Charles grimly. "We'll get your penknife back an' we'll wipe out the insult on my name. P'raps it's best not to challenge him. He's probably a coward and it gives him a loophole for escape. No, we'll – we'll hold him up. We'll hold him up and force him to give you back your penknife and apologise to me for slurring my ancestry."

"How'll we do it?" said Roger.

"He looks pretty strong," said Bill thoughtfully.

"Listen," said Charles. "He always goes home through the wood, so we could drop on him from a tree like commandos do. There's that big oak tree, you know, that one branch of goes right across the path. We could climb up that and crawl along the branch and then drop down on him and overpower him when he's got to just underneath us. We'll know it's him because of that awful check overcoat he always wears. It's quite easy to overpower people when you drop on them from trees. Then, when we've overpowered him, we'll make him apologise and give back the penknife."

"I don't think it's goin' to be as easy as all that," said Bill.

"All right," said Charles with dignity. "If you want to back out of it you can. I'm quite prepared to go through with it alone. He can only kill me, and I'd rather face death than dishonour."

"'Course we'll go through with it," said Roger.

"'Course we will," agreed Bill.

Charles still looked thoughtful.

"There's always the possibility, of course," he said, "that I might do him some vital injury. I'd have to fly the country then, so I'll bring all my money and my pyjamas with me in case I have to."

"We'll come with you if you do," said Roger.

"No, I think you'd better not," said Charles. "They'll have detectives at the docks and I may have to be disguised. I'd be safer alone. Of course, I may not be able to get out of the country. I may have to hide up in a cave or something, just kept alive by the food you bring me."

"By what?" said Bill.

"By the food you bring me," said Charles. "There'll probably be a secret path through the woods to my cave."

"I dunno what food I can bring you," said Bill, frowning perplexedly. "I never get enough to eat myself."

"I could bring you some breakfast sausage sometimes," said Roger. "We have it on Fridays an' I don't like it much."

"Neither do I," said Charles, "so you needn't bother. I expect I could live on wild herbs. For a time, anyway . . . I wish I lived in the sort of house that has a secret panel. I could hide up there without anyone knowing anything about it. I'd just come out at nights and eat whatever was in the larder."

"They'd get a bit suspicious, findin' the larder empty every mornin'," said Bill.

"Well, what about this hold-up?" said Roger, bringing them back to the matter in hand.

"Yes," said Charles. "We'll meet after school this afternoon at the oak tree. We ought to have masks like commandos to make us more terrifying and so that he won't know who we are till we've overpowered him. Let's take an oath of secrecy now and sign it in our blood."

"One minute!" said Roger. "Let's make sure that Jimmy isn't listening." He went to the door and opened it. "No, it's all right," closing it again. "He's at the bottom of the garden with Bobby Peaslake."

"I couldn't quite hear everything they said," Jimmy was saying. "But they're goin' to m-make a commando attack on Mr Jackson from the big oak tree in the w-wood when he's coming home from school this afternoon."

"Gosh!" said Bobby. "Why?"

"'Cause he's c-called Charles an emerald bog an' Charles has got to wipe it out with b-blood."

"Oh," said Bobby, after pondering on this explanation for some moments in silence.

"An' Charles is goin' to f-fly the country if he does Mr

Jackson a vital injury, but I think Mr Jackson's more likely to do Charles one than Charles him one. I think we'd better go, too, Bobby, case they all do each other v-vital injuries."

"They wouldn't let us."

"They c-can't stop us. We'll jus' go for a walk in the w-wood after school. There's no law against people goin' for walks in w-woods after school. There's plenty of bushes we can hide behind near that oak t-tree. Anyway, it sounds jolly excitin' an' I d-don't want to be out of it."

The Three Musketeers met under the oak tree soon after school. They were an impressive sight. Roger wore a mask that he had made from cardboard, cutting holes for the eyes and blacking the rest with ink; Bill, after trying to make a mask of an old saucepan that his mother had thrown away, finally gave up the attempt and simply rubbed soot over his face; Charles had tied a small chair-back cover across his face just beneath his eyes. Its only drawbacks were that the fringe kept slipping down and dangling about his neck. In addition Charles carried a small attaché case containing fourpence halfpenny, his pyjamas and a false moustache that he had got out of a cracker.

"The moustache is my disguise in case I have to fly the country," he explained.

"You wouldn't look like a man even in a moustache," said Bill.

"I'm as tall as a very short man," said Charles with dignity, "and any detective will tell you that it's not so much what you wear that makes the disguise. It's how you act the part. I've acted men in plays so that you'd hardly know the difference."

"Well, come on," said Roger, "or he'll be here before we've got up the tree."

The three climbed up the oak tree and crawled along the branch that overhung the path, retaining their positions with difficulty.

"I can't stay like this for long," said Bill. "This branch is a funnier shape than what it looks from the ground."

"Shut up!" said Roger. "He's comin'!"

The well-known check overcoat had appeared at the end of the path, making its way, unconscious of its doom, through the trees.

"Wait till I give the signal," whispered Roger, "then drop down an' overpower him . . . He's nearly here . . . wait a minute . . . *Now!*"

They dropped down from the tree on to the man in the check overcoat. But they didn't overpower him. With a series of strong blows he felled all three of them, then began to kick at them with large hob-nailed boots as they lay on the ground.

"'Obgoblins!" he shouted. "'Obgoblins!"

Jimmy sprang from his bush and ran to the rescue, followed more slowly by Bobby. He flung himself upon the man, but the man merely picked him up by the collar and threw him clear of the struggle. He landed unhurt in a bed of bracken and, when he had scrambled to his feet, saw in the distance another man in a fawn overcoat making his way along a parallel path in the wood. Breathless and panting, he ran up to him.

"Come quick!" he gasped. "Mr Jackson's m-murdering Roger."

The man looked down at him and, to his amazement, Jimmy saw that it was Mr Jackson. They ran back to the other path and Mr Jackson dragged the man in the check overcoat away from his victims.

"'Obgoblins, sir," panted the man. "Nearly got me, they did."

"It's all right, Weston," said Mr Jackson, helping the boys to their feet. "They aren't hobgoblins. They're friends of mine."

"Sorry, sir," said the man. He looked suspiciously at the Three Musketeers. Roger's mask had vanished in the struggle, leaving a trail of ink on his face, Bill's "mask" of soot had spread over his entire person, and Roger's chair-back cover had got pushed up into his hair, forming a fantastic-looking headgear. "They *looks* like 'obgoblins."

"That's all right, old chap," said Mr Jackson, patting his shoulder reassuringly. "They're friends of mine, I tell you. Now get along home."

"All right, sir. If you say so, sir," said the man and, still muttering, "'Obgoblins", shambled off down the path.

Mr Jackson helped the boys to their feet.

"He's a bit simple, poor old chap," he said. "His grand-mother used to tell him that there were hobgoblins in the wood and that they'd get him if he wasn't careful, and he's always on the look-out for them . . . I must say, you do look a bit – sinister. What's the idea?"

A little shamefacedly they told him.

"You'd insulted my race, sir."

"I wanted my penknife back, sir. It was mine. It wasn't Perkins's."

"We meant to overpower you and extract an apology."

"I didn't even *lend* it to Perkins, sir. He pinched it."

"It was to be an attack according to the rules of com-mando warfare. That's why we wore masks."

"His face was hidden by his hat, but we thought it was your overcoat."

"A natural mistake," said Mr Jackson. "Weston does jobbing gardening for me three or four days a week, and I gave him my overcoat yesterday when my new one arrived." He looked at them with a twinkle. "Well, I apologise for insulting you, Charles, and you can have your penknife back, Roger. You, I gather, have no grievance, Bill?"

"No, sir," said Bill after a short silence during which he tried to think of one.

"The insult is forgotten and forgiven, sir," said Charles, "and I apologise for any inconvenience I may have caused you. I shall always be under an obligation to you for saving my life."

"You owe that to Jim, partly," said Mr Jackson, "so suppose you all come along with me and have a cup of tea. I think my wife's been making jam tarts this afternoon."

The five walked slowly homeward through the wood – the Three Musketeers in front, Jimmy and Bobby a yard or two behind. Mr Jackson, it turned out, had a pleasant little house, with a stream running through the garden, and a wife of whom even the Three Musketeers, hardened women-haters though they were, could not help approving. The tea had been a sumptuous spread of sandwiches, jam tarts, chocolate biscuits, gingerbread, dates and ice-cream. Host and guests had parted on terms of cordial friendliness.

"I'm relieved in a way," admitted Charles, "not to have to fly the country. It might have presented difficulties I wasn't prepared for."

"I expect it would," said Roger, and added: "He's a lot nicer than he seems in school, isn't he?"

"Yes," said Charles. "He's a real gentleman and I consider that he's given me satisfaction."

Jimmy's mind went back over the jam tarts, chocolate biscuits, gingerbread and ice-cream.

"He has m-me, too," he said simply.

Chapter 8

Dangerous Drugs

"You know, Roger," said Jimmy thoughtfully, "I think Archie an' Georgie have joined the Society jus' so's they can m-mess it up somehow."

"I don't see how they can mess it up," said Roger. "Me an' Charles an' Bill will be there, so, if they do start anything, we can stop it."

"Y-yes," said Jimmy, "but I think they're only c-comin' so that they can p-play up Mr Fortescue."

"Oh, don't be such a chump," said Roger impatiently. "I tell you, they won't dare to do anything with me an' Charles an' Bill there."

Last term an enthusiastic master at St Adrian's had started a Nature Society, which a large number of the boys had joined. This term the master was away from school having his appendix removed, and a temporary master, Mr Fortescue, had come to take his place. Mr Fortescue was a cousin of Mrs Manning's – a state of things that gave ample scope to anyone who wanted to "score off" Roger or Jimmy.

So far, however, everything had gone smoothly. Mr Fortescue – a vague, absent-minded, rather shy young man – was, on the whole, popular, and Archie Mould and Georgie Tallow had had little chance of turning the situation to their account. But the autumn term Nature

Expedition was to take place tomorrow, and last week Archie and Georgie had joined the Society. Roger refused to see anything sinister in this move, but Jimmy was doubtful and more than a little apprehensive. He had seen Archie and Georgie sniggering together at Archie's gate in obviously conspiratorial fashion and was convinced that they were hatching some plot to expose to ridicule, not only Mr Fortescue, but – as members of the same family – Roger and himself. He went to bed that night hoping desperately that rain, snow, sleet and fog – however unseasonable – would put a stop to the expedition. But the day dawned bright and sunny, and the members of the Nature Society met at the entrance of the wood at the appointed time.

Mr Fortescue was to come in his car, and Jimmy's hopes, badly let down by the weather, were now fixing themselves on the possibility of a not too serious breakdown that would delay his arrival indefinitely. But, exactly at the right moment, Mr Fortescue's shabby little car drew up at the stile leading into the wood, and Mr Fortescue descended from it carrying his attaché case.

"C-can I take your case, please, sir?" said Jimmy, who had decided to constitute himself Mr Fortescue's bodyguard.

"Certainly," said Mr Fortescue, handing it to him, "And now, come along, boys. We'll fix our headquarters, as it were, and then scatter for observation."

The boys trailed along the woodland path behind Mr Fortescue. Then Archie and Georgie, after some furtive whispering and giggling, opened their campaign.

"Please, sir, I've been bit by an ant."

"Please, sir, I've been stung by a grasshopper."

"Please, sir, I think I saw a polar bear over there."

"Please, sir, isn't that an ostrich's nest up that tree?"

The attack petered out ignominiously. Though a few faint titters came from some of the younger boys, Mr Fortescue and the older boys ignored the humorists . . . and Jimmy's heart grew lighter.

"Please, sir, I've just been stung by a snake," said Archie, writhing in simulated agony and making a final effort to win over his audience. "A snake's bite's incurable, you know, sir."

"What can't be cured must be endured, then, Mould," said Mr Fortescue cheerfully, and the expedition proceeded on its way till they reached the clearing in the wood that Mr Fortescue had chosen as their headquarters.

"Leave anything you don't want here," he said. "I'll leave my case here. Then we'll all go off on our own. Make notes of anything interesting you see and bring back any specimens that you think will be interesting to the others. We'll meet here again in half an hour's time and compare notes."

"Shall I stay and g-guard the things, sir?" said Jimmy.

"No, I don't think that's necessary," said Mr Fortescue. "We shan't be very far away. I think they'll be quite safe here."

Jimmy, however, had seen the smile of anticipatory relish on Archie's face and was not so sure . . .

The boys scattered through the wood, but Jimmy hovered near the clearing, ready to defend Mr Fortescue's case against attack. He had not long to wait. After a few minutes he saw Archie and Georgie creeping back through the bushes. Georgie snatched up Mr Fortescue's case and Jimmy sprang to rescue it, only to be seized by Archie, who neatly twisted his arm (Archie was an expert at arm twisting) and flung him into the middle of one of the holly bushes that grew by the side of the clearing. By the time that Jimmy had extricated himself from the holly bush and made sure that his arm was still attached to his person, Archie, Georgie and the case had vanished. But he could hear voices, and he crept as silently as he could in the direction of the sound. Then suddenly he came upon them. Archie held the case, and Georgie held a rat-trap, containing a large rat. It was clear that this was the real plot, carefully planned and arranged beforehand. Jimmy remembered that Mr Fortescue had – perhaps unwisely – confided his dislike of rats to Archie's form when he was teaching them last week.

"I don't mind mice, cockroaches, or even bats," he had said, "but rats scare me stiff."

So they were going to put the rat into his case and enjoy his discomfiture when he opened it.

"We'll take these books out to make room for it," Archie was saying. "Gosh! Won't it be fun! We'll be able to rag Roger about it for the rest of his life."

"And Jimmy," said Georgie, chuckling happily. "I bet it'll bite ole Forty as soon as he opens it."

"Yes. I say! Have you got a bit of paper?"

"Yes."

"Good! I've got a pencil. Let's write that fool thing he said, shall we? – 'What can't be cured must be endured' – and put it in with the rat."

For a few minutes they were helpless with mirth, then Georgie took a packet from the case and opened it.

"What are these?" he said.

Archie examined one of the small white tablets and gave it an experimental lick.

"They're peppermint," he said. "I've seen him eating

them after lunch. Come on. Let's eat 'em all up."

They set to work on the peppermint tablets, and Jimmy crept away. An idea had suddenly occurred to him. He had seen a second case in Mr Fortescue's car. It would do, he thought, as well as the first for receiving the odds and ends of nature specimens that Mr Fortescue presumably intended to put in it. He would substitute it for the one with the rat in it and thus save both Mr Fortescue's and the family dignity.

He hurried down the path to the road, where the car still waited, took the other case and returned to the clearing with it, putting it down where Mr Fortescue had put the first. He would guard it carefully, he decided, till Mr Fortescue returned . . . He hadn't guarded it for more than a few minutes when a small harassed-looking man in a neat grey suit, with a pointed beard, came scurrying down the path. It was Dr Sykes, Jimmy's family doctor.

"Where's Mr Fortescue, Jimmy?" he said in his high-pitched penetrating voice. "A most unfortunate thing has happened. My car broke down on the main road, and Mr Fortescue kindly offered to take my case home for me after your nature expedition. I said that there was no hurry and, as there was nothing in it of any importance, it would do if he returned it any time during the evening, but I suddenly remembered that there were some dangerous drugs in it, and now I find it's gone from his car. If it's been stolen, it's a very serious matter."

"Is this it?" said Jimmy, holding up the case. "I'm afraid I t-took it by mistake."

"That's it," said the doctor, opening the case and examining its contents. "And nothing's been touched. What a relief! . . . Quite all right, my boy! All's well that ends well," and trotted off down the path again with his case.

Jimmy stood irresolute for a few moments, then a smile dawned slowly over his small round countenance. He strolled over to where Archie and Georgie were still munching peppermints among the bushes.

"Hello," he said innocently.

"Was that Dr Sykes talking to you just now?" said Archie.

"Yes," said Jimmy.

"I said it was," said Georgie. "No one else has a squeaky little voice like that."

"What did he want?" said Archie.

"Well," said Jimmy, "it s-seems that the c-case I carried for Mr Fortescue from his car wasn't Mr Fortescue's at all. It was Dr Sykes's an' he said it had some d-dangerous drugs in it."

Archie turned pale. Georgie's face was a mask of horror.

"Dangerous drugs?" gasped Archie.

"They – they – they tasted like peppermint," stammered Georgie.

"They didn't look dangerous," said Archie.

"Oo! I'm beginning to feel ill," wailed Georgie. "I'm going home to my mother."

"I am, too," said Archie on a high-pitched note of terror.

The two ran down the path. Georgie's wails floated back as he ran. Jimmy replaced the books and what was left of the peppermints, carried the rat-trap to the road, released the rat, and returned to the clearing, carrying the case.

Gradually the members of the Nature Society straggled back, laden with trophies of pine cones, wild flowers, birds' nests, leaves and brightly coloured fungi. One small boy carried with pride the decaying corpse of a weasel that he had found nailed by a keeper on to a tree trunk, another a disintegrating boot that he had found in a bush. Another returned empty-handed, though his mouth, wreathed in purple and wearing a smile of satisfaction, bore witness that he had discovered some interesting specimens of the wild blackberry.

Mr Fortescue counted his charges.

"Where are Mould and Tallow?" he said without much interest.

"They've g-gone home," said Jimmy.

"I told you they'd never dare to try anything with me an' Charles an' Bill here," said Roger to Jimmy with a superior smile.

At the end of the afternoon Jimmy went home by way of Georgie's house. Georgie hung over the gate. His face wore a woebegone expression and a greenish hue.

"It's all right about the d-dangerous drugs," said Jimmy.

"Yes, I know," groaned Georgie. "My mother rang up the doctor and he said he'd found the case with all of them in, but it was too late."

"Too l-late?" said Jimmy.

"Yes. She'd made me drink nearly a whole tin of mustard an' I feel awful. Archie's gone to bed. He feels worse than I do, even, 'cause his mother made him drink salt, too. I don't think I'll ever feel well again, an' my mother says she can't do anythin' to make me feel better."

"N-never mind," said Jimmy cheerfully.

He was going on his way when a sudden thought struck him and he turned with a grin to add:

"What can't be cured mus' be endured, m-m-mustn't it?"

Chapter 9

Government Surplus

Jimmy and Bobby stood with their noses glued to the shop window, gazing at a bewildering array of binoculars, telescopes, periscopes, goggles, transformers, induction coils, groundsheets, raincoats, police tunics, blankets, kitbags, tarpaulins, sleeping-bags, axes, shovels and soldering-irons. The shop had been empty for several months and had just been taken temporarily by an enterprising firm for a tempting display of bargains.

"Government Surplus Store," read out Bobby slowly, looking at the notice above the window.

"They don't look like s-surplices to me," objected Jimmy.

"P'raps it means diff'rent things at diff'rent times," said Bobby. "Like hair. Sometimes that means a sort of rabbit, you know, an' sometimes it means jus' hair."

"P'raps," agreed Jimmy. "I say! Look at that penknife. It calls it a j-jackknife."

"Yes. Three-an'-six. That's jolly cheap. If I had three-an'-six, I'd buy it, wouldn't you?"

"Yes . . . an' if we only had th-three-an'-six between us we c-could buy it an' sh-share it, couldn't we?"

"Yes, but we haven't, have we?"

"No. Come on, then. I bet it's about t-teatime."

"Yes, it is," said Bobby, consulting the large wrist-watch, devoid of works and fingers, that he always wore on his small bony wrist.

The two ran home and parted at the gate of Jimmy's house. Still thinking about the jackknife, Jimmy went indoors, washed his hands and entered the dining-room. His tea was laid on the table, and his mother sat by the fire, knitting. She was looking, he thought, a little harassed.

"Hello, dear," she said. "Come along. I've got some watercress for you."

"Th-thanks," said Jimmy, sitting down and setting to work upon it.

Suddenly Mrs Manning laid down her knitting.

"Jimmy," she said, "I've done a most dreadful thing."

"What?" said Jimmy.

"I've bought a telegraph pole."

"A w-what?" gasped Jimmy.

"A telegraph pole."

"W-w-why?" said Jimmy.

"I haven't the slightest idea," said Mrs Manning. "I bought it yesterday. I was passing that Government Surplus place and I saw them (they had a lot in the yard at the back), and I bought one. I can't think why I bought it and I can't think what to do with it now I've got it."

"Would it d-do for logs?" said Jimmy after a moment's thought.

"No. It's pine and pine spits."

"D-does it?" said Jimmy, interested by the mental vision the words summoned to his mind.

"Yes . . . I don't know *what* to do."

"Could you m-make something out of it?"

"No. I've thought of that. There's nothing I could

make. I've no excuse at all. I just lost my head. I'm afraid your mother's a born idiot, Jimmy."

"You're not," said Jimmy indignantly. "I say! C-could we send telegrams with it? It would be fun if we c-could."

"No, we can't even do that," said Mrs Manning. "I tried to forget it yesterday, but it came today. In two pieces. About seven feet each. It's in the garden. I must have been mad. What do I want with a telegraph pole?"

"It would do for the m-mast of a ship," said Jimmy thoughtfully.

"But we haven't got a ship," said Mrs Manning.

"No," said Jimmy, "but we could k-keep it in case we ever get one. It'd want a c-crow's nest on the top, but I 'spect we could f-find a crow's nest. We wouldn't need to buy a f-foghorn either, 'cause Bobby an' me can do a f-foghorn. We were practisin' yesterday."

"I know, dear," said Mrs Manning hastily. "No, please don't show me again. I remember it quite well."

"All r-right," said Jimmy regretfully. "Would it do to make a tent of? The telegraph pole, I mean."

"No, dear," said Mrs Manning. "I don't want a tent, anyway. I'm afraid it's quite useless. When you've finished your tea, I'd like you to help me hide it. I don't want your father to see it. He'd never stop teasing me about it."

"Where shall we h-hide it?" said Jimmy.

"Between the tool-shed and the hedge," said Mrs Manning. "I don't suppose he'll notice it there. Don't tell him about it, whatever you do, will you, darling? Then tomorrow I can find some way of getting rid of it."

After tea Jimmy and his mother carried the two poles down to the bottom of the garden and placed them in their hiding-place behind the tool-shed. Then Mrs

Manning returned to her knitting and Jimmy began his homework. But he was worried about the poles. They just protruded beyond the tool-shed at one end, and he thought that, with a little manipulation, he could conceal them altogether. He went down into the garden. Dusk was falling, and at first he did not see his father, busied about something near the compost heap.

"Hello, Daddy," he said. "I didn't know you'd come home."

Mr Manning stood up. He looked a little sheepish.

"I've just come in by the garden gate," he said.

Suddenly Jimmy noticed a round metal object by his father's feet.

"What's that?" he said.

"A Food Container," said Mr Manning bitterly, "whatever that may mean. Dunno why I bought the darn' thing. I was passing that Government Surplus place, and – well, I bought it. It's quite useless as far as I can see. I bought it simply and solely because it was cheap, and when you do find something cheap these days you're apt to lose your head."

"What are you d-doing with it?" said Jimmy.

"I was going to bury it in the compost heap," said Mr Manning, "so that your mother shouldn't see it. She'd never stop laughing at me if she knew I'd bought it. Don't tell her, whatever you do . . . On second thoughts, I'll leave it just behind the compost heap. She won't see it there, and I'll find some way of disposing of it tomorrow. You've got a fool for a father, you know, Jim."

"I h-haven't," said Jim stoutly.

Mr Manning's eyes were roving round the garden. They reached the tool-shed and stopped.

"What's that?" he said.

"What?" said Jimmy with a sinking heart.

"That – that pole sticking out."

"Oh, that!" said Jimmy. A determination not to betray his mother sharpened his wits. He looked round the garden for inspiration. The sight of two sagging rose poles in the front garden gave it to him. His small face cleared. "It's two poles that Mummy bought."

"What on earth for?" said Mr Manning.

"Well, those two rose poles, you know . . ."

"Good Lord, yes!" said Mr Manning. "They were pretty well done in by that last gale, weren't they? That was very thoughtful of her. Let's have a look at them."

He looked at them, then set to work taking down the old poles and putting up the new ones, afterwards nailing on to them the rope along which the roses were

"IT'S TWO POLES THAT MUMMY BOUGHT," SAID JIMMY.

trained. He let Jimmy hold the nails and even go up the ladder to drive one or two of them in. Then Jimmy returned to the house. He met his mother coming out with a basket.

"I'm just going to get the sprouts for dinner, dear," she said. "Would you like to come and help me?"

"Yes, p-please," said Jimmy.

They picked sprouts together till suddenly Mrs Manning stood upright, her eyes fixed on something that gleamed beyond the compost heap.

"What on earth's that?" she said.

Again Jimmy searched frantically for inspiration. Again inspiration came.

"Daddy bought it," he said.

"What on earth for?" said Mrs Manning, going to examine it.

"Well, you know you said the vegetable rack was too s-small an'—"

"Oh, yes, I remember," said Mrs Manning. She had taken it up. "It's a bit cumbersome, but it will do quite well to keep vegetables in. I didn't know your father had come back."

"Yes, he's in the f-front garden."

"What's he doing there?"

"F-fixing the rose poles."

Mrs Manning went round to the front garden, where her husband was tying up the roses to the poles.

"Darling, how nice of you!" they greeted each other.

Jimmy went indoors to finish his homework. A burst of laughter from the garden a few minutes later told him that his parents had discovered the real facts of the case. His father came in and stood looking down at him.

"You're quite an able tactician, Jimmy," he said.

"They weren't t-tacks," said Jimmy. "They were n-nails an' I only knocked one of them in."

"My food container makes an excellent vegetable rack annexe," said Mr Manning. "I displayed great wisdom in the purchase."

"There was a jolly good penknife at that place," said Jimmy wistfully. "It was three-an'-six."

"All right," said Mr Manning with a twinkle in his eye. He took a handful of loose silver from his pocket, counted out three-and-six and put it on the table by Jimmy. "You've earned it."

"Thanks awfully," said Jimmy. "May I go and buy it n-now before the shop closes?"

"Yes. Off you go!" said Mr Manning.

It was about half an hour later that Jimmy's owl-call brought Bobby down to his garden gate. Jimmy stood there, his face set and tense, one hand held behind his back. He didn't look like a boy who has been given three-and-six and bought a penknife.

"Daddy gave me three-an'-six for that knife," he said slowly.

"Good!" said Bobby. "Have you got it?"

"No. They'd sold them all, but—" He stopped.

"Yes?" said Bobby eagerly.

"Well, I b-bought something else."

"What?" said Bobby.

"Well, there were such a l-lot of things and I got a bit m-muddled. I dunno what we're goin' to d-do with it, but the man said it was the b-best value in the shop."

"But what was it?" said Bobby.

Jimmy brought his hand from behind his back. It held two large shapeless objects.

"A pair of g-g-gauntlets," he said.

Chapter 10

High Finance

"I think we ought to be th-thinkin' out what we're goin' to be when we're grown-up," said Jimmy. "I'm seven an' three quarters an' I don't want to leave it too l-late."

"I thought we were goin' to be chimney-sweeps," said Bobby.

"Yes, we w-were," said Jimmy, "but we got in a bit of a muddle when we tried it last an' I don't think there's much m-money in it."

"No, but goin' up chimneys an' messin' about with soot's more fun than money," said Bobby.

"Yes, I know," said Jimmy, "but I think we ought to t-try some other things, case chimney-sweepin' falls through."

"What other things?"

"Well, my father was talkin' about f-financiers las' night," said Jimmy. "They make so much money that they can have r-real yachts of their own."

"I'd like to have a real yacht of my own," said Bobby wistfully. "How do they start?"

"They buy things cheap an' s-sell them dear," said Jimmy.

"That sounds easy," said Bobby after a moment's consideration.

"He said you'd g-got to start young," said Jimmy.

"We could start now, couldn't we?"

"Yes," agreed Jimmy. "We're not v-very young but we're not old."

"What can we sell?" asked Bobby.

"There's that pair of g-gauntlets," said Jimmy. "I d-don't think it's any good keepin' them till we're grown up. Either we'll lose them or Sandy'll ch-chew them up."

"Yes, I s'pose so," said Bobby. "How much'll we charge for them?"

"Well, they c-cost three-an'-six," said Jimmy, "so we ought to charge four shillings."

"That's a lot," said Bobby.

"Well, f-financiers do charge a lot," said Jimmy. "That's why they're financiers."

"All right," said Bobby. "How'll we sell them?"

"We'll have to have a s-sort of shop," said Jimmy.

"A shop!" said Bobby, aghast. "We've not got enough money to buy a shop. They cost an awful lot."

"I know," said Jimmy. "We won't have a p-proper shop with a door. We'll have one of those w-wheel-barrow shops like the ones where they sell oranges an' cherries in t-towns."

"Yes," said Bobby, brightening, "an' we'll use that wheelbarrow I had for Christmas. It'll make a jolly good wheelbarrow shop."

"All right," said Jimmy. "Well, you go'n' fetch it now, an' I'll get the g-gauntlets an' write a notice about them."

Within quarter of an hour the "shop" was established on the grass verge by the side of the road. Bobby's wheelbarrow contained the pair of gauntlets and a sheet of paper, torn out of Jimmy's exercise book, bearing the words "CHEEP FOUR SHILINGS" printed in large irregular letters. Behind the wheelbarrow stood Jimmy and Bobby, anxiously awaiting their customers. The road was an unfrequented one and for the first ten minutes no one passed. Then a small boy, called Freddy Pelham, who attended the same school as Jimmy and Bobby, came strolling along.

He carried in his mouth a short twig, which he removed from time to time in order to exhale an imaginary cloud of cigarette smoke.

"Hello," said Jimmy.

Freddy stood in front of the wheelbarrow, surveying its contents in silence.

"Do you want to buy a p-pair of gauntlets?" said Jimmy ingratiatingly.

Freddy removed his twig to say "No", then replaced it. He was a boy of few words.

"Have you got any money?" asked Bobby.

"No," said Freddy.

"Go away, then," said Jimmy.

"No," said Freddy.

"All right, d-don't, then," said Jimmy.

At that moment Araminta Palmer came trotting down the road, holding her toy monkey, Sinbad, under her arm. She stopped and looked round the group.

"What are you doig?" she said.

"We're f-financiers," said Jimmy importantly. "We're s-selling things. It's a shop."

"It isn't a shop," said Araminta.

"It is."

"It isn't."

Araminta spoke with quiet enjoyment. Contradiction was the breath of life to her.

"Go away," said Jimmy. "We don't want you."

"I dode care," said Araminta, "ad I'b dot goig away. I'b

goig to stay. Ad it can't be a shop without a shop-lady. There's always a shop-lady id a shop."

"There isn't in this one," said Jimmy.

"Yes, there is," said Araminta calmly. "There's be. I'b goig to stop ad be the shop-lady." She looked at the gauntlets with dispassionate contempt. "Ad you can't have a shop with only one thig id it."

"Yes, you c-can," said Jimmy.

"No, you can't."

"All right," challenged Jimmy. "Get some m-more things."

"All right," said Araminta. "I will. I'll get theb frob by auntie. By auntie's got sub thigs for a jumble sale, but she'll give theb to be if I ask her. She likes be."

Jimmy and Bobby looked at each other, torn between reluctance to submit to Araminta's despotism and a desire to place their position as financiers on a sounder basis.

"She's got lots of thigs," said Araminta persuasively, "ad she lives just dear here."

"All right," said Jimmy, trying to preserve his dignity by assuming an air of aloofness. "You can fetch them if you like."

"I dode like," said Araminta. "You'll both have to cub ad carry theb. Shop-ladies don't carry thigs."

"Neither do f-financiers," said Jimmy. "Anyway, we can't leave the shop with no one to l-look after it."

"Freddy cad look after it," said Araminta. She turned to Freddy. "You wouldn't bind lookig after the shop, would you, Freddy?"

Freddy removed the twig from his mouth, emitted another imaginary cloud of cigarette smoke, said "No", and replaced the twig.

"Cub od, thed," said Araminta briskly.

She led Jimmy and Bobby down the road and in at the gate of a small, neat, semi-detached house.

"If by auntie's out, we won't get the thigs," said Araminta. "Her housekeeper's a dasty udkide woman. She doesn't like be."

She rang the bell. A woman with a dustpan in her hand and a harassed expression on her face opened the door.

"I've cub to see by auntie," said Araminta haughtily.

"Well, you can't," said the woman. "She's out."

"I want sub of the things she's got for the jumble sale," said Araminta in a calmly authoritative manner.

"Well, you won't get them out of me," said the woman, "and you won't get them out of her if she's got any sense. Off with you!"

She vanished, closing the door sharply.

"I told you she was a dasty udkide woman," said Araminta, unperturbed. "Let's go to by godbother. She lives dear, too. I'b sure she'll give us sub things for the shop. She likes be."

They trailed along to the further end of the village to Araminta's godmother's house. But that visit, too, was fruitless. Prolonged knocking and ringing at the door brought no response.

"She bust be out," said Araminta at last.

"Well, let's g-get back to the shop," said Jimmy, who was impatient to continue his financial career.

They began to walk back along the road, Araminta swinging her arms carelessly.

"I say!" said Jimmy in sudden concern. "You've lost Sinbad."

"No, I haven't," said Araminta. "I left hib at the shop. Freddy'll be lookig after hib. It's all right."

But it wasn't all right. The bend in the road showed them Freddy standing behind the wheelbarrow, still puffing away at his imaginary cigarette, and the pair of gauntlets reposing in solitary state in the wheelbarrow.

Freddy greeted them with an air of quiet pride.

"I've sold that toy monkey for one-and-six," he said.

Araminta's face darkened with anger.

"You've sode Sidbad! You daughty wicked boy!" She turned furiously on Jimmy and Bobby. "Ad you're wicked boys, too, to let hib sell Sidbad. I'll dever forgive you. Dever. I'll take your dasty old gloves and I won't give you theb till you've got Sidbad back for be!"

With that she snatched up the gauntlets and ran off down the road.

SHE SNATCHED UP THE
GAUNTLETS AND RAN OFF
DOWN THE ROAD.

The two financiers stared at each other blankly. Freddy watched them a little apprehensively.

"Well, you've made a m-mess of it, all right," said Jimmy sternly to Freddy. "Do you know who it was you sold it to?"

"No," said Freddy. "Here's the one-and-six." He put it down on the wheelbarrow and looked around, obviously anxious to extricate himself from the situation as quickly as possible. "Well, I think I'll be going now . . ."

He departed with an air of haste, recovering his aplomb sufficient as he reached the bend in the road to hold out his twig at arm's length and flick some imaginary cigarette ash from it.

"What are we goin' to do now?" said Bobby.

"We've got to get Sinbad b-back," said Jimmy.

Bobby was twisting his watch round and round his wrist – a process that always betokened deep thought.

"An' we've got to get the gauntlets back," he said at last. "Gosh! They cost three-an'-six."

"I know," said Jimmy, "but we've g-got to get Sinbad back first."

"How can we?"

"Well, someone that lives n-near must have bought him, so we've just got to g-go to every single house till we f-find the person that bought him an' buy him back."

"All right," said Bobby, adding bitterly, "If this is the sort of thing that happens to financiers, I'd rather do without a yacht."

"Oh, c-come on," said Jimmy impatiently.

A house-to-house search proved discouraging. Busy housewives shut the door in their faces before they had finished their lengthy and somewhat involved explanations. One boxed their ears. One threatened to send for the police . . . The spirits of the two financiers sank lower and lower.

"Well, the only house we've not been to is Araminta's aunt's," said Bobby at last, "an' we needn't go to that."

"Yes, we n-need," said Jimmy doggedly. "We're n-not goin' to leave a single one out."

They knocked at the door of Araminta's aunt's house. The harassed-looking woman answered their knock.

"Please, c-can we see Araminta's aunt?" said Jimmy.

With a shrug of mingled irritation and despair, the harassed-looking woman opened the sitting-room door and ushered them in. And there they stood, gaping in amazement. For Araminta sat on the sofa, surrounded by such dainties as her aunt had been able to rake up at a moment's notice – and that no mean array, consisting of grapes, biscuits, chocolates and a bottle of orangeade. On the chair next her sat Sinbad, his battered moth-eaten countenance wearing its usual sardonic leer. Araminta's aunt, a large woolly-looking woman, hovered about her – soothing, consoling, petting. As her eyes fell upon Jimmy and Bobby, the fond smile faded from her sheep-like face.

"Are *these* the boys, Araminta?" she said.

"Yes," said Araminta, through a mouthful of biscuit. "They're the dasty wicked boys that sode Sinbad."

Araminta's aunt turned her stern gaze upon Jimmy and Bobby.

"So it was *you* who played that cruel trick upon this dear little girl!" she said. "Luring her away so that that other little wretch could sell her beloved toy! It may interest you to learn that it was *I* who bought it. I recognised my darling's treasure and was determined to get to the bottom of the cruel trick that was being played on her. I hope you're ashamed of yourselves."

"But we didn't—" began Bobby.

"Tell her we d-didn't, Araminta," said Jimmy.

But Araminta was enjoying the situation and wasn't going to spoil it by any ill-advised statements of fact. By this time indeed she was convinced of the truth of her aunt's story and saw herself as its heroine.

She elevated her small nose contemptuously.

"I'll dever speak to you agaid," she said. "Dever."

"B-b-but—" began Jimmy again, and was again interrupted by Araminta's aunt.

"Don't dare to argue with me," she said. "Playing a trick like that on a child so much younger than yourself! It's disgraceful!"

But a thought had suddenly occurred to Bobby.

"Where's our gauntlets?" he said.

Araminta's aunt looked round.

"Oh, yes. Araminta quite rightly brought them here. Where are they, darling?"

"I dode know," said Araminta. Then she looked out of the window and gave a cry of delight. "Oh, look! Tinker's got theb."

They all looked out of the window. On the lawn a small puppy was romping about with the thumb of a gauntlet in his mouth. The remainder of the pair of gauntlets lay strewn about the lawn in small fragments.

"They're our g-gauntlets," said Jimmy indignantly, "an' they c-cost three-an'-six."

"It serves you right for your disgraceful behaviour," said Araminta's aunt. "I won't complain to your parents – though you richly deserve it – because I hope the loss of the gloves will be a sufficient punishment and impress the lesson on your minds. And now go home, both of you!"

"B-b-but—" began Jimmy again, then, suddenly, as it seemed, found himself standing with Bobby outside the closed front door.

They walked down the road in silence for some moments, then Bobby said:

"Well, I'm jus' about sick of bein' a financier."

"So'm I," agreed Jimmy. "Let's go b-back to bein' chimney sweeps."

Chapter 11

Christmas Waits

"Let's be waits this Christmas," said Charles, "but not jus' ordin'ry waits. Not jus' the sort that sing carols an' don't do anythin' else."

"What sort, then?" said Roger.

"Well, let's do some of the things that people used to do at Christmas in ye olden times," said Charles.

"What?" said Bill.

"Well, they did lots of things," said Charles. "They – they mummed."

"What's that?" said Roger.

"They were mummers. Mummin' means actin' old plays. They used to act a play about St George an' the Dragon at Christmas."

"Why?" said Bill.

"Oh, do shut up sayin' 'What?' an' 'Why?'" said Charles irritably. "That's what they *did*. I can't help it. I didn't make ye olden times, did I? Anyway, people always say they want a nice old-fashioned Christmas an' in a nice old-fashioned Christmas they – they mummed. I know, 'cause I read about it in a book. They acted St George an' the Dragon."

"All right," said Roger. "That's what we'll do, then."

"Where?" said Bill.

"Anywhere," snapped Charles. "We'll go round same

as waits do an' act it at people's front doors."

"When?" said Bill.

"On Christmas Eve, of course, you chump!" said Charles.

The Three Musketeers gave much time and trouble to their preparations. Charles appropriated the role of St George and Roger that of the Dragon. Bill was to be an ordinary mummer.

"You jus' dance about," explained Charles.

"How?" said Bill.

"Gosh!" said Charles in exasperation. "Don't you know what dancin' is?"

"Well, what is it?" challenged Bill.

"It's – it's sort of in between walkin' and runnin'," said Charles a little lamely. "Haven't you ever *learnt* dancin'?"

Bill considered.

"My aunt once taught me the Highland Fling," he said. "It was a long time ago, but I think I can remember it. Bits of it, anyway."

"That's all right," said Charles, mollified. "I should think the Highland Fling'd do jolly well for mumming."

At first the Three Musketeers had meant to keep the scheme secret from Jimmy and Bobby, but the preparations involved the borrowing of various domestic articles – such as saucepans and trays for St George's armour and a green curtain for the dragon – from the Manning household, and soon Jimmy and Bobby were hot on the scent. They approached the Three Musketeers with offers of help, while they were holding a meeting in the tool-shed.

"We could be m-m-mummers, too," said Jimmy.

"'Cause it's Christmas," said Bobby.

"An' the m-more the m-merrier," said Jimmy.

"That's a silly thing to say," said Roger. "It's the less

the merrier when you're anywhere about, so clear off."

"I've found out some more about Christmas in ye olden days," said Charles. "They had a boar's head."

"Well, we couldn't have that," said Roger.

"No, I s'pose we couldn't . . . An' they had a wassail."

"What's that?" said Bill.

"A sort of special Christmas drink."

"Well, we couldn't have that, either," said Roger. "We'll jus' stick to this mummin' business." Then he saw Jimmy and Bobby still hovering in the doorway and repeated: "Clear off, you two!"

The two cleared off.

"It's a rotten shame not to let us join in with them," said Bobby.

But a light was breaking over Jimmy's small countenance.

"I've g-got an idea," he said. "Let's have one of our own."

"How can we?" said Bobby. "They're doin' all the things."

"No, they're not," said Jimmy. "They're not doin' the b-boar's head or the wassail."

"Well, we can't do a boar's head."

"I d-don't see why not," said Jimmy. "Freddy Pelham's got a d-donkey's head. His father had it for a play an' gave it him afterwards, an' I know he'd lend it us."

"A donkey's not a boar."

"It's not f-far off a boar. They're both animals. I bet everyone in ye olden times couldn't get hold of a boar. I bet s-some had to put up with a donkey."

"Y-yes," said Bobby. "Then there's the wassail . . ."

"Yes," said Jimmy. "I dunno about the wassail."

It was the turn of Bobby's face to light up.

"I know!" he said. "My aunt's made some home-made ginger beer an' she's put it in bottles an' the corks keep poppin' off an' it's gettin' on her nerves an' she said I could have one if I liked."

"Good!" said Jimmy. "Ginger beer's a jolly fine wassail. I bet that's what people had in ye olden times. An' we'll keep it secret from the others. They'd only try to s-stop us if they knew."

And so affairs would have pursued their (presumably) uneventful course, had it not been for two things. One was that Archie Mould discovered the Three Musketeers' project and promptly set about forming a rival band of waits. The other was that Sir George Bellwater offered a prize of five shillings to the best band of child waits who should come to his house between the hours of six and eight on Christmas Eve.

"I bet we get it," said Roger confidently. "I bet no one else will be mumming as well as carol singing."

"What carol shall we sing?" said Bill.

"Let's sing 'Good King Wenceslas'," said Charles. "It's an easy one. It stays the same instead of going up an' down all the time like 'The First Noel'. Anyway, we won't need much of a carol with the mumming. It's the mumming that's the piece of resistance."

"What's that?" said Bill.

"Well, it's something that sheds lustre on your name," said Charles.

"Oh," said Bill.

Their preparations were by now well advanced. They had acquired all their "properties", and Bill had introduced a little variety into his "Highland Fling" by the addition of a few steps of the "Lambeth Walk" as danced by his mother's charwoman in her more light-hearted moments, with the Hoover as her partner. But they were rather worried about the Mouldies. Though they watched their activities closely, they could see no signs of preparation.

"They're not even practisin' singin' carols," said Roger.

"Well, they won't get the prize," said Bill. "Sir George'll jus' send them away."

"Pouring out the viands of his wrath upon them," said Charles a little uncertainly.

They were not quite happy about it, however. It was not Archie's wont to meet any contingency unprepared, and there was a look of sly triumph in the eyes of the Mouldies that certainly did not suggest unpreparedness.

"I 'spect they're jus' trustin' to luck," said Roger, and the others, though not quite convinced, tried to believe him.

Christmas Eve arrived . . . A few straggling bands of waits presented themselves at the front door of The Hall, sang the first verse of "Good King Wenceslas" and stood there hopefully.

Then Sir George appeared on the top step, eyes bulging with anger in a red face.

"Off with you!" he roared. "What d'you mean by coming carol-singing without learning the whole carol?"

And the waits departed hastily.

Then the Mouldies arrived, took up their stations, and – at once the air was filled with the strains of "The First Noel", sung so faultlessly, in such clear young voices that Sir George (who was rather sentimental at heart) felt the tears start to his eyes. He stood there looking down at them . . . the seraphic young faces, the young mouths opening wide as the strains poured forth. Verse after verse . . . faultless, word-perfect, not a single hesitation, not a note out of tune. As soon as they had finished, Sir George went down and shook Archie by the hand.

"Splendid, my boy! Splendid!" he said. Suddenly he noticed a wheelbarrow, piled high with holly, at the back of the group. "What's that?"

Archie bared his teeth in an ingratiating smile.

"We got some holly as we came through the wood, sir," he said, "and we're taking it round with us in case anyone's short of Christmas decorations. Would you like some, sir?"

"No, thank you, my boy," said Sir George, deeply touched, "but it's a kind thought. A very kind thought. The prize is most certainly yours, and I have some refreshments inside if—"

At that point the Three Musketeers arrived – a pale and woebegone group. The tragedy was so incredible that they still could hardly believe it. For on going to the box in the tool-shed, where they kept their "properties" for the mumming, they had found them gone. They searched tool-shed, greenhouse, garage without result. Dazed and bewildered by the catastrophe, they had decided that the only thing to do was to dispense with St George and the Dragon and just sing their carol as best they could.

Sir George looked at them coldly.

"Well, go on," he ordered. "Sing!"

Breathlessly, tunelessly, they sang the first verse of "Good King Wenceslas", then stopped.

"Off you go!" roared Sir George. "Off you go! . . . No, stop a minute and learn how a carol should be sung." He turned to Archie: "Sing your carol again, my boy, and let these boys hear how it ought to be sung."

Archie looked a little taken aback, but he did not lose his poise.

"Certainly, sir," he said, "but" – he glanced at the wheelbarrow – "let's just straighten that first. The holly's falling off and we don't want to mess up your drive."

The Mouldies crowded round the wheelbarrow, intent, apparently, on rearranging the branches of holly.

Then Sir George gave a start and stood staring in amazement at the point in the drive where a curious couple had just made their appearance. One was a small boy almost completely extinguished by a donkey's head, and the other was a small boy carrying a beer bottle. They walked slowly up to the flight of steps that led to the front door.

"What on earth—?" spluttered Sir George, when quite suddenly the cork popped off the beer bottle with a report like a pistol shot.

THEY WALKED SLOWLY UP TO THE FRONT DOOR.

Archie was startled – so startled that he lost his balance and fell backwards, dragging the wheelbarrow with him. And out of the wheelbarrow poured – not only the branches of holly, not only the St George and the Dragon equipment, but also a small portable gramophone. Sir George swooped upon it and took up the record. It was a record of "The First Noel", sung by a famous boys' choir.

The Mouldies did not stay to hear his comments. They took to their heels and fled into the dusk as fast as their legs could carry them.

Then Bobby stepped forward and made his little speech.

"Please, we've come a-wassailing," he said. "This," pointing to Jimmy, "is the boar's head, an' this," holding up his foaming bottle, "is the wassail."

Sir George burst into a roar of laughter.

"Well, that's the best I've ever heard," he said. "I think I'll count you the winning team. It's just on eight, so the competition closes now, anyway. Come along in."

Jimmy had by now managed to get his head off.

"We're all t-together," he said with a sweeping gesture that included Roger, Charles and Bill. "We're all the s-same team."

"All right," said Sir George. "Come in, all five of you, and share the supper and the prize."

For a moment the Three Musketeers were too much amazed to speak.

"Thank you, sir," said Roger at last, recovering himself with difficulty, "if we won't be too many for you."

"No, no," said Sir George, "that's all right."

Jimmy shot an expressionless glance at Roger.

"The more the m-m-merrier," he said.

Chapter 12

The Clue

"Look! There he is!" said Jimmy excitedly. "Come on!"

Every Monday morning Jimmy and Bobby hung over their garden gates, waiting for Mr Redwood to come down the road towards the station. Mr Redwood was a long, lank young man who lived at the end of the road and caught the eight-fifteen train every morning. Every morning he was in a hurry, but on Monday mornings his hurry was fast and furious. He always went away for the weekend, getting back so late on Sunday night that he overslept on Monday morning and had to run to catch his train. His run wasn't merely a hurried walk, as was the run of most of the train-catchers. It was an all-out Olympic sprint. Jimmy had invented the "Mr Redwood game" during a stretch of existence in which nothing exciting seemed to be happening, and it had added to life the zest that Jimmy demanded of it.

"Let's pretend he's a c-criminal running away," Jimmy had said, "and let's pretend to be p-p'licemen runnin' after him."

Mr Redwood, intent only on covering a quarter of a mile in two minutes, never noticed the two small boys who, every Monday morning, tore panting down the road behind him.

"What's he done today?" Bobby would ask breath-lessly.

"He's robbed the bank," Jimmy would pant in reply, or: "He's d-done a smash-an'-grab raid," or: "He's been s-smugglin'."

"Well, he's got away again," Bobby would say, as the long, lank figure was seen hurling itself over the bridge and flinging itself into the train as it moved off.

"We'll catch him one day," Jimmy would say grimly.

So real had the game become that by now the two were firmly convinced of Mr Redwood's criminal activities. His most innocent movements were watched closely and with deep suspicion by the self-appointed guardians of the peace.

"He's p-plannin' somethin' big for nex' Monday," Jimmy would say. "I could tell he was by his face. I shouldn't be surprised if he's plannin' to hold up the p-post office."

And next Monday, sure enough, Mr Redwood would come racing down the road, showing all the outward signs of a criminal fleeing from justice.

So engrossed were they by this interest that other local events passed by unnoticed. The news that a writer of thrillers called Miss Mellon had taken The Limes for the summer would normally have interested them, but, so occupied were they in trying to deduce Mr Redwood's next crime from his movements, that they did not even listen when the matter was discussed.

"I think he's goin' to r-rob the golf club," said Jimmy as the two walked back towards the village after pursuing Mr Redwood to the station. "He was up there yesterday nosing about. He l-looked jolly suspicious to me."

"I think he's goin' to steal Miss Pettigrew's hens," said

Bobby. "I saw him havin' a good look at them on Sat'day afternoon."

"Well, he stole the Vicar's rabbits last week," said Jimmy. "So I think he'll k-keep off animals for a bit. I think he's more likely to rob Mr Mince's t-till."

At this point their attention was distracted by a woman's voice upraised dramatically from a house they were passing.

"Gosh!" said Bobby, startled. "What's that?"

"Let's go 'n' see," said Jimmy.

They entered the gate of The Limes and crept up to the house, keeping well in the shelter of the hedge. From an open window on the ground floor the voice floated out again, becoming more shrill and dramatic with each word.

"My life is in danger while this murderer is in the neighbourhood. I have proof that I am the next victim on his list. Tomorrow will be too late . . . Very well! You leave me to my fate, but, let me warn you, my blood will be on your head."

The voice stopped abruptly.

Looking pale and shaken, Jimmy and Bobby crept back to the road.

"Gosh!" said Bobby again. "Who was it?"

"Dunno," said Jimmy, turning an awestruck gaze on the house. "It's someone that's goin' to be m-murdered asking someone else to come an' stop them bein' m-murdered."

"An' will they?" said Bobby anxiously.

"No," said Jimmy. "Didn't you hear? They're goin' to leave her to her f-fate with her blood on their heads . . . Well, I'm not *s'prised* he's a m-murderer as well."

"Who?" said Bobby.

"Mr Redwood, of course. Well, a man that robs a bank an' holds up p-post offices an' steals h-hens is jus' as likely to be a murderer, too. S-stands to reason. An' she said the m-murderer was in the neighbourhood an' Mr Redwood's in the neighbourhood, isn't he?"

Bobby considered this. He was apt to take a more realistic view of things than Jimmy.

"We don't axshully *know* he did those things," he said doubtfully.

"There's no proof he d-didn't," said Jimmy.

The logic of this seemed unassailable.

"Yes, I 'spect he did do 'em," said Bobby.

"An' this person his nex' v-victim was ringin' up won't help her, so *we've* got to," said Jimmy earnestly.

"How can we?" said Bobby, taken aback.

"Well, they do in b-books."

"Yes, I know," said Bobby, brightening. "Our gardener reads murder stories an' he sometimes tells me them. There's always a clue an' mos' people don't take any notice of it, but there's always one that does an' he's the one that catches the murderer."

"Well, we've got a c-clue, all right," said Jimmy, "so we'll be the ones that t-take notice of it an' catch the murderer."

"I don't see what we can do," said Bobby.

"Well, listen," said Jimmy. "I've g-got an idea. We could make a d-dummy same as Brer Fox did with the Tar Baby."

"But he didn't make it for a murderer."

"No, but we c-could. We could make a dummy an' then Mr Redwood would murder it 'stead of his nex' v-victim, an' it would s-save her life. It's a jolly good idea."

"Yes, but how can we make a dummy?" said Bobby.

"'S easy enough to make a d-dummy. You can make one of p-pillows. I made a dummy of myself once in bed to have a joke on my mother an' make her think I hadn't g-got up."

"We don't know when he's goin' to murder her."

"No, but she said tomorrow would be too late, so it m-mus' be today."

"I bet someone'll stop us if we start carryin' pillows an' things through the village. I bet my mother'll stop me before I've started."

"Well, we needn't c-carry them through the village. She'll have pillows an' things there. People in b-books aren't put off by little things like that, an' we've not got to be."

"It's all right for people in books," said Bobby. "They know it's goin' to be all right in the end."

"No, they don't," said Jimmy. "An' even if it's all right in the end, people g-get murdered while it's goin' on. Think of that story that Roger told us called Dr Jekyll an' Mr Hyde. He axshully murdered people an' I bet Mr Redwood's s-same as him."

"Gosh!" said Bobby apprehensively. "P'raps we'd better leave it alone."

"No, we can't," said Jimmy. "We've f-found the clue an' we've got to be the ones that take notice of it. If we let him m-murder her we'll be same as m-murderers ourselves."

"All right," said Bobby. "When shall we start?" He glanced at his fingerless watch. "I think it's jus' about dinner-time."

"Yes," said Jimmy, "I f-feel like that, too, so let's do it this afternoon. I don't s'pose he'll be murderin' her till this afternoon, 'cause he'll be wantin' his own dinner. They've got to eat – m-murderers have – same as other people."

"Yes, I s'pose so," said Bobby, interested by this aspect of the affair. "It mus' be nice, if a murderer's after you, to know that you're safe at meal-times."

"Well, come on," said Jimmy. "Let's m-meet here when we've had dinner."

The two met again in the road outside The Limes soon after two o'clock and cautiously inspected the premises.

"There doesn't seem to be anyone in," said Bobby.

"Let's knock at the door," said Jimmy. "We can say we've come to sweep the chimney an' then s-say we've forgotten our b-brushes or somethin'. Come on. We can't w-waste any more time."

They knocked at the front door. No one answered. They knocked at the back door. No one answered. Then Jimmy noticed that the window of a room on the ground floor was open an inch or two.

"Let's g-get in that way," he said.

Within a few minutes the two were inside a neat little study-sitting-room, the desk piled with manuscripts, a comfortable-looking wing armchair standing with its back to the bow window.

"Let's make the d-dummy quick," said Jimmy. "Mr Redwood'll be here any m-minute."

His eyes roved round the room. Armchairs and settee were all covered with gay cushions.

"We can m-make the dummy with those," he went on. "I've got some string."

They placed a small cushion on the seat of the wing chair and a long cushion leaning against the back, but, even with the string, which Jimmy tied round the imaginary neck of the dummy to form a head, it bore little semblance to the human frame.

"*Tell* you what!" said Jimmy. "Let's p-put some clothes on. It'll look all right with clothes on."

He went into the hall and returned with a long tweed coat and a hat. The coat wrapped round the cushions, and the hat perched on the "head", gave a vague, if slightly sinister, suggestion of humanity to the figure. Warming to his task, Jimmy took some newspapers from a newspaper rack and stuffed the sleeves of the coat, arranging it with an elbow resting on the arm of the chair.

"That's all right," he said at last. "It's as much l-like a person as anything could be that isn't a p-person."

"IT'S AS MUCH L-LIKE A PERSON AS ANYTHING COULD BE THAT ISN'T A P-PERSON," SAID JIMMY.

"It hasn't got a face," objected Bobby.

"I don't s'pose he'll notice that," said Jimmy. "He'll be in such a hurry he won't l-look to see if it's got a face. He'll jus' stick a dagger into it an' r-run away."

Bobby looked around nervously.

"I think we'd better go now," he said.

"All right," agreed Jimmy. "There's not much m-more we can do anyway. We've s-saved her life. Then we'll come back l-later an' look for some more clues."

Cautiously the two climbed out of the window again, leaving it an inch or two open as they had found it. At the gate they turned to survey their handiwork. The hat nestling against the corner of the wing chair and the glimpse of the tweed-coated elbow on the arm were certainly convincing.

"Gosh!" said Jimmy. "It looks jolly good. I think we ought to t-take it up as a sort of career. S-stoppin' murders, I mean. It's more excitin' than chimney-sweepin' an' the other things we've tried."

"Come on," said Bobby, his nervousness increasing. "Let's go a good way off, so's he won't know we've had anythin' to do with it."

They went down to the gate, looked cautiously up and down the road and, seeing no one, set off at a run towards the village.

It was about an hour later that a policeman, passing The Limes on his beat, noticed a suspicious-looking individual lurking among the bushes in the front garden, holding a sack. The policeman entered the garden, dragged the suspicious-looking individual from his hiding-place and demanded an explanation. Rather unexpectedly, the suspicious-looking individual gave him one.

"All right," he said. "I'm browned orf an' I'd as soon be inside as out. 'Er maid it was, wot give me the tip. Told me 'er missis 'ad a mink coat an' pearls worth I dunno wot. Said 'er missis was goin' up to London this afternoon an' she was goin' out herself as well, an' she'd leave the winder open for me. An' I've bin 'ere all afternoon, I 'ave, an' er missis 'asn't stirred a foot out of the place. Look at 'er – a-sittin' there in that there chair with 'er 'at an' coat on. Not 'ad a chance, I 'aven't, an' I'm browned orf."

The policeman stood, his hand on his captive's arm, gazing through the window at the rakish felt hat and the tweed elbow that was all he could see of the occupant of the chair. Before he had made up his mind what to do, there came the sound of voices . . .

Miss Mellon – a stout cheerful-looking woman, with grey hair and a large assortment of chins – was walking down the road with Mr Redwood. They had come back from London by the same train, and Mr Redwood was chivalrously seeing her home.

"Are you getting more used to your dictaphone?" Mr Redwood was saying.

"Just a little," said Miss Mellon. "But I haven't cured myself of shouting into it. This morning my heroine was supposed to be ringing someone up to tell them she was in danger of being murdered – I write the most frightful tripe, you know – and I found myself shouting so loud that everyone in the village must have heard me."

Mr Redwood laughed, then opened the gate of The Limes and stood aside for her to enter. Inside the gate, they stopped short, staring at the policeman and his companion. The policeman gaped at Miss Mellon, then turned to gape at the figure in the armchair. Miss Mellon's eyes followed his, and she gave a gasp of amazement.

"Good heavens!" she said. "What on earth's that?"

At that moment, Jimmy and Bobby arrived, anxious to witness the success of their scheme.

"Hi!" shouted Jimmy to the policeman. "You've got the wrong one." He pointed to Mr Redwood. "It's him that's the m-murderer."

Explanations were lengthy but not tedious. They were freely interspersed by chuckles from Mr Redwood and roars of laughter from Miss Mellon, and, in the general confusion, the suspicious-looking individual freed himself from the policeman's grasp and vanished from the landscape.

It was nearly bedtime when Jimmy and Bobby, fed and rewarded but still a little disconsolate, made their way homewards. They walked for some minutes in silence, then Bobby said:

"It was another mess-up, wasn't it?"

"Yes," agreed Jimmy dejectedly. The chuckles of Mr Redwood and the laughter of Miss Mellon still rang in his ears. "The nex' c-clue I find, I'm goin' to be one of the ones that d-don't take any notice."

Chapter 13

Cementing a Friendship

"What's this children's play that Miss Pettigrew's getting up?" said Mr Manning, taking his cup of tea from his wife.

"Some sort of fairy play," said Mrs Manning. "It's in aid of one of her pet charities. I've forgotten which. Sally, of course, is going to be the heroine."

"And who's going to be the hero?" said Mr Manning. "Roger?"

"Me?" gasped Roger, horrified. "*Me* act with a kid like that? Gosh, no!"

Mrs Manning laughed.

"No, the part was offered to Roger," she said, "but he turned it down."

"I should jolly well think so," said Roger.

"And what are you going to be, Jim?" said Mr Manning. "The villain?"

"No. I'm n-not goin' to be anythin'," said Jimmy, trying to imitate Roger's air of manly scorn but unable to prevent a note of wistfulness from creeping into his voice.

"It's the older children who're doing it," said Mrs Manning. "She only wants one small boy – for Sally's page."

"And who's the favoured small boy?" asked Mr Manning.

"She's leaving the choice to Sally. She says that if Sally chooses her own page, she can't object to him."

"She's an optimist," said Mr Manning. He looked at his sons with a twinkle. "Well, which of you is going to head that queue?"

"Huh!" said Roger contemptuously.

"Huh!" said Jimmy in a tone that was meant to imitate Roger's but that once again failed to hide the note of wistfulness.

After tea he walked slowly across the road to Bobby's. His brow was ravelled by thought, his hands plunged deeply into his pockets. A momentous decision was forming itself in his mind. Approaching Bobby's house, he gave the owl-call in such a preoccupied fashion that it sounded like the distant cooing of a dove. Bobby came down to the gate.

"There you are!" he said. "I've been waiting for you. Let's go 'n' play on that building place."

Some new houses were being erected just outside their village, and the two had adopted the spot as their playground. Scaffolding, ladders and piles of building materials afforded excellent practice as mountaineers, explorers and even navigators of ships in vast uncharted seas.

"N-no," said Jimmy. "I've got something very important to do."

"What?" said Bobby.

"I'm goin' to see Sally. I'm goin' to ask her to l-let me be her page in the play."

"Oh, Sally!" said Bobby in disgust. "I bet she won't let you be. I bet she'll choose Georgie Tallow."

"She once said she didn't l-like him," said Jimmy.

"Georgie can get round anyone he wants to," said Bobby.

Jimmy thought of Georgie – golden-haired, angel-faced, immaculately neat, with boundless self-possession and perfect manners – and heaved a deep sigh.

"I know, but I'm goin' to t-try all the same," he said.

"You're only wastin' time," said Bobby.

"I m-might not be," said Jimmy.

He hesitated for a few moments, then walked across the road to Sally's house and knocked at the door. Sally's mother answered his knock.

"P-please, c-can I speak to Sally?" said Jimmy.

"Yes, dear. Come in," said Sally's mother, ushering him into the sitting-room and leaving him there.

He stood uncertainly in the doorway. On the settee, in an attitude of easy elegance, sat Georgie, wearing a new suit and his most winsome expression. Next him sat Sally and on the table in front of them was a box of sweets, specially made for the occasion by Georgie's mother, who was as anxious as Georgie himself that he should secure the part of Sally's page. Sally was gazing at Georgie admiringly. There were times when she disliked Georgie as much as Jimmy did, but there were times when she fell a victim to his undoubted charm. She turned her eyes to Jimmy and looked at him coldly.

"Hello, Jimmy," she said. "What do you want?"

Jimmy gulped and blinked.

"I w-want to be your page," he blurted out.

Georgie broke into a peal of laughter.

"You'd look pretty comical in a page's costume," he said.

Jimmy blushed brick-red.

"I wouldn't sh-show much," he said to Sally. "I'd be standing b-behind you."

"It's very nice of you, Jimmy," said Sally with distant

"I W-WANT TO BE YOUR PAGE,"
HE BLURTED OUT.

graciousness, "but I've promised Georgie. He's really much more suitable."

"Yes, I s-suppose he is," agreed Jimmy dejectedly.

"Have a sweet if you like, Jim," said Georgie, pushing the box over to him.

"No, th-thanks," said Jimmy.

"Do go on telling me about Saturday," said Sally.

Georgie, it seemed, had been to London on Saturday to spend the day with an aunt, and Jimmy's entrance had interrupted the saga of his adventures.

"Well, we had lunch at the Ritz and then we went to a cinema," said Georgie. "We had a taxi there and the most expensive seats."

"How lovely!" said Sally. "What did you do after that?"

Jimmy continued to stand uncertainly in the doorway. They continued to ignore him.

"We went to tea at a very posh place my aunt knows," said Georgie. "A *terribly* posh place."

"What did you have for tea?" said Sally.

"Well, I've got to g-go now," said Jimmy, realising that, however long he stayed, they weren't going to take any notice of him. A wild desire to impress them came over him and he added: "I've got some s-scaffolding to climb."

But they weren't impressed even by that.

"All right. Goodbye," said Sally, without taking her eyes from Georgie. "Do go on, Georgie. What did you have for tea?"

Jimmy went down to the gate, where Bobby was waiting for him.

"Well, are you goin' to be her page?" said Bobby.

"N-no," said Jimmy. "Georgie Tallow is."

"I knew he would be," said Bobby. "Let's go to the building place now."

"All right," said Jimmy morosely. "I don't m-much care what I do."

They made their way to the building site. At the edge of it stood a half-built house covered by scaffolding.

"Let's try to get to the top this time," said Bobby.

"Yes, l-let's," said Jimmy, something of his depression vanishing at the prospect.

They began to ascend slowly and carefully.

"There's Toothy," said Bobby suddenly.

They looked down. Toothy was standing in the road, watching them disapprovingly.

"You'd better be careful, messing about like that," he

said in the tone of superiority that all Roger's friends adopted when speaking to Jimmy. "You'll be getting into trouble."

"No, we w-won't," said Jimmy, who resented the tone except from Roger, Charles and Bill.

Toothy shrugged his shoulders and went on down the road. Jimmy and Bobby continued the ascent. At the half-finished first-floor windows they paused.

"Have all the workmen gone home?" said Bobby.

"No," said Jimmy, peering down into the gloom of the interior. "There's that old d-deaf one mixin' cement in the tin bath. He hasn't s-seen us."

"He doesn't matter," said Bobby. "He doesn't mind what we do, anyway. Come on. Let's go on up."

Jimmy went on up. He wasn't climbing an inadequate piece of scaffolding. He was scaling a castle at the top of which Sally was imprisoned by kidnappers; he was climbing a mountain that no other mountaineer had ever succeeded in climbing, in order to give it Sally's name; he was drawing himself up the sheer side of a cliff to rescue Sally cut off by the tide. He stood poised for one glorious moment on top of the half-built wall; then, quite suddenly, he lost his balance and fell headlong into the bath of cement below. Miraculously unhurt, he climbed out and took to his heels, followed by Bobby and the angry shouts of the workman. At the corner of the road he stopped to draw breath and take stock of the situation.

"Gosh!" said Bobby, looking at him in horror. "You're covered with it."

"It feels awful," said Jimmy miserably. "What'll I d-do?"

"We'd better go home," said Bobby. "There's nothin'

else we can do. If it goes stiff on you, they'll never get it off. You'll have to go about lookin' like a stone statue the rest of your life."

"Gosh!" said Jimmy, appalled by this prospect.

"Yes," said Bobby, warming to his theme. "Jus' think of it! Gettin' on to buses an' goin' to school, lookin' like a stone statue. I don't s'pose you'll be able to sit down. You'll have to stand all the time like those statues of Nelson and people. I don't s'pose you'll grow, either. Statues don't."

"Oh, shut up!" said Jimmy miserably.

White and dripping, he set off homewards. The worst part of the whole situation was that he must pass Sally's house in this humiliating state. Dusk was falling, but there was enough daylight left to make him plainly visible. He tried to shrink into the hedge as he passed the house but, to his horror, he saw Sally looking out of the window, with Georgie standing just behind her. He imagined their mocking laughter, and his cheeks flamed beneath their covering of cement.

He slunk round to the back door of his own home and opened it slowly. Mrs Manning was in the kitchen. She looked at him . . . then sat down weakly on the nearest chair.

"What on earth—?" she began.

"I'm afraid I've had a b-bit of an accident," explained Jimmy apologetically.

Mrs Manning had not had eleven years' experience as a mother for nothing. She set to work on him without further questions and, by the end of half an hour, though he still looked somewhat patchy, he had lost his resemblance to an animated plaster cast.

"Now, Jimmy," she said when she had finished, giving

him a small pile of letters, "just run out to the pillar-box with those while I clear up the bathroom. I was just going out with them when you came in."

Jimmy's heart sank. He would have to pass the window of Sally's house again, exposing himself once more to her mockery.

Steeling himself to endure it, he took the letters and, cringing, cowering, head drooping, made his way towards the pillar-box.

"Jimmy!"

It was Sally, running down to him from her front door.

"Oh, Jimmy, is it really you?"

"Y-yes," said Jimmy.

"Oh, Jimmy, I'm so glad. I've been so miserable."

"Why?" said Jimmy.

"We were horrid to you, Jimmy, and you said you were going to climb scaffolding and Toothy saw you climbing scaffolding – he said he had done – and then I saw your ghost, Jimmy, and I thought you'd fallen down from the scaffold and been killed, and I felt it was our fault because we'd been so horrid to you. And I sent Georgie home and said I wouldn't have him for my page for anything because he'd laughed at you."

"Well, axshully," said Jimmy, reluctant to abandon his spectral importance, but unwilling to sail under false colours, "it wasn't so much g-ghost as c-cement."

"I don't care what it was," said Sally. "I saw you – all white and ghostly – and I was so terribly sorry I'd been horrid to you. I'm so glad you're all right, Jimmy. You will be my page now, won't you?"

"Th-thanks awfully," gasped Jimmy.

"I must go now," said Sally. "Mother's calling me. Good night, Jimmy."

"G-good night," said Jimmy.

She turned and ran indoors.

It had been a miserable small boy who had crept abjectly out of the Manning gateway to post the letters; but it was Sally's page, jaunty, swaggering, devil-may-care, who dropped them into the pillar-box.

Chapter 14

A New Career

"We still haven't decided what we're goin' to be when we g-grow up," said Jimmy.

The two were sitting on the bank of the river, idly throwing stones into the water.

"Well, we keep tryin' things," said Bobby, a little despondently. "We tried bein' chimney-sweeps an' it didn't come off, an' we tried bein' financiers an' got into a muddle . . . I say! That nearly went right to the other bank."

"It didn't quite," said Jimmy. "There! Mine went farther . . . Well, there's other things besides chimney-sweeps an' f-financiers."

"What is there? . . . That was a jolly good splash, wasn't it? I bet if any ole fish was asleep jus' there it got woke up all right."

"You prob'ly hit it right on the head. It's prob'ly feelin' m-mad . . . Well, my father knows a m-man that's a newspaper man an' it sounds jolly int'resting."

"What do they do?" said Bobby.

"They go to places free," said Jimmy. "They go to c-circuses an' pantomimes an' don't have to pay any money."

"Who lets them?" said Bobby, so startled by this information that he put down the stone he was just preparing to throw into the river.

"Newspapers do. They've got to write about the things they go to, but I b-bet that's jolly easy. I bet I w-wouldn't mind writin' about circuses an' pantomimes an' things if I could go to them free."

"What do they do when there aren't any circuses an' pantomimes?" said Bobby.

"They go to other things. There's always somethin'. Some of the other things aren't as excitin' as c-circuses an' pantomimes, but they go to them to keep in practice for circuses an' pantomimes."

"Doesn't anyone try to stop them?"

"No. They jus' say 'Press' an' p-people have to let 'em in."

"What do they say 'Press' for?"

"It's another word for a newspaper man."

"Yes," said Bobby thoughtfully. "It'd be better than chimney-sweeps an' financiers 'cause you wouldn't get in such a muddle. When shall we start?"

"Let's start n-now," said Jimmy.

"What shall we start on?"

"We'd better s-start on somethin' small and sort of w-work our way up to circuses an' pantomimes."

"Yes, but what?" said Bobby, throwing a stone so absent-mindedly that it lodged in the tree above his head.

"That was a rotten throw," said Jimmy. "Well, anythin' that's g-goin' on."

"There's nothin' goin' on jus' now."

"I know there isn't, but there m-might be soon. We've got to keep our eyes open. Come on. It's time we w-went home for tea."

Bobby consulted his watch.

"Yes, it is," he said. "I'll just have one more throw."

He took up a stone and threw it with such violence that he overbalanced and fell in the river.

"I meant to do that," he said with an air of dignity as he scrambled out. "I knew I'd have to get right into the river for a throw like that."

"Well, it wasn't a b-bad throw," admitted Jimmy, "but you've got jolly wet. Come on. Let's go home."

They walked back along the river bank.

"It's an int'restin' sort of feeling," said Bobby. "Water squirtin' through your toes."

"Yes, I know," said Jimmy. "I had it when I f-fell through the ice into the pond last winter. Will your mother be cross?"

"No," said Bobby. "She says she doesn't mind anythin' but tar."

"Mine says she doesn't mind anythin' but c-cement," said Jimmy, remembering his recent immersion.

They parted at Bobby's gate and Jimmy went home.

There were crumpets for tea and for some minutes Jimmy gave them his undivided attention, then suddenly he heard his mother mention "that tiresome affair at Miss Tankerton's" and pricked up his ears.

Miss Tankerton had only recently come to live in the village. She was a tall, thin woman with untidy hair and piercing eyes who considered it her mission in life to raise the standard of culture in whatever place she happened to find herself. Already she had organised lectures on "New Art", "The Early Civilisation of Egypt", and "Ceramic Discoveries of the Third Century". They were sparsely attended, but Miss Tankerton was an expert in harassing her acquaintances into attendance and allowing no excuses whatsoever.

"What is it at Miss Tankerton's?" said Jimmy.

"A lecture, dear," said Mrs Manning. "Tomorrow afternoon. On Chinese Art. Someone who's just back from China and has brought a lot of exhibits with him. I don't want to go, but I'm afraid I shall have to. She came round last night, and I had to promise I'd be there."

"Oh," said Jimmy.

He finished his tea as quickly as he could and ran across the road to Bobby. Bobby came out at the sound of the owl-call. He was wearing his best suit, because his other suit was drying before the kitchen fire.

"I s-say, Bobby," said Jimmy excitedly, "there's somethin' at Miss Tankerton's tomorrow. A l-lecture on Chinese Art. Let's g-go to that."

"They wouldn't let children in," said Bobby. "They don't."

"Yes, but this m-man my father knows said somethin' about that. He said that sometimes people don't want to let him go into p-places but he always goes. He said you can always find a w-way of getting into them. L-let's find a way of getting into them, same as real ones do. It'll be good p-practice for bein' the Press."

"All right," said Bobby.

But the next morning Bobby was in bed with a streaming cold. Jimmy was tempted to give up his enterprise, then decided that it might be a long time before such a chance came his way again and that his whole future might suffer in consequence.

The lecture was to begin at five o'clock, and at half-past four Jimmy set out as unostentatiously as possible for Miss Tankerton's house. Looking through the drawing-room window, he noticed that the curtains were drawn across the recess formed by the big bay and that just inside the curtains was a small statue on a stand. The curtained recess seemed an ideal hiding-place. The window was slightly open, and Jimmy was soon inside. Peeping through the curtains he saw the table at which the lecturer was to sit and, facing it, rows of empty chairs awaiting the audience. Then he considered his own arrangements. He had made his simple preparations – a crumpled piece of paper and a stubby pencil in one pocket, and in the other a toffee apple in case he should feel the need of sustenance. The statue was rather in his way, so he moved the stand to one side and took his seat in an armchair that was conveniently placed near the centre. Then, taking paper and pencil from his pocket, he waited.

He heard the murmur of conversation and the movement of chairs as the audience took their places . . . the high-pitched, neighing voice of Miss Tankerton as she introduced the lecturer . . . the deep droning voice of the lecturer . . .

Jimmy sat there, frowning, the stubby pencil poised over the crumpled piece of paper . . . He couldn't make head or tail of it. Words like "Han Dynasty" . . . "Chou Dynasty" . . . "Yuan Dynasty" . . . "Kuan-yins" . . . "Tiao Ch'i" . . . "Huan Te" . . . floated round him. He couldn't spell them and he didn't know what they meant. Gradually he gave up the unequal struggle, abandoning himself to mingled boredom and apprehension. Retreat was impossible, as any movement might betray his presence. He must just wait till the end and escape under cover of the applause. Then he remembered his toffee apple and his spirits rose. Taking it out of his pocket and assuming as comfortable position on his armchair as possible, he began to lick it with slow enjoyment. The voice of the lecturer droned on . . . then reached what was evidently some sort of climax.

"At the risk of seeming somewhat theatrical, I have reserved a surprise for the end of my lecture. I did not want to show you this exquisite little figure till I had explained the various aspects of this particular form of art and told you what to look for in it. This figure belongs to one of the later dynasties and is, I think, the most beautiful I have ever seen. Draw the curtains, please."

Someone drew the curtains, revealing to the startled gaze of the audience a small boy, tousled and grubby, seated in an inelegant attitude on an armchair – heels on the edge of the seat, shoulders hunched against jointure

SOMEONE DREW THE CURTAINS, REVEALING TO THE STARTLED GAZE OF THE AUDIENCE A SMALL BOY, TOUSLED AND GRUBBY.

of seat and back – licking a toffee apple. The statue was hidden by the curtain.

The lecturer did not immediately turn to look at his exhibit. He continued to read from his notes.

"The delicacy and beauty of this figure are obvious to the most casual observer. The points I wish to press home—"

The expressions on the faces of his audience told him that all was not well. He turned to the alcove – and his mouth dropped open.

"Press home . . ." he repeated automatically.

Jimmy sat up and looked about him, panic-stricken.

"Press home . . ." murmured the lecturer again faintly, as if hypnotised by the amazing sight.

"All r-right," said Jimmy apologetically, gathering up his cap and swallowing what was left of his toffee apple. "I'm j-jus' g-goin'."

Chapter 15

The Birthday Present

Jimmy and Bobby walked down the road towards the village. An air of heavy responsibility hung over them. It was Mrs Manning's birthday and Jimmy, with Bobby's assistance, was going to buy a birthday present for her. The responsibility would have been heavy enough in any case, but it was made heavier by the fact that Roger was in bed with a cold and had deputed Jimmy to buy his, Roger's, present as well as his own. They were going to have the birthday tea in Roger's bedroom and give Mrs Manning the presents when she cut the cake. In his small, hot palm Jimmy carried four sixpences, one shilling, one threepenny piece, five pennies and eight halfpennies.

"Four shillings!" he said. "Gosh! What a lot of money! I'll have to be jolly careful. I hope there aren't any of those smash an' g-grab people about."

At first Bobby was inclined to discuss the details of a paper chase that the two had planned for next Saturday, but Jimmy sternly brought him back to the matter in hand.

"We've not got to think of anythin' else but this birthday present," he said. "It's a matter of life an' d-death till we've got it. Roger said I was too much of a k-kid to do it prop'ly an' I've got to show him I'm not."

Four shillings had seemed unbounded wealth, but a close inspection of the several shop windows slightly modified that view.

"If I'd got ten shillings," said Jimmy, "I could get that blue vase from Roger an' that c-case with note-paper an' envelopes from m-me."

"Well, you haven't," said Bobby, "so it's no good goin' on looking at things. Let's go to Mr Prosser's. He has cheap things."

They went to Mr Prosser's shop and stood, flattening their noses against the window. There were several articles that could be purchased with the sum of money at Jimmy's disposal. There was a broken birdcage, an oil lamp with a once-pink shade, a straw hat with a portion of the brim missing, a pair of motorcycle goggles, a mutilated cricket pad, a saddle with the stuffing coming out, the top part of a basket chair, an Indian club, a tarnished spirit kettle and a couple of croquet mallets.

"You can see that birdcage's *been* a good one," said Bobby judicially. "You could mend that place where the bars are broke with a bit of string."

"But she hasn't got a b-bird," objected Jimmy.

"She could keep her knitting or something in it," said Bobby vaguely. "An' look at those goggles. There's nothing wrong with them."

"She hasn't got a m-motorcycle," said Jimmy.

"You could paint the glasses blue an' she could use them for sunglasses," said Bobby. "An' look at that Indian club thing. She could use it for a rolling pin if she chopped a bit off one end."

"Oh, shut up!" said Jimmy. "We can't give her old r-rubbish like that. Not for a *birthday* present."

At that moment they saw Georgie Tallow, spruce and

immaculate as usual, coming down the street towards them. Jimmy gave him a guarded look. He was prepared for hostilities from Georgie. Miss Pettigrew's play had been performed the night before, and Jimmy had played his insignificant part of Sally's page – standing behind her chair and carrying her train – without incident, while Georgie had sat in the front row with his mother, wearing his most angelic expression. But Jimmy had a vague idea that Georgie wasn't going to let it stop at that.

"Hello," said Georgie. "You out shopping?"

"Yes," said Jimmy, disarmed by the friendliness of Georgie's tone. "I'm tryin' to f-find a birthday present for my mother. I've to g-get one for her from Roger, too, 'cause he's got a cold. I've g-got four shillings, but—"

He ended the sentence with a sigh and a speculative glance at a butterfly net with several large holes in the netting.

"You could mend them," said Bobby, following the direction of Jimmy's gaze.

"She doesn't c-catch butterflies," said Jimmy, and added: "I wish we'd even got f-five-an'-six. You can get things for five-an'-six that you c-can't for four shillings."

"I'm awfully sorry," said Georgie. "I just haven't any money at all or I'd lend you some."

With that he proceeded on his way down the street.

"That was jolly n-nice of him," said Jimmy, deeply touched. "I thought he'd have been m-mad with me for bein' Sally's page. Well, come on. We can't waste any more time here."

Bobby was loath to leave the fascinations of Mr Prosser's shop.

"That meat safe's got quite a lot of the wire stuff left

on," he said, "and there's only a bit of the head broke off that statue."

"Oh, come on," said Jimmy again impatiently. "She's g-got a meat safe an' she doesn't want a statue. L-let's look somewhere else."

They flattened their noses against a few more windows, but by the end of a quarter of an hour the situation was unchanged except that Georgie Tallow was again approaching them. He carried a plant pot containing a small hydrangea with a pinkish-bluish bloom.

"Look!" he said. "I don't know if you'd like this. You can have it for four shillings. They cost much more than that in the shops. You could give it her from you and Roger together."

The two looked at the plant with eager interest.

"Gosh!" said Jimmy. "It's l-lovely. An' she likes flowers. They l-last a long time, don't they?"

"Oh, yes," said Georgie. "If you keep them watered they last indefinitely. You can put them out into the garden when they're too big for the pot. Would you like it?"

"Yes. Th-thanks awfully," said Jimmy.

He poured the moist, hot coins into Georgie's hand and took the plant pot carefully in his arms.

"Well, goodbye," said Georgie. "Glad I've been able to help."

With that he went on down the village street and the two set off homewards.

"I know she'll l-like it," said Jimmy, "an' I bet Roger'll be pleased."

In his eagerness to get home and show the plant to Roger, however, he did not see a large stone that lay in the middle of the road, and fell headlong. The plant pot was unbroken, the bloom uninjured, but Jimmy,

HE POURED THE MOIST, HOT COINS INTO GEORGIE'S HAND AND
TOOK THE PLANT POT CAREFULLY IN HIS ARMS.

scrambling to his feet, stood and gazed at them with
dawning horror. The trick that Georgie had played on
him was now revealed in all its iniquity. For the "plant"
was no plant at all. It was a single hydrangea bloom, cut
from some larger plant and stuck into the soil in the pot
to look as if it grew from it.

"It's a s-s-swindle!" said Jimmy furiously.

"Gosh!" gasped Bobby. "Let's go after him an' get our
money back."

"No," said Jimmy. "There isn't time. He'll be h-hiding
somewhere where we can't find him an' he'll have
h-hidden the money somewhere. Gosh! All Roger's
money gone on that old s-stalk!"

"Well, what'll we do?" said Bobby.

Jimmy considered. His small face was tense and set.

"We'll have to g-get some more money," he said at last.

"How?" said Bobby blankly.

"We'll have to earn it," said Jimmy. "There m-mus' be ways of earnin' money . . . C-come on. Let's look at the notices in the p-post office window."

The post office window offered a rich choice of articles wanted and for sale, missing pets, a tricycle that wanted to be exchanged for an incubator, an incubator that wanted to be exchanged for a sewing machine, a sewing machine that wanted to be exchanged for an electric cleaner.

"Look!" said Jimmy excitedly, pointing to one of the notices. "'Wanted: Boy of fourteen for garden work'."

"We're not fourteen," objected Bobby. "We're seven."

"Yes, but we're t-two boys of seven," said Jimmy, "an' that makes us one b-boy of fourteen. It's a house called Crossways at Eckton. C-come on."

"Yes, but—" began Bobby.

"Oh, s-stop arguin'," said Jimmy impatiently. "Do you want to be a b-boy of fourteen with me or d-don't you?"

"All right," said Bobby resignedly.

The two made their way across the fields to Eckton – a village about three miles away – and presented themselves at the front door of Crossways. It was a large square house with steps up to the front door and an air of rather weary dignity. Repeated knocking and ringing produced no answer.

"They mus' be out," said Jimmy. "Come on. L-let's start bein' a garden boy. If they come back an' find us bein' a g-good one, they won't stop us."

They wandered round to the back of the house and

down to the bottom of a straggling, tree-surrounded garden.

Bobby's eye fell on a large rubbish heap under one of the trees, and his air of gloom left him.

"Let's have a bonfire," he said. "That's the mos' excitin' part of gardenin'."

"All right," said Jimmy. "We'll try 'n' find something that l-lights easy."

They began to turn over the pile of rubbish. In the middle were some bundles of small paper leaflets.

"I'm goin' to bag those for the paper chase," said Bobby, putting them on one side.

"I wish you'd shut up about the ole p-paper chase," said Jimmy irritably. "I tell you it's a m-matter of life an' death till we've got this b-birthday present."

They found a box of matches and some old newspapers in the tool-shed and collected some twigs from beneath the trees.

It was just as they were for the tenth time coaxing a reluctant and obviously expiring flame, a sea of spent matches about their feet, that they raised their blackened faces to find a young man standing watching them. He was a vague-looking, untidy young man with a thin, pleasant face.

"Hello," he said.

"Hello," said Jimmy.

"Who are you?" said the young man.

"We're the g-garden boy," said Jimmy.

"You hardly look old enough," said the young man.

"Well, we're two b-boys of seven an' that makes us one boy of f-fourteen," said Jimmy.

"I see," said the young man, as if completely satisfied by the explanation.

"Do you l-live here?" said Jimmy.

"No," said the young man. "My aunt lives here and I'm staying with her. It's a depressing visit. She has a bee in her bonnet about tobacco in all its forms, and she deluges every house in the neighbourhood with pamphlets on the subject. She's got hold of a dreadful little model of perfection, called Georgie Tallow, who lives somewhere near. Do you know him?"

"Yes, we d-do," said Jimmy bitterly.

"I see you share my opinion of him. Well, she sends him round to every house within reach, distributing her pamphlets. He makes quite a good thing out of it, I believe, and – oh, here they are!"

An elderly lady of upright build and unprepossessing appearance was coming to them across the lawn, accompanied by George Tallow.

"Who are those children?" said the lady majestically.

"They're a boy of fourteen," said the young man.

"We're s-seven each an' f-fourteen altogether," explained Jimmy.

But the lady had lost interest in them. She was gazing with incredulity and dawning wrath at the little piles of pamphlets sodden with damp, encrusted with leaves and weeds, that Bobby had salvaged and put on one side. For the first time Jimmy noticed their titles: *Nicotine the Poisoner* . . . *Suicide by Smoke* . . . *The Weed that Kills* . . . It was obvious what had happened. Georgie, in order to save himself trouble, had "distributed" the pamphlets by the simple means of thrusting them into the heart of the rubbish heap, taking for granted that they would be destroyed without trace or question. They all turned to look at him. The angelic smile had frozen on his face and he was looking wildly round for escape.

"So *this* is how you performed your trust!" said the lady sternly. "*This* is how—"

But Georgie was already vanishing through a convenient hole in the hedge.

The lady turned her gaze upon Jimmy and Bobby.

"I was going to give that wretched boy ten shillings for helping me with my work," she said, "but I'll give it to you, instead. I see by the way you have saved my little pamphlets that you realise the importance of the work I am engaged on."

"Th-thanks awfully," said Jimmy, taking the ten-shilling note she held out to him.

"And now perhaps you'll—"

But Jimmy and Bobby had followed Georgie's example and, still murmuring thanks, were vanishing through the hole in the hedge.

"I think they're simply lovely, children," said Mrs Manning. "I adore the vase, and the note-paper's just what I needed."

They were sitting round the dining-room table (Roger was so much better that he had been allowed to get up) and Mrs Manning had just cut the cake – a pink iced cake with three and a half candles on because Mrs Manning was thirty-six.

"I can't think how you did it on the money, Jimmy," said Roger with an unwilling note of admiration in his voice.

Jimmy's mind went over the events of the afternoon.

"Well, I did s-stretch it a bit," he said.

Chapter 16

The Inventors

"We've simply *got* to decide what we're goin' to be when we're g-grown-up," said Jimmy. "We're gettin' older an' older every day an' we haven't d-decided yet."

The two were sitting on the top rung of a stile by the roadside, gazing idly at the empty road.

"Well, we've tried things," said Bobby. "We've tried bein' chimney-sweeps an' financiers an' newspaper men an' we only got into muddles."

"Yes, but there's other things," said Jimmy. "There mus' be somethin' we wouldn't get into m-muddles over."

"There's – there's sailors," said Bobby vaguely.

"I don't want to be a s-sailor," said Jimmy. "I went to sea once an' it gave me the most awful f-feeling."

"Well, there's soldiers."

"You've got to have a gun to be a s-soldier," said Jimmy, "an' I bet my father'd take mine away every time it b-broke anything."

"There mus' be *somethin*'," said Bobby.

"Yes, there mus'," said Jimmy. "Let's think."

"All right," said Bobby.

They sat in silence for some minutes – elbows on knees, hands on chins, faces set and tense. Gradually Jimmy's face lightened.

"I've got a s-sort of idea," he said.

"What?" said Bobby.

"We could be inventors."

"Yes, that's a jolly good idea," said Bobby.

"I dunno." Jimmy's face had clouded over again. "When you come to think of it, everything's *b-been* invented."

"Yes, it does seem to 've been," agreed Bobby, "but there mus'—"

They broke off the discussion to watch a group of land workers who were coming down the road. The land workers consisted chiefly of students and office workers, who were spending their holiday assisting the local farmers and were housed in an agricultural camp just outside the village.

"My back's half-broken," one of them said as they passed the stile. "There'd be a fortune for anyone who invented something to collect those darned potatoes when the plough's turned them up."

Jimmy and Bobby stared after them open-mouthed, then looked at each other.

"*That's* what we'll invent," said Jimmy in a tone of finality. "We'll invent something to p-pick up potatoes."

Bobby considered, turning his watch round and round his wrist.

"What sort of a thing?" he said at last.

Jimmy knit his brows.

"I know!" he said. "We'll have something like that s-scooper thing they use for mendin' roads. It'll be a jolly good invention. It'll make us f-famous for the rest of our lives."

"Yes, but how will it pick up potatoes?" said Bobby.

"Well," said Jimmy slowly, "it'll have to have sort of

holes in to let out the soil an' k-keep in the potatoes."

"Sounds a bit difficult," said Bobby.

"Well, everything's d-difficult," said Jimmy. "You've not got to mind a bit of d-difficultness if you want to be an inventor. Come on. Let's go home an' see if we can f-find anythin' that'll do for it."

They got down from the stile and walked along the road, still discussing the affair.

"I still don't see how it's goin' to work," said Bobby.

"We'll have to try it d-diff'rent ways till we get it r-right," explained Jimmy a little irritably. "I bet that's what real inventors do. I 'spect the man that invented gas had a lot of sh-shots before he got it right."

They were passing Toothy's house and stopped by tacit consent to look through the hedge into the garden to see if anything interesting was going on. The garden was empty, but right at the bottom beneath a tree was a heap of leaf mould; by it stood a bucket, rusted and worn into holes, that had obviously been turned out as of no further use in the house.

"I *say*!" said Jimmy in sudden excitement. "We could 'speriment with that. If we got a rope we could fix the b-bucket over that branch an' try scoopin' out the leaf mould. It'd be a sort of s-start. Come on. Let's see if there's any rope in their tool-shed."

They crept through the hedge and carried out a cautious reconnoitring expedition in the tool-shed. A length of rope hung on a hook on the wall.

"Let's b-borrow it," said Jimmy. "Toothy's mother won't mind. She never minds anything. We can p-put it back afterwards."

"Perhaps we ought to go an' ask her," said Bobby nervously.

They looked towards the house and for the first time became aware of signs of unusual activity.

"Gosh!" said Jimmy. "I b'lieve Roger's there. An' Charles an' Bill . . . Let's go an' see what's happenin'."

"They'll be mad with us if we go bargin' in," Bobby warned him.

"We'll creep up so's they won't know we're there. We'll creep up same as Red Indians. C-come on."

Crawling on all fours, keeping to the shade of the hedge, they made their way to the house and then stood gazing through the open kitchen door. Mrs Forrester (Toothy's mother) was there, with Toothy, Roger, Charles and Bill. The kitchen was in a state of wild confusion – the contents of every drawer and cupboard overflowing on to table and floor. The forms of Toothy, Roger, Charles and Bill could be seen fitfully, as they dived into various receptacles, scattering oddments of all kinds around them, while Toothy's mother watched with an air of serene detachment, and Selina, Toothy's two-year-old sister, sat on the floor, gurgling with delight and putting things into her mouth.

"What's the m-matter?" said Jimmy, so interested in the situation that he forgot his Red Indian role.

"I've lost something, dear," said Mrs Forrester placidly, "and they're helping me look for it."

Nothing ever disturbed Mrs Forrester's placidity. She was a vague, good-tempered little woman who spent most of her life hunting for things she had lost and singing to herself as she did so. Only her choice of songs betrayed her state of mind. When she was happy she sang mournful little songs like "Just a Song at Twilight" or "Poor Old Joe". When she was depressed she sang gay little songs like "A Bicycle Made for Two" and "D'you ken John Peel?"

She broke into "D'you ken John Peel?" now as she emptied a tin containing string, nails, sealing-wax, pen-nibs, gas-lighters, flints, matches, nutmegs, clothes-pegs and various other objects on to the dresser, from which they fell to the floor in a sort of cascade. Selina put a stick of sealing-wax into her mouth, taking out an india-rubber and a moth-ball to make room for it.

"What is it you've lost?" said Bobby.

"The petrol coupons, dear," said Mrs Forrester, break-ing off her song. "You see, my husband's been away on business for a week and he told me to go to the post office and get the new issue of petrol coupons, to be ready when he came back, so I did, and I put them away very carefully, but I don't remember where, and he's coming home this afternoon and they're the first things he'll ask for and – well, we're looking for them. We feel that it would be nice to find them before he knows we've lost them."

Jimmy thought of Mr Forrester and understood the feeling. Mr Forrester was a large irascible man with a loud voice that, on the slightest provocation, would break into a bellow of rage, audible from one end of the village to the other. He disliked children, except his own (to whom he had had of necessity to resign himself), and Toothy's friends generally fled in terror at his approach. The only person who was not frightened of him was his wife, and even she found him a little tiring.

"I do wish you could remember where you put them, Mother," said Toothy.

Toothy was burrowing in a confused welter of sauce-pans at the bottom of a cupboard, Roger was head and shoulders in a rag bag that hung behind the kitchen door, Charles and Bill were emptying the paper salvage sack into the sink, prior to a thorough examination of its contents.

"Well, I know it was a safe place," said Mrs Forrester with a touch of pride in her gentle voice, "because I always put things away in safe places. Herbert dear (Toothy in his home circle was Herbert), don't let Selina eat that fire-lighter. It's the last one we've got. Put it right out of her way. In the teapot or somewhere." Suddenly she clapped her hand to her head. "I *remember* where I put them now. I put them in that silver teapot my grandmother left me."

"Good!" cried six eager voices. "Where's the teapot?"

The radiance of Mrs Forrester's countenance clouded over.

"I don't know," she said. "I put that away in a safe place, too."

"But where, Mother?" said Toothy desperately.

"I haven't any idea," said Mrs Forrester.

"It used to be on the sideboard."

"I know, dear, but it isn't now. You remember Aunt Letty came over to see us on Sunday, and she'd been furious when Grandmother left me the teapot and it always put her into a bad temper to see it, so I thought I'd hide it. I've no idea where I hid it, but she's very nosy, you know, and I remember thinking: 'Well, even Letty will never find it here'."

"Can't you remember anything about it?" said Roger, coming out of the rag bag and removing a few wisps of stray sheeting from his mouth.

"No, dear," said Mrs Forrester serenely. "I might have put it anywhere. I do put things in the oddest places. I once hid the ration books in the coal-shed and didn't find them for months, and I once hid my diamond ring in the flour bin . . ."

Humming "You Should See Me Dance the Polka", she opened the clothes-boiler and began to ferret among the heterogeneous collection of domestic articles that had taken refuge there.

"Come on," said Roger. "I'm going to try the coal-shed."

"Where shall I l-look?" said Jimmy.

Roger seemed to realise Jimmy's presence for the first time.

"Nowhere," he said severely, "and clear off. We don't want you here."

He advanced so threateningly upon Jimmy and Bobby as he spoke that they turned and fled down to the bottom of the garden again.

"Let's g-get on with our invention," said Jimmy, "an' stop bothering about the ole teapot. Come on . . . There's two pieces of rope here. That's all right. Now we'll fasten this end of the rope to the handle of the bucket an' take the other end over this branch. Then we'll fasten the other rope to this hole so's you can pull it along."

"Well, how does it work?" said Bobby.

"Gosh! Haven't you any sense?" said Jimmy sternly. "Listen! You p-pull it along the ground with your rope so's it'll pick up potatoes an' then I'll pull it up by my rope that's over the branch an' it'll come up with the potatoes in. I don't see why it s-shouldn't, anyway. Let's try."

They tried, with no results but the dislodging of a neg-ligible amount of leaf mould. Then suddenly a series of ferocious bellows filled the air. It was evident that Mr Forrester had returned to discover the loss of his petrol coupons and the chaos of his home. There was a rush of three terror-stricken boys to the gate – Roger and Bill streaked with coal, Charles coated with flour.

"Gosh!" gasped Bobby. "Let's go, too."

"We c-can't," said Jimmy. "It's too l-late. He'd see us."

For the large form of Mr Forrester had appeared at the door, cutting off their retreat.

"Let's f-freeze," went on Jimmy. "L-like animals. If we d-don't move p'raps he'll think we're part of the l-landscape."

But a fresh bellow of rage showed them that Mr Forrester had seen them and had not mistaken them for part of the landscape. He plunged down the garden to the heap of leaf mould and stood looking at the strange contraption that Jimmy had fixed up. Threatening rumbles of rage issued from his large form.

"What in Heaven's name is the meaning of this?" he roared at last.

"It's an inv-vention," said Jimmy, standing his ground in spite of his terror.

Mr Forrester waved his arms, inarticulate with fury.

"Messing up the place . . . tramping about . . . trespassing! An *invention*? What d'you mean by an invention, you young hooligans?"

Bobby's courage had deserted him and he was making for the gate, without even stopping to disentangle himself from his rope and bucket. They trailed after him, dislodging yet more of the leaf mould, revealing a tarnished silver teapot and jerking open the lid to show a book of brand new petrol coupons inside . . .

Jimmy looked at it, and a smile of triumph spread slowly over his countenance.

"An invention for finding l-l-lost things," he said.

Chapter 17

Minding the Baby

"It's goin' to spoil the whole afternoon," said Jimmy indignantly. "You can't do anythin' int'restin' with a b-baby."

"I don't want to do anything interesting with it," said Mrs Manning, "and I hope you won't try. I just want you to walk quietly down the road with it."

"But Bobby an' me were goin' exploring in the w-wood," protested Jimmy.

"I can't help that, dear," said Mrs Manning. "You must just give up this one afternoon to your little cousin."

Jimmy threw a baleful glance at the occupant of the pram.

"It's never d-done anythin' to me," he said bitterly, "'cept pull my hair an' yell at me an' scratch my f-face, so I don't see why I should waste a whole afternoon out of my l-life on it. Why can't it stay in the garden in its pram? It did this morning."

"Auntie Jean likes him to go out in the afternoon," said Mrs Manning. "It's better for him than staying in the garden all day. She can't take him herself because she has a headache, and I have to stay in for the laundry. I'm surprised at you, making a fuss about a little thing like this, Jimmy."

Jimmy sighed. Auntie Jean was Mrs Manning's sister,

who had come on a week's visit with her baby. Jimmy was finding the week a long one. Not only was he always getting into trouble for waking the baby, but he was expected to endure without retaliation the baby's assaults on his person and destruction of his property.

"All right," he said bitterly. "I s'pose I'll have to, but I hope it'll remember all its life that it's stopped the only chance we might ever g-get of 'splorin' that wood."

"Of course it won't," said Mrs Manning. "And don't be so ridiculous, Jimmy. What's to prevent you going to the wood tomorrow?"

"Anythin'," said Jimmy. "The end of the world might come. It's g-got to come sometime, an' I've always had a f-feelin' it'd come when I wanted to d-do somethin' special . . . All right," seeing that his mother's patience was rapidly nearing exhaustion, "I'll take it."

"Wheel it carefully," said Mrs Manning, "and bring him back about teatime. There's a cold wind, so keep the cover right over him as it is now. Goodbye."

"Goodbye," said Jimmy in a voice that was hoarse with self-pity.

Slowly, gloomily, he wheeled the pram out of the gate and across the road to Bobby's house. Bobby came out in answer to his owl-call, carrying a large stick with which he intended to clear a path through the more impenetrable parts of the wood. His mouth dropped open in horror when he saw Jimmy.

"Gosh! What on earth have you got *that* for?" he said.

"I can't come 'splorin' with you," said Jimmy dejectedly. "I've got to take this r-rotten ole baby out. You'd better g-go without me."

But Bobby was not capable of such a betrayal.

"No," he said, putting down his stick. "I'll go with you,

but it's a shame. There ought to be laws about babies."

"Come on, then," said Jimmy. "We'll jus' walk it up an' down the road till teatime."

They pushed the pram slowly down the road. Sandy accompanied them, walking dejectedly at their heels, as if he shared their humiliation.

"Can't we play a game with it?" suggested Bobby. "You can't see its face. It might be anything."

"No," said Jimmy, clinging to his martyrdom. "It'd spoil any g-game. It's a rotten baby." He stopped and peeped under the hood. "It's asleep now. It seems to go on sleepin' on an' on an' on. Doesn't seem to know what's n-night an' what's day. I think there's s-somethin' wrong with it."

THEY PUSHED THE PRAM SLOWLY DOWN THE ROAD.

"They're all like that," said Bobby. "My cousin once had one."

"Well, I'm g-glad it is asleep," said Jimmy. "It's jolly s-savage when it's awake. I've still got a scratch on my nose it did yesterday. An' its m-manners are awful. Gosh! The way it *eats*. I'd get into a row all right if I ate like that, but it can squirt food all over the place an' they jus' say it's sweet. *Sweet!* Huh!"

So absorbed was Jimmy by his grievances that he failed at first to see Araminta Palmer coming down the road, pushing her dolls' pram.

"Gosh!" he groaned when he saw her. "There's Araminta Palmer. An' I bet she's got that awful c-cat in that pram."

For the Palmers possessed a ginger cat, called Marigold, who not only allowed itself to be dressed in dolls' clothes and taken out in Araminta's dolls' pram, but seemed to enjoy the process.

"Where are you goig?" said Araminta, stopping in the middle of the road.

"Mind your own b-business," said Jimmy, who was in no mood to dally with Araminta.

"I'll cub with you," said Araminta, turning her pram round.

The movement showed the yellow face of Marigold reposing on a lace-trimmed pillow, wearing a red knitted cap, tied under its chin by blue ribbons.

Araminta began to walk down the road with them. Sandy growled softly and Marigold raised her head to spit languidly from the pram, but they knew each other too well to show much interest. Marigold was one of the cats who didn't run away from Sandy, and Sandy never quite knew what to make of cats who didn't run away from him.

"That's a dice prab," said Araminta, looking at the pram that Jimmy was wheeling.

Jimmy ignored the remark. There was a silence during which Araminta's countenance settled into lines of resolution.

"I'll swop you," she said abruptly.

"Swop what?" snapped Jimmy.

"I'll swop by prab for yours," said Araminta. "Barigold's gettig too big for this ad you could get the baby idto it dicely, ad it wouldn't be so heavy to push. I want a big prab like that for Barigold."

"Well, you can't have it," said Jimmy, "so go away."

"Why?"

"'Cause we don't w-want you."

"I dode want you, either," said Araminta serenely, "ad I'b goig away, adyway. But" – again the look of resolution tightened her small features – "I'b goig to have a big prab like that for Barigold. I'b *goig* to."

With that she turned her pram round again and proceeded on her way down the road, pursued by a parting growl from Sandy. Jimmy and Bobby also went on their way, looking back as they went, to eject their tongues in an ungentlemanly fashion at her retreating figure and almost colliding with a small boy who was coming round the bend in the road. He was in the same form as Jimmy and Bobby at school and bore the name of Peregrin Pollitt. He carried a newspaper under his arm and there was an expression of anxiety – almost of anguish – on his face.

"Hello," said Jimmy and Bobby.

"Hello," said Peregrin.

He looked from Jimmy and Bobby to the pram, and hope seemed to shine suddenly through the gloom of his countenance.

"I say! Lend me yours, will you?" he said persuasively. "Just till I've found mine."

"L-lend you our what?" said Jimmy.

"Your baby."

"Why?" said Jimmy, startled. "What do you want it for?"

"Well, you see, I've lost mine," said Peregrin. "You see, a friend of my mother's stayin' at our house with her baby an' this afternoon my mother sent me down to the post office to fetch the newspaper 'cause it hadn't come an' she told me to take the baby out in its pram to make it go to sleep 'cause it goes to sleep better when it's movin' about an' I left it outside the post office while I went in to get the newspaper an' – an'—"

He stopped and the look of horror returned to his face.

"Yes?" said Jimmy and Bobby breathlessly.

"Well, when I got home I found that I hadn't got the pram. I'd forgot to bring it back from the post office, so I went back for it an' – it wasn't there."

"Gosh!" said Jimmy.

"Wasn't your mother mad?" said Bobby.

"She doesn't know yet," said Peregrin. "She'd told me to leave it in the garden when I came back, so I want one to leave in the garden till I've found ours to stop her makin' a fuss." He looked at the pram again. "They've both got blue covers with white rabbits. She'll never know the difference."

Jimmy considered. The arrangement seemed to solve his problems. The pram would be safe in Peregrin's garden, and he and Bobby would have their long-projected afternoon of exploring the woods.

"All right," he said at last, "if you'll promise to t-take care of it."

"'Course I will," said Peregrin.

The transaction thus settled to the satisfaction of all parties, Jimmy handed the pram over to Peregrin and set off with Bobby for the woods.

The afternoon surpassed their highest expectations. They found a fox's hole, an owl's nest and distinct traces of an aboriginal tribe of bushmen, whose presence in the wood Jimmy had long suspected, while Sandy chased imaginary rabbits and worried sticks. They could hardly believe that it was four o'clock when the four notes floated out from the church tower.

"Gosh," said Jimmy. "It's teatime. We'd better go an' c'lect that baby now."

Tired, dirty, happy, they made their way down to Peregrin's house. Peregrin stood at the gate.

"We've come for our baby," said Jimmy.

"I'm afraid I don't know where it is," said Peregrin apologetically. "You see, a woman had found ours outside the post office and brought it back. Gosh! My mother was pretty mad with me."

The explanation, satisfactory though it was up to a point, did little to dispel Jimmy's anxiety.

"Yes, but where's ours?" he demanded.

"Well, you see," said Peregrin, "when I got ours back I didn't need yours any longer, so I got it out of the garden as quick as I could before she saw it. I'd have got in a worse row if she'd seen it."

"Yes, but where is it?" said Jimmy.

"Well, I don't quite know," said Peregrin. "I lent it to Billy Frensham."

"Lent it to Billy Frensham?" said Jimmy, open-mouthed with dismay.

"Yes," said Peregrin. "He and Micky were playing at

being tramps an' they wanted a pram to be tramps with so I said they could borrow it if they brought it back by teatime. It was a piece of luck for me that they were jus' passing when I was taking it out of the garden."

"Yes, but what about m-me?" said Jimmy indignantly. "Where is it now, anyway?"

"Dunno," said Peregrin vaguely. "I can't think why they've not brought it back. Perhaps they've lost it. They're always losing things. Or p'raps they've just got tired of pushing it an' left it somewhere."

Jimmy's throat was dry. He could only gasp "Gosh!" in a faint whisper.

"Well, I've got to go now," said Peregrin. "I 'spect it'll turn up."

With that he vanished into the house, closing the door. Jimmy and Bobby stared at each other, their faces blank with horror.

"What'll we do?" said Bobby.

Jimmy gulped and swallowed.

"We've got to look for it," he said. "We've got to look for it till we find it."

"We'll never find it," said Bobby. "All prams look jus' alike, anyway."

"No, this one doesn't," said Jimmy. "It's got a scratch down one side. I'd know it if I saw it. C-come on."

They searched the village without success, looking into gardens and shops, examining ditches, barns and outhouses. Sandy, aware that a search of some sort was afoot, did his best to help, bringing them an old boot out of a ditch and a bristleless hearth brush that he had discovered by somebody's dustbin. It was just as they were deciding to go home and confess the crime that, passing the Palmers' house, they suddenly saw the pram –

scratch, blue cover, white rabbits and all – standing at the gateway. With a great relief at his heart, Jimmy seized the handles and ran down the road with it to his home. Auntie Jean was standing at the gate, looking anxiously up and down the road. Her face cleared when she saw Jimmy and Bobby with the pram, and she opened the gate to admit them.

"I thought you were never coming," she said, then, changing her voice to a cooing sound, "And where's Mummy's darling, 'ickle, precious babykins, then!"

She drew back the cover to reveal the yellow face of Marigold reposing on the lace-edged pillow.

Bobby, who had fled in terror at the sight, came furtively back to look for Jimmy. He found him sitting on a log behind the greenhouse, gazing dolefully into the distance. Sandy sat by him, his head on Jimmy's knee, obviously offering sympathy and comfort.

The baby had been discovered, safe and unharmed, crawling round the Palmers' back garden, but Jimmy had been docked of his pocket money, condemned to early bed and forbidden to go out of the gate. And there he sat – an outcast, a pariah, a boy so lost to all sense of right and decency that no one of his family would have any dealings with him.

"It was rotten," said Bobby, sitting down by him. "It was Billy Frensham that messed things up."

"Yes," said Jimmy bitterly. "Fancy sellin' it to Araminta Palmer for a s-stick of rock!"

There was a long silence. Jimmy's hand moved slowly over Sandy's head.

"Babies are a w-wash-out," he said at last. "I'd sooner have d-dogs any day."

Chapter 18

The Test

It was Aggie, Bobby's family maid, who first drew Bobby's and Jimmy's attention to Miss Tressider's affairs of the heart. To Aggie, affairs of the heart were the only affairs worth anyone's attention. She read love stories in all her spare time and went to the pictures three times a week. Having brought her own affair of the heart to a satisfactory conclusion by becoming engaged to the dustman – in ordinary eyes an undersized uncomely man, but in Aggie's eyes a combination of Clark Gable, James Mason and John Mills – she was ready to take an interest in other people's. And she began with Miss Tressider's.

"I've seed 'er out with a dark man, an' I've seed 'er out with a fair man," she said, "an' I've seed 'er out with both together. It's my belief 'er 'eart's divided."

"It couldn't be," said Bobby, stretching out his hand to the sultanas that Aggie had just weighed on the scales. "She'd die if it was. You couldn't live with your heart divided."

Jimmy and Bobby were hanging about on the kitchen table, "helping" Aggie make a cake by the simple means of eating everything within reach.

"I don't mean that," said Aggie. "I mean 'er destiny 'angs on a thread, an' – now, where's that bag of sugar?

– she's torn between them. One of 'em'll mean 'appiness to 'er an' the other won't – 'ere's the syrup spoon for you to lick – an' she can't make up 'er mind. If she chooses the wrong one, she's doomed to a life of misery."

"Gosh!" said Jimmy aghast. "Can't she find out which is the nicest?"

"It ain't always easy," said Aggie, shaking her head mysteriously as she emptied the sultanas into the mixture. "I tried to do 'er tea-leaves the las' time she come to tea 'ere but there was only one left in 'er cup, so I couldn't do nothin' with it."

"But she must know which she likes best," said Bobby.

Again Aggie shook her head.

"Sometimes they don't," she said. "Sometimes Fate blinds them. You can scrape out that basin I've 'ad the syrup in. I've left a good wallop for you."

"What can you *do*, then?" said Jimmy, setting to work on the syrup. "It's awful to think of her d-doomed to a life of misery."

"I read a story once," said Aggie, "about a woman 'oos 'eart was tore between two men, an' she told them both she'd lost all her money an' one of them gave 'er up an' the other stuck to 'er an' 'e was rewarded 'cause she 'adn't lost 'er money. Pass me that tin of bakin' powder, ducks. I never trust this 'ere self-raisin' flour. Self-sittin'-down more like, I call it."

"It was a jolly g-good idea, to pretend she'd lost her money," said Jimmy, frowning thoughtfully as he passed the tin. "I'll r-remember it."

"You've gotter 'ave some sort of test to tell gold from dross," said Aggie. "It's the only way . . . A woman's 'eart can't always tell 'er the truth. 'Ere's some more sultanas for you. Yer ma'll never know. An' I'll 'ave the whole thing mixed in a minute now an' there'll be a nice lot of scrapin's."

"It's jolly d-decent of you," said Jimmy.

"Well, that's wot kids is for – to eat – ain't it?" said Aggie, slapping the cake mixture with her wooden spoon in a hit-or-miss, happy-go-lucky fashion.

"But listen," said Jimmy, struck by a sudden idea, "s'pose they're b-both nice."

"That never 'appens," said Aggie, with an air of dark and mysterious knowledge. "One's gold an' one's dross. Stands to reason." She slapped the mixture into a cake tin, put the cake into the oven and slammed the oven door.

"Now finish up that there bowl an' let me get on with me washin'-up," she said. "I've got other things to do than waste me time talkin' to you two."

They finished the bowl, scraped some syrup off the table, licked out the bottom of the carton of icing sugar, sampled the vanilla essence, divided what was left of the candied peel and mixed it with what was left of the ground almonds . . . then Jimmy set off homewards. He was strongly fortified by cake ingredients, but the feeling of well-being that the process usually induced was absent. The thought of Miss Tressider's unwittingly marrying the one that was dross and being doomed to a life of misery weighed heavily on his spirit. He stood for a moment, looking up and down the road . . . And there at the bus stop, only a few yards away, he saw Miss Tressider. She was standing with two young men – one dark and one fair. Jimmy gazed at them with interest, wondering which was the gold and which the dross. Then the bus arrived. Both the young men got on to it, and Miss Tressider set off towards the village alone.

Coming to a sudden decision, Jimmy ran after her and began to walk by her side.

"Hello, Jimmy," said Miss Tressider.

"Hello," said Jimmy. He cleared his throat nervously. "I s-say, Miss Tressider."

"Yes?"

"You – you don't want to be doomed to a life of m-misery, do you?"

Miss Tressider looked at him in some surprise.

"No, Jimmy," she said, "I don't think I do."

"Well," said Jimmy, "if you want to choose between two people an' you don't know which is d-dross, it's – it's a good plan to – to pretend that you've l-lost your money."

"But I haven't any money to lose," said Miss Tressider simply.

Jimmy sighed.

"That's a p-pity," he said.

Frowning thoughtfully and replying absently to her questions about his doings and the health of his family, he accompanied her to the gate of her cottage, then returned to Bobby's house.

Bobby was in the front garden, practising pole-jumping, and had just landed his solid person into the middle of a rather prickly berberis bush.

"Hi, Bobby!" called Jimmy, leaning over the gate.

Bobby extricated himself from the berberis bush, and went down to the gate.

"Yes?" he said.

"I've been t-talkin' to Miss Tressider," he said, "an' she can't p-pretend to lose her money, 'cause she hasn't got any."

"Well, we can't do anythin' more about it," said Bobby.

"Yes, we must," said Jimmy earnestly. "We don't want her to be doomed to a l-life of misery. We've got to think out another t-test."

"Could we get them to fight a duel?" said Bobby after a moment's thought. "I've always wanted to watch someone fight a duel."

"No, that's s-silly," said Jimmy. "We want to find which is the nicest of them."

"Well, I still think *she* ought to know which is the nicest," said Bobby.

"But she *doesn't*," said Jimmy. "She can't. Aggie said Fate b-blinded them . . . We've *got* to think out another test. Let's sit down an' think hard!"

They sat side by side on the grass, and Jimmy screwed up his face into an expression suggestive of deep thought, while Bobby twisted his wristwatch round and round his wrist . . .

"I've got a s-sort of idea," said Jimmy at last, relaxing the tension of his facial muscles.

"What?" said Bobby.

"Well, we could ask her to come d-down to the old quarry with us an' then g-get her to shout 'Help!' an' I'll throw a stone in the pond there that'll make a splash so's they'll think she's f-fallen in and then see which of them c-comes to rescue her first."

Bobby considered this.

"Where will they be?"

"They'll be up on the road. The road j-jus' over the quarry."

"It'll take a bit of arrangin'," said Bobby doubtfully.

"'Course it will," said Jimmy. "We've got to take a bit of trouble to save her bein' d-doomed to a life of misery. It's an idea, anyway."

"I don't think much of it," said Bobby.

"All right. Think of a b-better one," said Jimmy huffily.

"No, I can't," said Bobby. "I'm not much good at thinkin' . . . All right. We'll do it. How shall we start?"

"We'll have to get 'em all three on that r-road that goes over the old quarry."

"That's not goin' to be easy," said Bobby.

"We may have to w-wait a bit for it," admitted Jimmy.

They had to wait for about a week. During the week they followed Miss Tressider's movements so closely that it caused that lady no slight bewilderment. Wherever she went and whatever she did, the figures of Jimmy and Bobby seemed to be hovering in the background. On Monday evening she went for a walk with the fair young man, and on Wednesday afternoon they saw the dark young man having tea with her in her cottage, but on the Saturday afternoon she set off for a walk along the road that led past the quarry with the fair young man on one side of her and the dark young man on the other.

"Now," said Jimmy, "we've gotter do the plan. C-come on! Quick!"

Miss Tressider and her escort were surprised to find the two small boys planted firmly in the middle of the road just above the quarry, barring their road.

"Hello," said Miss Tressider.

"Hello," said Jimmy. "Will you – will you come down to the quarry with us? I'll f-find you an easy way down."

"Why?" said Miss Tressider.

"We want to show you s-something," said Jimmy.

"We'll all go down," said the fair young man.

"Yes, I don't see why we should be left out of it," said the dark young man.

"No, you c-can't come," said Jimmy. "It's a s-secret. Only Miss Tressider can c-come."

Miss Tressider laughed.

"All right," she said. "I'll come, but I can only stay a minute."

She followed Jimmy and Bobby lightly down the winding path to the bottom of the quarry, in a corner of which a pool of stagnant water had collected.

"What's the secret?" she said.

"W-w-well," said Jimmy, stammering more than usual in his excitement, "there's an echo, and we w-want you to try it."

"'Cause we want to find out which is the nicest," said Bobby.

"Shut up," said Jimmy. "The w-word that does the echo best is 'help', an' we want you to shout 'Help!' so's you can hear the echo."

Miss Tressider looked mystified but amused.

"All right," she said and, drawing a deep breath, called "Help!"

Jimmy had run to the pond and taken hold of a boulder that he had put already on a ledge of the quarry just above the water.

He never knew quite how it happened . . . but, instead of throwing the boulder into the water, he slipped on the rocky ledge and fell into it himself. He never even knew who got him out. He only knew that he was led – a dripping, unsightly object – sneezing copiously, down the road to his home.

That evening Miss Tressider came to see him. He was in bed, still sneezing copiously.

"I can't think how you came to fall in like that, Jimmy," she said.

INSTEAD OF THROWING THE BOULDER INTO THE WATER, HE
SLIPPED ON THE ROCKY LEDGE.

"Which of them came down to the p-pond first?" said
Jimmy anxiously.

Miss Tressider knit her brows, trying to remember.

"I think they both came down together," she said at
last.

"Gosh!" said Jimmy in dismay. "So we still don't know
which one you ought to m-marry."

"Marry?" said Miss Tressider. "But they're my brothers."

"Brothers?" gasped Jimmy.

"Yes. One of them has a job near here, and the other's
staying with him, and they've both been coming to see
me whenever they could."

"Oh," said Jimmy blankly.

"The man I'm going to marry," went on Miss Tressider, "is in Kenya. He's coming home next year, and we shall be married then."

Jimmy was silent, trying to sort out the situation.

"Is he n-nice?" he said at last.

"I think so," smiled Miss Tressider, "and most people seem to agree with me."

"Good!" said Jimmy with a sigh of relief. "Then you've not been b-blinded by Fate."

"What are you talking about, Jimmy?" said Miss Tressider.

"It d-doesn't matter," said Jimmy, who was beginning to feel rather sleepy. "If you're not d-doomed to a life of misery, that's all that matters."

With that he let the test and everything connected with it slip into the limbo of the past and turned his attention to the bunch of grapes that Miss Tressider had put on the table by his bedside.

Chapter 19

Befogged

"M-m-me?" said Jimmy, indignation intensifying his stammer. "Me go to Araminta's party?"

"I'm afraid you must, dear," said Mrs Manning. "Her mother particularly asked you, and you've no reason for refusing."

"Reason?" said Jimmy passionately. "Why, she's a kid in a k-kindergarten."

"She's only two years younger than you are," said Mrs Manning, "and I've promised that you should go, so I'm afraid you must."

Hands plunged in pockets, spirits sunk in dejection, Jimmy wandered across the road to Bobby Peaslake.

"I s-say," he said. "I've g-got to go to Araminta Palmer's party."

"So've I," said Bobby with a bitterness that rivalled Jimmy's. "A rotten ole kid like that!"

"Yes," agreed Jimmy. "Jus' the one kid in the w-world that we wouldn't want to go to's party."

They were silent for some moments, meditating on the cruel stroke that Fate had dealt them.

"I wish we lived in the days when people ran away to sea," said Bobby. "I'd jolly well run away to sea to get out of this."

"Yes," said Jimmy thoughtfully. "I once read a t-tale

where someone did that. He found an island of savages an' they m-made him king."

"I'd like to be made king by savages," said Bobby wistfully. "Or we might find a country no one'd ever discovered before. They call it after you when people do that. They'd call it Bobbypeaslakeland or something like that."

"Jimmymanningland," murmured Jimmy. "If we found it together, I s'pose they'd call it Bobbypeaslakeandjimmymanningland, only it's a bit long."

"Or we might find a gold mine," said Bobby, "and come back millionaires."

"Yes," said Jimmy. "There's a lot of things I'd like to buy if I was a m-millionaire. There's that model jet-propelled fighter in the t-toy shop window."

"You'd have to be a jolly big millionaire to buy that," said Bobby. "It's twenty-five shillings."

"Well, m-millionaires do have t-twenty-five shillings," said Jimmy. "That's why they're c-called millionaires."

"And 'stead of that," said Bobby disgustedly, "we've got to go to Araminta Palmer's party." An expression of determination came over his face. "I'm jolly well going to try an' have a cold."

"I'll have a s-sore throat," said Jimmy. "It's easier to do than measles. I t-tried measles once, but I couldn't d-do the spots."

The day of Araminta's party, however, found the two of them in their usual robust health. In vain did Bobby produce what was known as his "dancing-class cough" (he hated his dancing class). In vain did Jimmy give a masterly display of difficulty in swallowing. Bobby's family ignored his symptoms so completely that he soon tired of the sheer hard work needed to produce them, and Jimmy, told to open his mouth, revealed organs of such perfect normality that his family lost interest in him. To make things worse, a fog hung over everything, dripping from the bushes in the garden, seeping into the house, deepening Jimmy's already deep dejection . . . and, to make things worse still, Roger began to tease him at lunch about Araminta's party.

"Going to the babies' tea party?" he said in what was meant to be kindly mockery, but that turned Jimmy's small countenance brick red. "Don't forget your bib."

It was that remark which drove Jimmy to his momentous decision. He allowed himself to be prepared for the party with a docility that made his mother think he had forgotten his objections to it, then slipped across the road to Bobby's house. Bobby loomed through the fog in answer to his owl-call – washed and cleaned and in his best suit.

"I'm goin' to d-do it," said Jimmy.

"What?"

"R-run away to sea. I'm sick of bein' made to d-do things like g-goin' to kids' parties. Are you comin' with me?"

Bobby considered.

"Mr Mince is goin' to have some choc-ices in tomorrow," he said. "What about putting it off to the day after tomorrow?"

"No. We've g-got to do it now," said Jimmy. "Besides, what's a choc-ice to bein' king of a s-savage island or findin' a g-gold mine?"

"All right," said Bobby, convinced by Jimmy's argument. "Shall I go back for my pyjamas?"

"No," said Jimmy. "We'll be sleepin' in b-barns an' hedges an' things. We won't n-need pyjamas."

"All right," said Bobby a little doubtfully. "D'you mean, start straight away now?"

"Yes," said Jimmy. "We'll try 'n' g-get to the sea tonight."

"What do we do when we get there?" said Bobby.

"We find a sh-ship to take us abroad. They f-found ships in all the tales I read. We might have to work our ways as c-cabin boys or something."

"I'd rather work my way as a captain," said Bobby. "I've always wanted to be captain of a ship."

"Well, we m-might," said Jimmy vaguely. "How much money have you g-got?"

"Threepence halfpenny."

"I've got twopence halfpenny. That's sixpence. That ought to t-take us to the sea."

The two walked for some time in silence down the road through the thickening fog.

"What'll you call yourself if they make us king of this savage island?" said Bobby suddenly.

"Dunno . . . I'd like to be called Someone the T-Terrible," said Jimmy.

"I'd like to be called something like Chief Eagle Eye."

"That's Red Indian," objected Jimmy.

"Well, it might be a Red Indian island," said Bobby. "How long d'you think we've walked now?"

"Miles an' miles."

"I can't s-smell the sea yet, can you?"

"I can smell something."

"It's the f-fog."

"I say!"

"Yes?"

"I hope we're goin' in the right direction. To the sea, I mean."

"It doesn't matter," said Jimmy. "England's an island. We'll g-get to the sea sooner or l-later, whichever way we go."

"Yes, but I think we ought to know which way we're going."

"How can we? You can't see anythin' in this f-fog. I don't even know where we are, do you?"

"We're jus' comin' to a shop."

The light of a shop window showed faintly through the fog. They stopped and pressed their noses against the glass. Dimly they saw a familiar expanse of broken cricket bats, stringless tennis rackets, gas brackets, Indian clubs and headless china figures.

"Gosh!" said Jimmy. "It's Mr P-Prosser's. I thought we'd got farther than this, didn't you?"

"Yes," said Bobby. "We mus' be almost as far off from the sea as when we started."

"Look!" said Jimmy in sudden excitement, pointing to a tray that stood in the middle of the window, marked "Everything 6d." "It's a compass. We ought to have a c-compass. They tell you where you are."

"It'd take all our money," objected Bobby. "We shouldn't have any left for food."

"That doesn't matter," said Jimmy. "We'll b-beg our way. People do in books. We must have a c-compass."

"All right," agreed Bobby doubtfully.

They entered the little shop, which was almost as full of fog as the street outside. At the summons of the jangling bell, Mr Prosser came out of an inner room, his jaws moving rhythmically in the manner of one who has been interrupted at his tea, and peered at them over his steel-rimmed spectacles.

"Good afternoon, Mr Prosser," said Jimmy politely.

Mr Prosser swallowed with an air of ceremony, then addressed himself to the matter in hand.

"Good afternoon," he said. "A dreadful day. And what can I do for you?"

"We want to buy the c-compass, please," said Jimmy. "The one in the sixpenny tray."

It was an idiosyncrasy of Mr Prosser's to lose interest in any object that a customer actually wished to buy and to press the claims of its rivals.

"Yes," he said. "A nice little compass. Good value, too. A very nice little compass. But what about this game of Ludo? Only a few pieces missing. Always good fun on a wet day."

"No, thank you," said Jimmy. "It's the compass we want."

"Or this toasting fork. Make a nice little present for your mother on her birthday. It should pull out into three sections but it's got wedged. Quite a nice length as it is, of course."

Jimmy shook his head.

"No, th-thank you."

"Or this goldfish bowl. Not seriously cracked. You needn't put the water above the crack. There'd be quite enough room for the little fellow to swim about in most happily. Very pretty they look, swimming about in it. Decorations as well as pets."

"No, th-thank you," said Jimmy.

"You wouldn't like this little album? Filled with very pretty scraps. Views of foreign countries and so on. Educational as well as entertaining. You can have that for sixpence. It's a bargain. Must have taken someone years to assemble. Arranged very artistically."

"No, th-thank you," said Jimmy.

"If you could rise to ninepence, here's a very neat little picnic spirit lamp. The handle that adjusts the wick is broken off but otherwise it's in perfect condition."

"No, th-thank you," said Jimmy. "It's the c-compass we want."

"Very well," said Mr Prosser in a rather dispirited manner, as he stretched out his hand to take the compass from the tray.

Jimmy gave him the sixpence, but Mr Prosser continued to call his attention to the other "bargains" scattered about the shop, dwelling almost tenderly on the charms of a moth-eaten "mechanical bird" in a cage, whose singing apparatus had long since ceased to function. It was as if he felt lonely in his fog-enshrouded shop and were anxious to prolong their visit. When finally they took their leave he stood watching them wistfully till the fog swallowed them up, then returned to his interrupted tea.

The two went to the nearest street lamp and inspected their purchase in its faint rays.

"How do you work it?" said Bobby.

"Dunno," said Jimmy, "but it's s'posed to tell you where you are."

"Well, it doesn't."

"No, it jus' w-wobbles about."

"Perhaps the fog's got into it."

"Let's wait till the fog's cleared an' try it again. Come on. We mustn't waste any more t-time if we're goin' to discover those countries an' things."

They didn't waste any more time, but the fog grew thicker, and the road, which they thought they knew so well, seemed to wind about more and more confusedly. It was just as Bobby was saying that he believed he could smell the sea that Jimmy stood stock still, staring at a gate they were passing.

"Gosh!" he said. "It c-can't be!"

"What?" said Bobby.

"It l-looks like Araminta's gate. We can't have g-got back there."

"P'raps we've been right round the world," said Bobby. "You do get back to the same place if you go right round the world."

"Yes, but we'd have gone over the sea if we'd d-done that," said Jimmy, "an' we haven't d-done."

A figure loomed suddenly out of the fog, and Mrs Palmer's voice said: "Oh, there you are! I couldn't think what had happened to you. Come along in. The party's just beginning."

Blinking and bewildered, Jimmy and Bobby were led into a brightly-lit nursery, full of children. In the middle stood Araminta, wearing a white frock with a blue ribbon in her hair.

"What have you got in your hand, Jimmy?" said Mrs Palmer.

Jimmy opened his hand, disclosing the pocket compass. Mrs Palmer fell upon it with a scream.

"How sweet of him! He heard Araminta say she wanted a clock for her dolls' house and this is the nearest he could get. Fancy going out into the fog for it, the little pet! Say 'Thank you', Araminta."

"Thag you," said Araminta.

"Do try to speak nicely, darling," said Mrs Palmer. "You know you've had them out."

"Thag you," said Araminta again.

The grown-ups opened the door of the dolls' house and clustered round it, fixing up the compass on the little chimney piece.

JIMMY OPENED HIS HAND, DISCLOSING THE COMPASS.

"How sweet!" they cooed.

"He's always been devoted to Araminta," said Mrs Palmer with a fond smile. "Her little sweetheart, I always call him!"

Jimmy stood in the background, scowling, hands thrust into pockets . . . He didn't see the brightly-lit room, the crowd of children or the dolls' house.

He saw Jimmy the Terrible, Jimmy of Jimmy-manningland, Jimmy the Millionaire, vanishing slowly into the distance.

Chapter 20

The Glorious Fifth

"It's the Fifth of November on Friday," said Jimmy gloomily, "an' I haven't g-got any fireworks."

"It's your own fault, Jimmy," said Mrs Manning. "Roger saved up his pocket money to buy some, and you ought to have done the same."

"Well, I didn't know the Fifth of November was so n-near," said Jimmy. "It seemed to come s-suddenly."

"I hope it will teach you a lesson," said Mrs Manning.

"It would be a b-better lesson if you gave me some money for fireworks," said Jimmy hopefully. "I'd never f-forget it then."

"No, Jimmy," said Mrs Manning firmly.

At first the obvious solution of the problem seemed to be a working arrangement with Roger, but Roger, approached by Jimmy and Bobby, showed little enthusiasm for the idea.

"We only want to h-help," said Jimmy.

"No, we don't want you messing about at all," said Roger. "The whole gang's coming as well as a lot of others, and we don't want kids. You can watch if you like, but you'll have to keep right at the back."

In silence Jimmy and Bobby contemplated the bleak prospect of watching Roger's firework display from behind the stalwart forms of Roger's friends. Then they trailed disconsolately over the fields and sat down on a stile to discuss the situation.

"It's goin' to be rotten," said Bobby. "We shan't see anythin' at all an' I bet they won't let us touch anythin'."

But the gloom was gradually fading from Jimmy's round rosy countenance.

"T-tell you what," he said. "Let's have somethin' of our own."

"What can we have?" said Bobby. "We haven't any money for fireworks."

"No, but there's other th-things," said Jimmy. "They do fireworks to c-celebrate this ole Guy Fawkes man that let off f-fireworks in the House of Commons in hist'ry. Well, let's f-find somethin' else in hist'ry. There mus' be lots of other things in hist'ry."

"They didn't all make bangs," objected Bobby.

"Some of them d-did," said Jimmy, "Let's think, any-way."

They thought for some moments . . . Bobby twirled his watch round his wrist in silent concentration, then said:

"They cut off people's heads in hist'ry, but I don't s'pose it made much of a noise."

"No, I don't s'pose it did," said Jimmy, and again the two abandoned themselves to thought. It was Jimmy who broke the silence this time.

"There was a bubble once in hist'ry called the South Sea Bubble," he said, "an' it burst, but I don't know if it made much of a b-bang."

"No, bubbles don't," said Bobby. "I've made bubbles that burst an' they don't make a bang at all."

"*Tell* you what," said Jimmy. "There was a place in hist'ry that got burnt an' someone played a fiddle while it was b-burnin'."

"What place?" said Bobby.

"D-dunno," said Jimmy. "I've forgot."

"An' why did they play a fiddle?"

"I've forgot that, too," said Jimmy.

"An' was it in November?"

"I've forgot that, too," said Jimmy, adding a little irrit-ably: "We'll never get it settled if you k-keep on makin' objections."

"I'm not makin' objections," said Bobby, "but I don't see how we can do it, anyway, if we don't know what place it was an' haven't got a fiddle."

"Well, I bet I'll remember the place if I th-think a bit more," said Jimmy.

"There's somethin' in hist'ry called Bannockburn," said Bobby, uncertainly, "but p'raps that's where Alfred burnt the cakes."

"No, I don't think it is," said Jimmy, brightening. "I think it means they burnt a place called Bannock an' someone played a fiddle while they did it."

"Well, that's settled, then," said Bobby. "We'll have a bonfire for it an' play a fiddle 'stead of fireworks. It'll be jolly excitin'."

"Yes, it will," agreed Jimmy. "Guy Fawkes'll be n-nothin' to it." Then something of his eagerness faded as he added: "But we haven't got a f-fiddle."

"Perhaps we could borrow one," suggested Bobby.

"We d-don't know anyone who has one," said Jimmy, "an'—"

He stopped and got off the stile to give passage to a tall grey-haired man who had been making his way across the field.

"Good day to ye," said the man politely.

"G-good day," said Jimmy. Then, encouraged by the kindly expression in the blue eyes, he continued: "Do you know anything about B-Bannockburn, please?"

"Bannockburrn," said the man slowly, "is the most glorrious event in the history of the worrld."

"Oh," said Jimmy, impressed. He was silent for a moment, then said:

"Was it in N-November?"

"It took place," said the man, "on the twenty-fourrth of June, thirrteen hundred and fourrteen."

"Oh," said Jimmy again and added, "I suppose we couldn't c-celebrate it in November?"

"Ye can celebrate Bannockburrn," said the man, "at any season of any yearr."

"Good!" said Jimmy. "We'll celebrate it on Friday, then. Did – did they play a f-fiddle at it?"

"They played an eenstrument," said the man, "more glorrious than any feedle everr made."

"I – I suppose you haven't g-got one?" said Jimmy, tentatively.

"Aye, I have, that," said the man.

There was a silence, during which Jimmy summoned all his courage.

"I suppose you couldn't l-l-lend it us?" he said.

"I never lend it," said the man with a twinkle in his blue eyes. "But I'll come and play it for ye."

"Gosh! Will you *r-really*?" said Jimmy excitedly.

"Aye. Sure as me name's Angus McTavish, I weel. And noo I'll be on me way."

They watched his tall upright figure till it was out of sight.

"Well, that's settled," said Jimmy. "It was jolly k-kind of him."

"He'll prob'ly forget," said Bobby. "Grown-ups gen'rally do."

"I bet he won't," said Jimmy. "I wonder if it's a m-mouth organ."

"It might be a saxophone," said Bobby. "They make a jolly good noise."

They decided to hold their "celebration" in a corner of the field where Roger and his friends were having their bonfire.

"We mus' have a b-bonfire," said Jimmy. "Let's go' n' collect stuff for it."

Their search was not very successful. Bobby's mother refused to let them have the wooden box on which he had set his heart. Jimmy's mother stopped him taking an armful of firewood that had been chopped up for lighting fires. Finally Bobby collected a few shavings from his uncle's carpentry shed and Jimmy some nondescript packing that had come with a set of saucepans, given by his father to his mother on her birthday. To this they added some rather damp twigs from the wood and a derelict "moth-bag" that had once sheltered Mrs Manning's fur coat and that she had put out for salvage because it was coming into holes. This not very inflammable material they piled up in a corner of the field where Roger and his friends were having their firework display and bonfire. It looked a paltry affair indeed beside the magnificent structure that Roger had built, culminating in a tarred barrel and a guy.

As dusk fell Roger put a light to his pile and it blazed up gloriously. Rockets shot into the air. Catherine wheels sent out cascades of sparks. Roman candles made sheets of flame.

Jimmy's moth-bag smouldered sulkily. The shavings

caught fire, glowed fitfully then died away altogether. The twigs refused to light at all.

"He's not brought that m-mouth organ," said Jimmy.

"Saxophone," said Bobby. "I knew he wouldn't."

"It's r-rotten, isn't it?" said Jimmy miserably.

A few of Roger's friends turned round and began to laugh at Jimmy's "bonfire." They pointed it out to others and soon all were joining in the laughter. Jimmy, his cheeks burning with shame, tears not far away, poked and prodded his fire. The last sputtering flame died away . . .

And then suddenly Angus McTavish appeared. He strode on to the field in full piper's regalia, kilt swinging,

WITHOUT WORD OR GREETING, ANGUS McTAVISH APPROACHED
JIMMY'S FIRE AND BEGAN TO MARCH ROUND IT.

plaid flying in the breeze. The thrilling notes of the bagpipes cut sharply through the air. Without word or
greeting, he approached Jimmy's smoking "bonfire" and
began to march round it, his eyes fixed in front of him, his
distended cheeks hardly seeming to move as he drew
forth the inspiriting strains. A sudden silence fell over
Roger's group. One by one its members straggled over to
Jimmy's fire, watching the piper spellbound. He was no
longer the elderly Scotsman who had recently taken the
cottage adjoining the field. He was a heroic being from
the legendary world of adventure and romance. Soon
Roger's bonfire was entirely deserted. So engrossed was
Jimmy in watching the piper that at first he did not notice
that Roger had approached him and was addressing him
with unusual deference and humility.

"I say, Jimmy," he said. "Would – would you mind if he
came over to our fire?"

"N-no," said Jimmy, "if Bobby an' me can march with
him."

"Yes, of course," agreed Roger.

Jimmy approached the piper.

"Would you m-mind coming over to the b-big fire?"
he said. "There's more r-room for you to march there."

The piper gave a slight inclination of his head, then,
still continuing his majestic march – kilt swinging, plaid
flying, bagpipes sending out their heartening strains –
made his way over to Roger's bonfire. An excited trail of
boys followed him.

"It's awfully good of you, sir," said Roger. "Would you
mind walking round it like you did round Jimmy's?"

The bonfire blazed, the rockets rocketed, the Catherine
wheels span. The circle of boys pressed closer, eyes agog,
craning their heads over each other's shoulders. They

watched – not the bonfire or the rockets or the Catherine wheels, but the glorious figure that marched round in the red light of the fire. And behind it went Jimmy and Bobby, marching with a swagger, swinging imaginary kilts, holding imaginary bagpipes to their lips . . .

Jimmy had been right.

Guy Fawkes was nothing to it.

Chapter 21

The Haunted House

Roger strolled idly round the garden, hands in pockets, whistling untunefully. Though he would not have admitted it to himself, he was feeling rather at a loose end. It was the last week of the holidays . . . He had done all the things he had intended to do in the holidays, and now school loomed so near that it didn't seem worthwhile making any further plans. He had arranged to meet Charles and Bill immediately after tea, but till then time lay heavy on his hands and he was wondering whether to start a fresh series of experiments on the rain-tub (his attempts to turn it into an ornamental fountain had ended disastrously a few days ago) or to go on with the miniature log cabin that he was building behind the tool-shed. This was a somewhat thankless task, as, whenever the edifice seemed to be well and truly laid, someone always seemed to come down and carry away an essential part of it to put on the sitting-room fire. He still hadn't made up his mind what to do when suddenly Sally's face appeared over the hedge that divided the two gardens. It wore a wistful, woebegone expression.

"Hello, Roger," she said mournfully.

Ordinarily Roger would have muttered a curt greeting and passed on his way, but today he felt that even Sally might provide a diversion.

"Hello," he said and added rather reluctantly, for he looked on any converse with Sally as a confession of weakness. "What's the matter?"

"It's Aunt Lucy," said Sally.

Roger thought of the vague, kindly aunt who had been staying with Sally's mother for the last few months.

"What about her?" he said.

"She can't get into her house," said Sally.

"Oh, yes," said Roger, with hazy memories of grown-up conversation. "She's let it to someone, hasn't she?"

"Yes, to Miss Morland," said Sally, "and she wants to get it back, and Miss Morland won't go out and the law won't let Aunt Lucy turn her out, and she's terribly unhappy . . . We're a bit unhappy, too," added Sally as an afterthought, "'cause we're a bit tired of having her staying with us."

"Hard lines," said Roger shortly and was going on down the path when Sally heaved a deep sigh and said:

"*Please*, Roger!"

He stopped.

"Yes?"

"Won't you do something about it?"

"*Me?*" said Roger, taken aback. "What can *I* do?"

"You're so clever, Roger. Can't you get Aunt Lucy back into her house?"

Roger looked at her. The blue eyes held admiration and appeal. The small mouth drooped exquisitely at the corners. Roger was not quite so impervious to Sally's appeal as he liked to imagine he was. He didn't want her to think that any exploit was beyond his powers. He hesitated . . .

"Well, I s'pose I *might*," he said in an elaborately off-hand manner.

"Oh, Roger, I'm *sure* you can. You can always do things if you try. You're so clever. You're the cleverest person I know."

"Well," temporised Roger, looking gratified but a little dubious, "I can't actu'lly *promise*, but—"

"Oh, *thank* you, Roger," interrupted Sally fervently. "I kept saying to myself: 'I know Roger could do it,' but I didn't dare ask you till now."

"Yes, but—" said Roger. "I don't know – I mean – Well – well, what I mean is – Where is her house, any-way?"

"It's called The Laburnums and it's on the main road of the new estate. Oh, Roger, *thank* you!"

"That's all right," said Roger airily, swaggering a little in spite of the foreboding at his heart. "I 'spect I can do it. I'll have to think it out a bit, but—"

"Oh, thank you, *thank* you," said Sally, hopping about on one leg with delight. "I'll go and tell Aunt Lucy that it's going to be all right now."

With that she danced across the lawn and into the house.

Roger blinked at her retreating figure, then set off in search of Charles and Bill. He met them just coming in at the gate.

"We thought we'd come round a bit early," said Bill. "There doesn't seem much to *do*, does there?"

"Nothin' to beguile the tedium of our lives," said Charles.

"There's somethin' to *do*, all right," said Roger grimly. "Come into the tool-shed an' I'll tell you about it."

They went to the tool-shed and took their usual seats – Roger on the roller, Bill on the mowing machine, Charles on the upturned wheelbarrow; and Roger told them of the task he had undertaken. The other two listened with mingled consternation and interest.

"Gosh!" said Charles. "It's goin' to be jolly difficult even with turnin' every stone an' explorin' every avenue."

"But we *can't* get people out of houses," said Bill. "We aren't earthquakes or removers."

"We'll have to," said Roger. "I promised."

The light of hero-worship in Sally's eyes had gone to his head, and he felt that any fate would be preferable to admitting defeat.

"Well, how *can* we?" said Bill.

"People do go out of houses," said Charles. "I once read a story about a volcano, and they went out of their houses without even stopping to put their hats on. They jus' fled like – like – like mornin' dew."

"Well, we can't make a volcano," said Bill. "You need stuff called lava to make volcanoes an' we haven't got any."

"Well, I read another story once," said Charles, "where the people went out of a house 'cause it was haunted."

"That's an idea," said Roger. "We could haunt it."

"How?" said Bill.

"Jus' put sheets on an' – an' – an' sort of flap about in 'em."

"But ghosts haunt at night."

"We'll go there at night, then."

They looked at each other in silence. The adventure so lightly undertaken, seemed to be assuming immense proportions.

"How'll we get in?" said Bill.

"There's always a way of gettin' into houses," said Charles carelessly. "People always leave a window or a door open. When my mother forgets her key, I climb up the scullery roof an' in at the bathroom window. You can do that in most houses. Bathroom windows are nearly always open. So that's what we'll do. We'll jus' go in an' haunt it."

"When?" said Bill.

"Tonight," said Roger. "We want to get her out as quick as possible."

"Strike while the iron's hot," said Charles.

"Can I come, too, p-please?" said Jimmy.

They stared at him indignantly, aware for the first time that he was standing at the half-open door of the tool-shed, listening, and had probably been there all the time.

"No!" said Roger. "Clear off! We don't want you in on this. You're too young."

"I could be a y-young ghost," suggested Jimmy tentatively.

"No," said Roger again, "and clear off!"

Jimmy cleared off. He cleared off to Bobby's house and told him what was happening.

"Well, we can't be ghosts if they won't let us," said Bobby.

"I'd like to watch them bein' g-ghosts," said Jimmy wistfully.

"How could we?"

"We could f-follow them an' see what they d-do," said Jimmy. "We won't be ghosts, of course, an' they won't know we're there. We'll jus' w-watch."

"Yes," said Bobby a little uncertainly. "We could do that, all right."

Dusk was falling when Roger set off stealthily out of the gate, his sheet bundled under his arm. Sally, who had been told of the plan, waved to him from her bedroom window, and Roger gave her in return a stiff military salute vaguely intended to convey the dangerous nature of the enterprise on which he had embarked.

Charles and Bill, each with a sheet under his arm, were waiting for him at the corner of the road, and together the three set off towards the new estate. Having reached it, they made their way a little uncertainly along the main road. So engrossed had they been in preparing their spectral disguises, that they had omitted to ascertain the exact position of the house, and it was too dark now to read the names on the gates.

"She jus' said 'The Laburnums on the main road'," said Roger.

They walked along to the end of the road.

"Look! That must be it," said Charles suddenly. "It's got a laburnum tree in the garden an' it's the only laburnum tree in the road. Come on!"

Collars turned up, shoulders hunched, the Three Musketeers crept round to the back of the house.

"Yes," whispered Roger excitedly. "It's jus' like ours. You can climb up the scullery roof to the bathroom window."

"It's shut," said Bill.

"I bet it's not fastened. I'll go first an' try."

Draping his sheet round his shoulders in the manner of a scarf, he climbed up the drainpipe, then up the sloping scullery roof. He tried the window. It slid open.

"It's all right," he said in a sibilant whisper. "Come on."

After several false starts, considerably hampered by their sheets, the other two finally clambered up drainpipe and roof and all three vanished inside the house.

Jimmy and Bobby emerged from their hiding-place in the shelter of the hedge. They had followed their quarry so silently that not even Roger had suspected their presence. They stood looking at the house into which the three had vanished. No sounds came from it. It seemed to have swallowed the intruders up completely, leaving no trace.

"Gosh!" said Jimmy. "I wish we could go in with them, an' help them h-haunt."

"We can watch them."

"No, we can't. The curtains are drawn . . . 'cept the ones at the side of the house . . . I *say*!"

"Yes?"

"There's a window in the nex' house that looks right into the ones at the side where the curtains aren't drawn. If we got into the nex' house we could look right in an' watch them h-hauntin'. No one would know we were there. We wouldn't make a s-sound."

"I don't think we ought to," said Bobby nervously.

"Oh, c-come on," said Jimmy. "I want to do it s-same as they did. I want to go up a roof an' in at a window s-same as they did."

And a few seconds later Bobby, still protesting feebly, was following Jimmy up the sloping scullery roof of the next-door house and in at the open bathroom window. It was Jimmy who knocked over the tin of bath salts that stood on the window-sill, sending it on to the floor with a re-echoing clash. They waited, holding their breath, but there was no sound or movement in the house. They crept on to the dark landing, and there, too, it was Jimmy who walked into a small table, upsetting it and sending a book-trough and a cascade of books down the stairs. And then a woman's voice, deep and vibrating, called "Who are you?" from below . . . They looked wildly about them. In the dim light they could just see a ladder set against a trap-door in the ceiling. It seemed their nearest way of escape. Bobby swarmed up it, followed by Jimmy, who lost his foothold at the top and sent the ladder hurtling down on to the landing. For a moment he hung precariously, then swung himself up into the tiny attic. They closed the trap-door and stood gazing at it fearfully, but still no sound came from the house.

"Gosh!" panted Jimmy. "We've got to get out of this, quick!"

"I'm not goin' down there again," said Bobby. "I bet she's waitin' for us."

Jimmy looked round the room. It was evidently used as a box-room. There were trunks, suit-cases, packing-cases. In the roof was a fair-sized skylight.

"We'll get out that way," said Jimmy. "We'll pile up these trunks an' boxes, so's we can reach it. It's got a thing to open it, an' then we can get down by a drain-p-pipe or somethin'."

They piled up the trunks and suitcases and began to climb. But the erection was top-heavy and fell, with a series of loud thuds, before they reached the top. Again they listened in terror. Again only silence answered them.

"P'raps she's fetchin' the p-p'lice," said Jimmy. "Let's try that big packing-case. Quick!"

Standing on the packing-case, they swung themselves up to the window . . . on to the roof . . . down a drainpipe . . . and home through the dusk as fast as their trembling legs could carry them.

The meeting next morning between the Three Musketeers on their side of the hedge, with Jimmy hovering in the background, and Sally on her side, was a stormy one.

"We haunted an' haunted," said Roger, "an' there wasn't anyone there. The house was empty."

"You went to the wrong house," said Sally angrily. "That isn't Aunt Lucy's house. The people in that house are away."

"But you said The Laburnums an' there was a laburnum tree in the garden."

"Well, there isn't a laburnum tree in the garden of The Laburnums. It's called The Laburnums, but there isn't a laburnum tree in the garden. There's a laburnum tree next door, and that's all."

Suddenly, Aunt Lucy, vague and amiable, floated across the lawn to them.

"Well, Sally," she said, "you told me that I might have some good news about my house this morning, but I haven't had it so far."

"I'm sorry," pouted Sally. "It's *their* fault," pointing to the Three Musketeers. "They made a silly, stupid mistake. They—"

"Oh dear!" interrupted Aunt Lucy. "Here's Miss Morland."

They turned to see a tall woman, with a beak-like nose, deep-set eyes and jutting chin, come in at the gate of Sally's house and stride in a purposeful manner across the lawn to the hedge.

"I am vacating your house today," she said to Aunt Lucy.

Aunt Lucy gasped.

"But why?" she said.

"I passed through a most shattering experience last night," said Miss Morland. "A poltergeist – I repeat, a poltergeist – was in possession of the house. A tin of bath salts was hurled across the bathroom floor by no human hands. Books were thrown down from the top of the stairs to the bottom by no human agency. A loft ladder was flung across the landing. Trunks in the box-room were precipitated from one end of the room to the other. Nothing would induce me to spend another night in that house, and I warn you that you return there at your peril."

"I don't think I'd mind a poltergeist," said Aunt Lucy mildly. "It would be sort of company."

"Well, I have warned you," said Miss Morland. "I do not lack courage, but courage against the supernatural is of no avail. I do not mind admitting that I hid under the dining-room table during the greater part of the manifestations. I am going now to pack my things. I will not spend another night under that roof."

With that she turned abruptly and left them.

"Oh, Roger!" said Sally, dancing about gleefully. "You did it, after all. I knew you would. You're so clever. I'm sorry I was horrid. I didn't know that you'd really done it, after all . . . Come on, Aunt Lucy, let's go and pack your things."

The two disappeared into the house. The Three Musketeers looked at each other blankly.

"What *is* a poltergeist?" said Bill.

Jimmy cleared his throat.

"It's m-m-me," he said.

Chapter 22

Jimmy is Hypnotised

"My cousin went to the theatre las' week," said Bill, "an' there was a hypnotiser there."

"I think I saw one at the circus," said Roger a little uncertainly. "He swung on a sort of bar from the roof. He was jolly clever."

"He was Breathtaking and Spectacular, the Eighth Wonder of the World," said Charles. "It said so on the poster."

"No, that was a trapezer," said Bill. "This is somethin' quite diff'rent. This man jus' wished people to do things an' they did them."

"Well, that's happened to me sometimes," said Roger. "It did on Sunday. I was wishin' there'd be jelly for supper an' there was. So I mus' be one."

"No, but this is *diff'rent*," said Bill impatiently. "This man *made* people do things jus' by wishin' them to do them. He made them turn somersaults an' pretend to be dogs an' things like that."

"Well, what was the point of that?" said Roger. "If they weren't real dogs they wouldn't be much fun. Dogs are all right as dogs—"

"The noblest friends of man," put in Charles.

"– but they've got to be real ones. People pretendin' to be dogs are jus' silly."

"No, but *listen*," said Bill irritably. "I keep tellin' you. This man made people do anythin' he wanted jus' by wishin' they'd do it an' hundreds of people came to watch him an' he got paid money for it an' my cousin said it looked as easy as easy an' I don't see why we shouldn't do it."

"Yes, let's," said Charles. "I could do with a bit more money. I keep tryin' to explain this devaluation of the pound to Mr Mince an' he jus' won't understand that he ought to give me more sweets for less money."

"Well, come on, then," said Bill. "Let's have a try."

"How shall we start?" said Roger. "Shall we start wishin' each other to do things?"

"No," said Bill. "We mightn't be much good till we've had some practice. I think we ought to find someone else to do it on – someone fairly small to start with – an' all wish together hard. Then p'raps, when we've had a bit of practice, we can do it sep'rately an' on bigger people."

"Who'll we start on?" said Charles.

Roger looked out of the window of the tool-shed, where they were holding their meeting. At the end of the lawn he could see Jimmy and Bobby engaged in fixing up a "tent" with a walking stick of Mr Manning's and a couple of old sacks.

"Jimmy an' Bobby," he said. "They're small. They ought to be easy enough."

"What shall we wish them to do?" said Bill.

"Climb the church tower an' stop the clock," suggested Charles. "Like the woman in po'try who said 'The curfew shall not toll the knell of parting day'."

They considered this with the respect they generally accorded to Charles's suggestions.

"That's a bit too difficult to start with," said Roger.

"We've got to start with easy things an' work our way up gradu'ly."

"Let's wish them to cross the river by the stepping stones an' bring back one of those pebbles from the other side to show they've done it," said Bill.

"Yes, that's a good idea . . . *Jimmy!*"

Jimmy and Bobby abandoned the tent (which collapsed as soon as their backs were turned) and made their way to the tool-shed.

"You're goin' to be hypnotised," said Roger.

"We're goin' to wish you to do something an' you've got to do it."

"What do you want us to d-do?" said Jimmy.

"We're not goin' to tell you that."

"Well, how can we do it if we don't kn-know?" said Jimmy.

"That's the point," said Bill in exasperation. "You've got to go out an' then go on walkin' down the road thinkin' about nothin' an' then when a feelin' comes over you that you want to do somethin' that means you're hypnotised an' you've got to do it."

"G-got to do what?"

"The thing you've got a feelin' you want to do. That means you're hypnotised . . . Gosh! You are stupid. Don't you understand?"

"Y-y-yes," said Jimmy doubtfully.

"Well, go on out, then we can start wishin'. Remember to think of nothin'."

The two wandered off down the road.

"Are you thinkin' of n-nothin'?" said Jimmy.

"I'm tryin' to," said Bobby, "but when you think of nothin' it keeps turnin' into somethin', doesn't it?"

"Yes, it d-does," agreed Jimmy.

They walked on for some minutes in silence. They were walking in the direction away from the river.

"I don't feel hyp – hyp – hyp— What's the word?"

"Hypnotised," said Bobby.

"Well, I don't f-feel it yet, do you?"

"No, not yet. Perhaps we're goin' too quick for it. Let's walk slower."

They walked on more slowly. Suddenly a small black kitten crossed the road and began to rub itself against their shoes, purring and arching its tail. They stopped to stroke it. Jimmy picked it up. It nestled against him, purring resonantly.

"I've got a s-sort of feeling comin' over me," he said.

"What sort of a feeling?" said Bobby.

"A feeling I'd like to t-take it. I've always w-wanted a kitten an' I 'spect Sandy'd soon get used to it. He's gettin' k-kinder to cats."

"I don't think you ought to," said Bobby.

"They said we'd not g-got to think," Jimmy reminded him. "They said we'd jus' got to do what we'd got a f-feelin' to do an' I've got a feelin' I want to take this k-kitten . . . Well, I've started gettin' hyp – hyp – hyp— What's the word?"

"Hypnotised," said Bobby.

"Well, I've started gettin' hypnotised, all right."

"I've got a feeling I'm goin' to start soon, too," said Bobby.

They walked on through the village – the kitten rubbing its face against Jimmy's chin and purring more loudly than ever – and on to the new building estate. Then, as they were passing a gate, they both stopped again. The French window of a downstairs room stood open, and through it they could see a tea-table and on the tea-table a plate of cream buns.

"I've got another f-feelin' comin' over me," said Jimmy.

"Yes," admitted Bobby. "I've got a bit of one, too."

They walked up to the open French window.

"Have you got a f-feelin' you'd like to go in?" said Jimmy.

"Yes, I have," said Bobby.

A look of satisfaction spread over Jimmy's face.

"We're bein' hyp – hyp—"

"Hypnotised."

"Yes, we're bein' hypnotised, all right, now."

They stood in the little dining-room, looking down at the cream buns.

"I've got a very s-strong feelin' now," said Jimmy, "have you?"

Bobby looked round nervously.

"I don't think—" he began.

"But we've not g-got to think," Jimmy reminded him again. "They said so."

Each stretched out a hand for a cream bun . . . then another . . . then another . . . till the plate was empty.

"I've got another f-feelin' comin' on," said Jimmy, looking at a plate of biscuits.

But at that moment they saw two women – both tall, both gaunt, both elderly – coming in at the gate.

"Gosh!" panted Jimmy. "I've got a sort of feelin' to g-get away quick. Come on."

They went into the hall and through an open back door into a little garden. A high fence surrounded the garden, and there was no gate. In one corner, however, was a little summer-house – a small square wooden room with windows and a door – and into this the two plunged, urged by the strongest "feeling" that the process of hypnotism had yet provided. Jimmy closed the door and looked about him. Evidently the little hut was being redecorated. The walls were half whitewashed and on the floor stood a pail of whitewash. Deck-chairs were stacked against the wall, and there was a pile of cushions in a corner. Jimmy put down the black kitten on the floor and looked about him. The black kitten sprang sideways at a cobweb and began to tear it to pieces.

"I've got another f-feelin' comin' over me," said Jimmy.

"What?" said Bobby apprehensively.

"I've got a f-feelin' that I'd like to finish the whitewashin'. It looks jolly easy an' they s-said we'd got to do what our feelings t-told us to do."

Bobby looked at the pail of whitewash and his scruples vanished.

"Yes," he said. "The same feelin's comin' over me, too."

For the next quarter of an hour a blinding blizzard of whitewash filled the hut, falling impartially on everything within it – on walls, floor, deck-chairs, cushions, and the black kitten – and coating Jimmy and Bobby from head to foot. Finally, when their joint efforts had upset the bucket so that the wash flowed in rivulets all over the floor and trickled under the door out on to the grass, they drew breath and surveyed their efforts.

"Gosh!" said Jimmy. "It's a b-bit of a mess, isn't it? We're bein' hyp – hyp – hyp—"

"Hypnotised."

"Yes. It's acting very s-strong now, isn't it? I've got a f-feelin' to get away, haven't you? To get right away qu-quick."

Bobby looked out of the window.

"We can't," he said. "There's a woman sittin' writin' at a table at the window, where she'd see us if we went out."

"If anyone comes," said Jimmy, "I'm goin' to p-pretend to be asleep. People can't do m-much to you if you're asleep. *You* don't n-need to pretend." For Bobby was a boy who could fall asleep on the slightest provocation.

"Well, I do feel a bit tired," said Bobby.

"Look, the k-kitten's gone to sleep already."

The black kitten – black no longer – exhausted with chasing cobwebs, had curled up on a cushion and was sleeping soundly.

"I'm feelin' a bit tired, too," said Jimmy. "I 'spect it's with bein' hyp – hyp – hyp—"

"Hypnotised."

"Yes, hypnotised." He spread the cushions out on the floor. "Come on. Let's have a r-rest."

The Misses Cranston had got their tea ready and then taken a stroll to the end of the road. On their return Miss Henrietta had looked at the tea-table with an air of mystification.

"I'm getting more and more absent-minded," she said. "I could have sworn I put the cream buns on that plate. I did, didn't I, dear?"

"I really don't remember," said Miss Charlotte mournfully, "and it doesn't matter as far as I'm concerned. I'm so worried about Blackie that I couldn't eat a thing."

"He may turn up yet," said Miss Henrietta.

"I'm afraid not," said Miss Charlotte. "He's been gone the whole day. A little black kitten like that! Anything might have happened to him. If he wandered on to the main road he might have been run over."

"Oh, no, dear!" said Miss Henrietta, then, trying to turn to more cheerful subjects, "Let's go out after tea and see if the workmen have finished whitewashing the summer-house."

"Very well," agreed Miss Charlotte with a sigh. "I have a few letters I must write first."

When Miss Charlotte had finished her letters, the sisters went out into the garden.

"Yes, I think they've finished it," said Miss Henrietta as they approached the hut. "I can see the inside through the window." She went nearer and gave a scream. "It's Blackie . . . No, it can't be . . . it's white . . . Yes, it *is* . . . Good *Heavens*!"

She flung open the door.

On a whitewashed floor on whitewashed cushions two whitewashed boys lay asleep. Between them curled up a whitewashed cat.

And at that moment the Three Musketeers arrived.

"'Scuse me," panted Roger, "but we're lookin' for Jimmy an' Bobby. You see, we were hypnotising them an' we wished them to go over the river by the stepping stones an' we stopped hypnotising for a bit—"

"'Cause we were watching a dog fight in the road," explained Bill.

"An' now we can't find them—"

"They've disappeared, leaving no trace," said Charles.

"An' we're afraid they fell into the water when we stopped hypnotising," said Roger.

"And got carried away by the roaring torrent deep and wide," said Charles.

"And a boy said he'd seen them come into your

ON A WHITEWASHED FLOOR ON WHITEWASHED CUSHIONS
TWO WHITEWASHED BOYS LAY ASLEEP.

house," said Roger, "so—" He saw Jimmy and Bobby and stopped short.

Jimmy sat up and looked round the circle of accusing faces.

"It's not our fault," he said. "We were – hyp . . . Bobby!" Bobby was slowly awakening. "What's the word, Bobby? Hyp – hyp – hyp—"

"Hurray!" said Bobby sleepily.

Chapter 23

The Highwaymen

The Three Musketeers were strolling aimlessly down the road when the figure of Toothy suddenly appeared, coming towards them and wearing that slightly forlorn look that the figure of Toothy generally wore. They stopped.

"Hello," said Roger. "Where are you going?"

"I'm going out to tea," said Toothy.

"Where?" said Charles.

"I don't know yet," said Toothy. "It depends who asks me."

"Why?" said Bill.

"Well, you see, she said I'd got to go out to tea 'cause there's a man comin' to tea at home to see my father on important business an' this man's got to be put into a good temper 'cause of this important business, so," simply, "I've got to go out to tea."

"Well, why should you have to go out to tea jus' 'cause of that?"

"Well, I s'pose this man doesn't like children," said Toothy, adding with an air of philosophic melancholy: "Not many people do."

"I think it's a shame," said Charles. "Turning you out like – like a worn-out glove."

"I don't mind," said Toothy. "This man came over to see us one day las' week an' I didn't like him. He was awful. He talked a lot of nonsense an' said he wished he'd lived in the good old days when life was full of danger an' excitement an' stuff like that. He said that danger was the only thing that made life worth living, and he said that his motto was 'Live dangerously'. He had a red face an' a big yellow car with black lamps like a huge insect, an' he patted my head an' called me a little man, so I'm jolly glad I'm not goin' to be in to tea . . . An' she's in an awful muddle, gettin' things ready for him, so I'm jus' as well out of it."

"Yes, but how can you go out to tea, if you don't know where you're goin'?" said Bill.

"I do know where I'm goin'," said Toothy. "I'm goin' wherever anyone asks me."

"You could come to tea with us," said Roger, "but I think there's only bread and jam."

"You could come to us," said Bill. "There was goin' to be crab sandwiches but the crab's gone bad."

"We've got nearly three-quarters of a jelly," said Charles. "It was left over from lunch an' we're goin' to finish it up for tea."

"Thanks awfully, Charles," said Toothy.

The four wandered off together down the road.

Jimmy and Bobby, who had come up while the discussion was going on and had hung about on the outskirts of the group as usual, stood watching them till they vanished round the bend in the road.

"I bet Toothy eats most of that jelly," said Bobby. "He can eat quicker than anyone else I know."

"P'raps it's b-because of his teeth," said Jimmy.

"Well, come on," said Bobby. "Let's go to the brook an' catch some tiddlers."

But the state of affairs in Toothy's home as described by

Toothy had struck Jimmy's imagination and he felt an irresistible desire to go and see it for himself.

"Let's go an' have a l-look at Toothy's," he suggested.

"No, let's go an' catch tiddlers," said Bobby.

"We can catch t-tiddlers afterwards," said Jimmy. "Let's go to Toothy's first."

"All right," said Bobby resignedly.

Treading warily, ready to flee at sight of Toothy's father, they made their way to the back premises of Toothy's house. The kitchen door stood open, and the kitchen was empty except for Toothy's mother, who was moving about among a wild confusion of crockery and cooking utensils, singing "Hearts of Oak" to herself.

"Hello," she said. "You'd better not come in. I'm in an awful muddle getting ready for a visitor."

"Yes, Toothy was t-tellin' Roger about him," said Jimmy, eyeing the chaos with interest.

"Herbert doesn't like him," said Mrs Forrester, picking an eggshell up from the floor, "and I don't much, but if he can put my husband in the way of making a little money – well, Heaven knows we can do with it."

She sighed and began to hum "You Should See Me Dance the Polka".

"When is he c-coming?" said Jimmy.

"He'll be here any minute now," said Mrs Forrester. "I've made a cake, but it's not turned out right, so I shall have to use the one I bought last week. If I cut off the end pieces it won't seem as dry as it is. Look! Here's the one I made. There's no two ways about it, is there?" She dived into the sea of heterogeneous articles on the table and brought out a cake, so heavily depressed in the middle that there was practically no middle left. "Well, I couldn't ask anyone to eat that, could I?"

"C-c-couldn't you?" said Jimmy wistfully.

She laughed.

"All right. You take it. I'll be glad to get it out of the way. I'd have given it to Herbert but he'd gone when I took it out of the oven. Here it is!"

"Thanks awfully," said Jimmy gratefully, taking it from her.

"That's all right," she said, "and run off now. I've got the tea to see to and I want to get straight before this man comes."

They left her singing "Clementine", and made their way down to the road, dividing the cake as they went. They munched blissfully as they walked along.

"It's jolly g-good, isn't it?" said Jimmy indistinctly.

"Yes, it is," said Bobby. "I like the sunk part the best, too, don't you?"

"Yes, I do," said Jimmy. "It gives it a sort of t-taste of toffee."

"Well, now let's go an' catch those tiddlers," said Bobby when the last crumb had vanished. "I want to try an' get a hundred before bedtime."

"N-no," said Jimmy slowly. "I want to do somethin' to h-help Toothy's mother. It was jolly good c-cake an' it was jolly decent of her to give it us."

"Well, what *could* we do to help her?" said Bobby.

"We could do somethin' to help put that m-man in a good temper."

"What?" said Bobby.

Jimmy considered.

"Well . . . He said he'd like to have lived in the g-good ole days when excitin' things happened. Let's – let's give him somethin' excitin' out of the g-good ole days."

"What could we give him?"

"That's what we've got to think out."

"What about a boar's head an' a wassail? We got a prize for that once."

"No, that's only a Christmas thing. Besides, he wants d-danger, an' there's no danger in b-boars' heads an' wassails . . . I *know*!" with a burst of inspiration. "Highwaymen!"

"Highwaymen?" said Bobby, bewildered.

"Yes, listen," said Jimmy excitedly. "We could be highwaymen an' hold up his car an' say 'Your money or your life,' an' then he'd feel he'd l-lived dangerously an' it'd put him in a good temper."

"I dunno," said Bobby doubtfully. "It doesn't *sound* the sort of thing to put people into good tempers."

"But I k-keep tellin' you," said Jimmy. "This man l-likes danger."

"Well, anyway, he won't b'lieve we're highwaymen. We don't *look* like highwaymen."

"We'll have to get m-masks an' pistols, of course. We'll look like highwaymen, all right, when we've got those."

"How'll we get them?"

"Well, let's go home an' see what we can f-find. I bet we find somethin'."

The preparation of masks and pistols took some time, but the final result was undeniably impressive.

Jimmy wore a piece of black chiffon that he had found in the rag-bag. It completely covered his face except for two large and jagged holes that he had cut out for his eyes. He carried a clothes-peg, painted black, that, held at a certain angle and at a certain distance, gave, he considered, a realistic impression of a pistol. Bobby, having tried in vain to make a mask of a piece of cardboard, had finally given up the attempt and inked the top part of his

face. He carried a carrot that he had long treasured because of its likeness in shape to a pistol.

"You look j-jolly good," said Jimmy as they made their
way to the point in the road, near Toothy's house, that
they had fixed on for the "hold-up". "I do, too, d-don't
I?"

"Yes," said Bobby. "I think we both look like real
ones."

"Let's get into the d-ditch," said Jimmy, "an' wait till
he comes along, then we'll d-dash out an' hold him up."

They clambered into the ditch and crouched among
the grass and mud at the bottom.

All the romance of Jimmy's romantic soul was aroused
by the situation. The real facts of the case – exciting
though they were – were too tame to satisfy him. He
wasn't just trying to put Toothy's father's visitor in a good
temper because Toothy's mother had given him a cake.
He was trying to rescue a beautiful princess called Sally
from a cruel tyrant. The cruel tyrant had locked her up in
a lonely fortress, and Jimmy was going to conquer the
tyrant and rescue her. The tyrant was on his way down
the road now and Jimmy was going to leap out with a
shining sword and beat him to his knees.

The black-and-yellow car hove suddenly into sight.

"Here he is," said Jimmy. "C-come on."

Bobby leapt from the ditch brandishing his carrot . . .
then lost his footing and fell sprawling in the middle of
the road. The car drew up with a screeching of brakes a
few inches short of him, and a large man with a red face
and shaggy eyebrows got out of it. As he got out, a rain-
coat that had been hanging over the back of the driving
seat fell into the road and out of its pocket dropped – a
bunch of keys. Keys! The keys of the fortress where the

princess was imprisoned! Without a second's thought Jimmy seized them, scrambled over a stile and set off at a run over the field. The large, angry man pursued him.

The race was an unequal one . . . Before Jimmy reached the gate leading to the next field, the man had caught up with him, taken the keys and boxed his ears with such violence that for a few minutes all he could see was a constellation of dancing stars. By the time they had vanished, both the large, angry man and the car had vanished, too.

Jimmy made his way slowly back to the road. Bobby was just climbing out of the ditch. They stood for a moment or two silently considering the situation. Jimmy had lost his "mask" in his flight across the field and Bobby's had spread over his face in a series of curiously

JIMMY SET OFF AT A RUN WITH THE LARGE, ANGRY
MAN IN PURSUIT.

shaped smudges. Both clothes-peg and carrot had disappeared in the confusion.

"Well, we weren't much g-good as highwaymen," panted Jimmy.

"Yes, we were," said Bobby. He dived into the ditch again and emerged, dragging a large attaché case. "I took this out of the back of the car while he was running after you. I highwaymanned him, all right."

"But gosh!" said Jimmy, horrified. "You oughtn't to've d-done that. We'll get into an awful row."

"Well," admitted Bobby, looking a little crestfallen, "I did sort of get a bit carried away. I sort of forgot it wasn't real."

"We'll have to take it to Toothy's, that's all," said Jimmy, "an' it'll p-prob'ly put him in a bad temper 'stead of a good one . . . Jus' think if we've put him in a b-bad temper 'stead of a good one after her givin' us all that cake!"

They made their way along the road towards Toothy's house, carrying the suitcase.

"Gosh!" said Jimmy as the church clock came into sight through the trees. "It's nearly six o'clock."

Bobby consulted his watch.

"Yes, so it is," he said.

"We took longer than we meant gettin' those masks an' pistols. He mus' have been goin' away from Toothy's when we held him up – not to Toothy's. He mus' have h-had tea an' been goin' away."

"Yes, he must," agreed Bobby. "'Course he must when you come to think of it. He *was* goin' away from Toothy's."

Jimmy heaved a sigh of relief.

"It can't have put him in a bad temper before he went

there, then. It won't matter so much p-puttin' him in a bad temper when he's goin' home 'cause they'll have fixed up this important business that Toothy had to go out to tea because of. We'll get in a row for t-takin' his case, but p'raps Toothy's mother can get it back to him without Toothy's father knowin' about it. She will, if she can, I know."

As they neared the house they heard the voice of Toothy's father upraised on its usual stentorian note . . . and their courage failed them.

"Let's *creep* up an' find out what's happenin' before we take in the c-case," said Jimmy.

Bobby nodded agreement, and they crept stealthily round to the open back door, hovering in its shadow as they surveyed the scene.

Toothy's mother was coping with the chaotic kitchen in her own vague fashion, taking things up, putting them down in different places, then moving them back to where they had been before, humming "Oh, for the Wings, for the Wings of a Dove", softly to herself as she did so. Toothy's father strode to and fro about the room, declaiming exultantly.

"A red-letter day, my dear!" he was shouting. "A red-letter day! It isn't every day in the week that your husband turns fifty pounds into two hundred. I think I may congratulate myself I—"

The telephone bell rang and he went to answer it. His voice rumbled in the distance, then rose to a bellow that made his wife stop short at "– far away would I fly" and drop the handful of soda she had meant for the washing-up water into a jug of milk. The bellow grew louder as her husband strode back into the kitchen.

"I've been fleeced!" he roared. "Fleeced! Sold!

Swindled! That was Smithson warning me that the man's a crook and a scoundrel. There's a warrant out for him tonight. He says I'll never see a penny of my fifty pounds again."

"But can't you stop the cheque, dear?" said Mrs Forrester.

His bellow made the china on the shelves rattle.

"Cheque? I paid the blighter in cash. He said the banks would be closed and it was very important that the deal should go through at once and I'd got the notes ready in case he—"

He suddenly espied Jimmy and Bobby lurking in the doorway. With a fresh bellow of rage he bore down on them and dragged them into the kitchen, a hand on the collar of each.

"What do you mean by coming round here like this?" he roared. "Who are you? How dare you? What do you mean by it?" He accompanied each sentence by a shake so violent that the attaché case fell from Bobby's hand to the floor. "What's that? What have you got there? How dare you bring your rubbish round here? Take it away. Take it—"

He picked up the case and opened it. On the top lay a packet of banknotes.

"My notes!" he shouted. "My notes!"

Jimmy and Bobby walked slowly homewards. They still felt bewildered and deafened. Toothy's father had bellowed thanks and congratulations at them in the intervals of berating them for taking cases from people's cars, coming to houses uninvited, having ink on their faces and mud on their shoes. Finally he had dismissed them with a roar that still rang in their ears.

"Well, we'd better g-go home now, I s'pose," said Jimmy. "It's jus' about b-bedtime, I 'spect."

"Yes," agreed Bobby with a sigh. "We've never got those tiddlers, after all."

Jimmy was silent for a few moments.

"No," he said at last, "but we've l-lived dangerously."

Chapter 24

The Newspaper

It was Charles who suggested publishing a newspaper. "Lit'rature's goin' to be my career," he said, "so I want to get started in good time."

Roger and Bill considered the idea in silence. The three were in the tool-shed on their usual seats of roller, mowing machine and wheelbarrow.

"All right," said Roger at last, "but I'm the head of the gang, so I've got to be captain."

"You call it editor when it's a newspaper," said Charles with an air of superiority, "an' you can be. I'm goin' to write a serial to be continued in our next every day an' I'm not goin' to waste my insp'ration on anythin' else. Shakespeare wasn't an editor an' I'm jolly well not goin' to be."

They looked at him, deeply impressed.

"Well, what am I goin' to be?" said Bill, realising suddenly that he alone held no office.

"You can write a leading article," said Charles.

"What's that?" said Bill.

"It tells people what they ought to be thinkin' about things."

"Why can't they think that for themselves?"

"Well, why should they," said Charles, "if they can pay a newspaper to do it for 'em?"

"What shall I tell 'em to think?" said Bill with a harassed frown.

"Anythin' you like."

"All right," said Bill, his brow clearing. "I'll tell 'em to think that they ought to give sweets in schools 'stead of milk, 'cause milk's got a rotten taste an' sweets haven't. Is that all right?"

"Yes . . . but they gen'rally tell the government how to save money as well."

"All right," said Bill. "They can save money by stoppin' printing all those Latin and French books that we have to do in school. That'll save money all right."

"Yes, that's a good idea," said Charles in grudging approval.

"An' what do I do?" said Roger.

"Oh, you just tell us how much to write," said Charles, drawing a grubby exercise book out of his pocket. "I brought this along so's we could start on it at once. Look! There's jus' three pages left. You have columns for news-papers an' I've divided the pages into two columns each."

"That's easy, then," said Roger. "Bill can do two columns and you can do two an'—"

"I've got to have three columns," broke in Charles indignantly. "My serial's goin' to be full of hair-raisin' adventures an' breathtakin' escapes an' – an' people's lives hangin' by threads an' – an' deathly dangers an' murders an' kidnappin's an' ghostly hauntin's, an' if you think I can get all that into two columns you're jolly well mistaken."

"Oh, all right," said Roger, bowing before the storm of Charles's artistic temperament, "have your own way. Have three columns."

"Well, that leaves one," said Bill. "What'll we do with it?

A small head peeped round the door.

"Please, c-can we have it?" said Jimmy. "We once tried havin' a newspaper an' bein' reporters an' it didn't come off, so we'd l-like to try again."

"Have you been listening all the time?" said Roger in a tone of august displeasure.

"Yes," said Jimmy, entering the shed, followed by Bobby.

"Have you no self-respect?" said Charles sternly.

"N-not much," said Jimmy, after giving the question a moment or two's honest consideration.

"Well, we ought to have reporters, you know," said Bobby. "They do in newspapers."

"All right," said Roger, yielding. "You can try. We'll let you have one column to try."

Jimmy and Bobby hurried to Jimmy's home.

"Let's look in the newspaper an' see what sort of things they r-report," suggested Jimmy.

He took the local paper from the newspaper rack and spread it out over the table. The two heads bent over it.

"This part's all about weddings," said Jimmy. "It keeps sayin' what the bride wore for a g-going-away dress. Listen. 'Pale blue dress an' beige (he pronounced it "beege") coat an' hat.' It's all that s-sort of thing."

"Well, here's a robbery," said Bobby. "Look. 'Thieves broke into the premises of Mr John Dawson early yester-day morning' . . ."

"Here's another wedding. All about another g-going-away dress. Look. 'Blue-an'-white spotted silk with a smoked neck—' Gosh! It s-sounds awful."

Bobby craned his head over Jimmy's neck.

"'Smocked neck line,'" he corrected, looking at the words.

"It s-still sounds awful," said Jimmy.

"Look! Here's another robbery. It's all weddings an' robberies."

"Well, we'll have to have t-two columns. One for weddings an' one for robberies."

"Yes . . . Let's go back an' tell 'em."

"Wait a minute," said Jimmy. "I'll g-get a note-book. Reporters have g-got to have note-books. I've got an old one that my father gave me. I'll g-get a pencil, too."

A few minutes later the two presented themselves at the tool-shed. The editorial staff was hard at work. Roger, who had decided to include the weather report among his duties, was just writing "A troff of low preshure" . . . Bill was biting his pencil over his leading article, and Charles had already reached the end of his first chapter (headed "The garstly krime, a cereal storey"). The final paragraph read: "And so we will leeve our herro knashing his teath and taring at the crule feters that chaned him by the waste to the flor of the dunjun littel did he guess what the next day would bring fourth to be kontinyoud."

"What do you want?" said Roger irritably.

"Please, c-can we have two columns?" said Jimmy, "'cause we've got t-two sorts of reportin' to do."

"No, you can't," said Roger.

"B-but—"

Charles ran his hands wildly through his hair.

"Go away," he shouted. "You're messing up all my insp'ration."

"B-but—"

"Go away," said Roger threateningly.

The two went slowly and despondently out of the gate and into the road. Then gradually Jimmy's face brightened.

"T-tell you what!" he said. "We could sort of j-join them together."

"Join what together?"

"Weddings an' robberies."

"How could we?"

"Well, we could f-find a thief an' see what c-clothes he wore for g-going away in an' that'd get them both in, wouldn't it?"

"Yes," said Bobby, doubtfully.

"Well, come on. Let's s-start."

They walked through the village and out to the building estate. As they approached a house at the end of a short row of houses, the front door opened and a young man came out, carrying an attaché case.

"P'raps he's a thief," said Jimmy hopefully.

"No, he isn't," said Bobby. "He lives there. You can see he lives there."

"Well, I'm goin' to make n-notes about him, anyway," said Jimmy, pulling out his note-book.

At the gate the young man turned to the window of the house and took off his hat with a smile and a flourish.

"There, you see!" said Bobby. "I told you he lived there."

"I d-don't care," said Jimmy doggedly. "I'm goin' to g-go on makin' notes about him."

The young man got on to a motorcycle and went off.

"Oh, come on," said Bobby impatiently. "Let's go on an' try to find a real one."

They wandered on to the end of the estate without any result, then slowly retraced their steps. At the gate of the house from which the young man had emerged stood two women and a policeman. One of the women was talking excitedly.

"WELL, I'M GOIN' TO MAKE N-NOTES ABOUT HIM,
ANYWAY," SAID JIMMY.

"I've come back to find the whole place ransacked,"
she was saying. "He's taken everything of value – all my
jewellery and my precious bits of Georgian silver. He had
the effrontery to take off his hat as he reached the gate as
if he'd been paying a call. My next-door neighbour here
saw him and thought he was just a visitor and she can't
describe him at all."

"I'm sorry, dear," said the other woman apologetically.
"I just saw him casually and didn't notice anything about
him. I've always been unobservant."

Jimmy gave a modest cough and took out his note-
book.

"I can tell you what he was g-goin' away in," he said.
He turned the pages. "He'd got a blue hat an' a blue-an'-

r-red tie an' a sort of grey coat an' blue trousers an' blue socks an' brown shoes."

"Good Heavens!" gasped the policeman.

Jimmy turned another page.

"I can tell you the g-goin' away number of his motorcycle, t-too," he said.

Quarter of an hour later, when the thief had been caught as the result of Jimmy's description, Jimmy and Bobby burst excitedly into the tool-shed.

"We've caught a thief in his g-goin' away clothes," panted Jimmy, "so you've g-g-got to give us two columns."

Chapter 25

Midsummer Night's Dream

"What's this play you're g-goin' to do about, Roger?" said Jimmy.

He and Roger were filling in an idle hour after tea sitting under an apple tree in the garden, munching windfalls.

"Oh, jus' a play," said Roger vaguely.

Roger, as one of the elder pupils of St Adrian's, had been chosen to take part in the school play, and Jimmy, too young and insignificant even to hand out programmes, was very curious about it.

"Well, t-tell me about it," pleaded Jimmy.

"You're only a kid," said Roger in a tone of elder-brother superiority, muffled by a mouthful of Worcester Pearmain. "You wouldn't understand it."

"I m-might," said Jimmy, taking a bite and spitting it out. "That one's all maggoty . . . I s-sometimes do understand things. T-try me an' see."

"Well," said Roger, "it's a play called *Midsummer Night's Dream*. Charles is a king called Theseus."

"An' what are you?" said Jimmy.

"I'm a man called Bottom."

"An' what do you d-do?" said Jimmy. "Gosh! I nearly swallowed a wasp. You'd have an awful time with it buzzing about inside an' stingin' your stomach if you swallowed it, wouldn't you? . . . What does this man do?"

"He has a magic donkey's head," said Roger, "that makes people fall in love with anyone that's wearing it . . . Look! We've finished all the decent windfalls. Let's make some more."

"All r-right."

They attacked the trunk of the tree, and by means of a process that Mr Manning always referred to as a synthetic cyclone, brought down another shower of "windfalls" on to the grass. Then they sat down again and set to work on them.

"Why do grown-ups peel them?" said Jimmy suddenly. "Apples, I m-mean."

"Haven't a clue," said Roger, taking a crisp bite into a particularly promising specimen.

"Roger . . ."

"Yes?"

"About this d-donkey's head . . . I wore a donkey's head when I was a wait at Christmas an' no one fell in l-love with me."

"That ole thing of Freddie Pelham's!" said Roger contemptuously. "That was only cardboard. This is the real thing."

"Do you mean a *really* magic one?" said Jimmy in an awestruck voice.

"Of course," said Roger, winking at his half-eaten apple for want of anything else to wink at.

"Well, who falls in l-love with you?"

"A woman called Titania falls in love with me in the play, but anyone that saw me would fall in love with me when I'd got it on."

"Gosh!" said Jimmy. "Where is it?"

"Bill's bringing it round here this evening. We're goin'

to keep my donkey's head an' his lion's head in the spare bedroom till the dress rehearsal, so's they won't get messed up."

"Is there a l-lion in it, too?" said Jimmy.

"Yes, but it's not important," said Roger.

"Don't people fall in l-love with it?"

"No, they only fall in love with the donkey's head," said Roger. He aimed his apple core at a sparrow (who gave a squawk of derision as it missed him by several inches), filled his pocket with apples, and rose to his feet. "Well, I've got to go and do my homework now."

"I've g-got some to do, too," said Jimmy.

"You!" said Roger contemptuously. After one of his recurrent spells of fraternising with Jimmy he always liked to reassert his position of superiority. "A kid like you doesn't know the meaning of the word."

"Yes, I d-do," said Jimmy. "I've got a whole l-lot of Arithmetic homework."

"Twice two are four," jibed Roger as he went indoors.

In no way abashed by this (for Roger's superiority in every way was as much an article of faith with Jimmy as it was with Roger himself), Jimmy went in search of Bobby and told him about the donkey's head. Later, goggle-eyed with excitement, they watched two magnificent heads being carried into the house and put on to the floor in the spare bedroom. The thrill of this would have lasted for several days had it not been dwarfed the next morning by a new and greater excitement. For a fair had appeared overnight in Three Acre Meadow, with caravans and lorries and their attendant crowds of men, dogs, women and children – all, even the dogs, wearing, in Jimmy's and Bobby's eyes, the air of beings from a world of glamour and romance.

"I bet my father'll take us to it," said Jimmy. "He likes f-fairs an' things."

Mr Manning, approached by his sons at lunch, agreed to take them to the fair – but with reservations, for Jimmy, practising with his bow and arrow before breakfast, had shot an arrow into the air and it had fallen to earth by way of the postman, who was just coming in at the gate. The postman had delivered his complaint together with a pile of bills, and Mr Manning was not in the best of tempers.

"Any more trouble from you, young man," he said, looking darkly at Jimmy, "and the fair's off as far as you're concerned. In other words, you'll have had it. Understand?"

"Y-y-yes," said Jimmy.

He meant, of course, to go very carefully, but, chasing Bobby through the village in a rather complicated game in which Bobby was an enemy paratrooper and Jimmy a commando, he forgot everything else in the thrill of the chase and plunged through the hole in Miss Pettigrew's hedge, intending to take a short cut over her lawn and fall upon Bobby from the ambush of the side gate. It was unfortunate that he tripped as he crossed the lawn and fell spreadeagled over a bed of tulips. It was still more unfortunate that Miss Pettigrew happened to witness the disaster from her kitchen window. She swooped down upon him, her face set and tense with anger.

"I'm s-s-sorry," stammered Jimmy, scrambling to his feet and removing a clod of earth from his mouth.

"You naughty boy!" said Miss Pettigrew. "And just when I have my niece staying with me and particularly want the place to look its best! I shall ring up your father this very evening and tell him. And now go away at once!"

Jimmy went away at once, meeting Bobby at the gate. Realising from Jimmy's expression that he had stopped being a commando, Bobby stopped being a paratrooper.

"What's happened?" he said.

Jimmy told him what had happened.

"An' now I shan't be able to g-go to the fair," he ended mournfully, as they began to walk slowly back along the road.

"Gosh!" said Bobby in sympathetic dismay. "Isn't there anythin' we can do about it?"

"Let's th-think," said Jimmy.

They thought. Gradually the gloom vanished from Jimmy's countenance.

"I've g-got an idea," he said.

"What?" said Bobby.

"Listen. You know that m-magic donkey's head that Roger's got that makes people fall in love with the one that's wearing it?"

"Yes?"

"Well, if I wore it an' Miss Pettigrew fell in l-love with me, she wouldn't tell my father, would she?"

"No, I s'pose not," said Bobby doubtfully, "but I can't imagine her fallin' in love with you."

"She would if I had the head on," said Jimmy confidently. "Roger s-said so."

"Well, I'll wear the lion's head," said Bobby. "If you're going to wear an animal's head, I don't see why I shouldn't. I've always wanted to wear a lion's head."

"All right," said Jimmy, "but I don't think anyone'll fall in l-love with you."

"I don't want them to," said Bobby.

Events proved favourable to Jimmy's plan. He and Bobby took the heads from the spare bedroom and transferred them to Miss Pettigrew's cottage without meeting anyone. They stopped at the hole in the hedge and cautiously inspected the garden. In the middle of the lawn stood a deck-chair with a book on the grass beside it. At the edge of the lawn were two small laurel bushes.

"L-look," said Jimmy. "I 'spect she's been sittin' there readin' an' she's jus' gone in an' she'll be comin' b-back in a minute. Let's hide behind these bushes an' then when she comes back I'll put my head out an' – an' – an' she'll fall in l-love with me."

"And what then?" said Bobby.

"Then I'll ask her not to tell my father an' she won't, 'cause she'll be in l-love with me."

"All right," said Bobby. He was a boy who accepted most situations philosophically and without question.

They put on their heads, took up their positions behind the bushes and waited. Very soon the French window of the sitting-room opened and a pretty girl came out, accompanied by an angular and somewhat peevish-looking youth. Jimmy recognised the girl as Miss Pettigrew's niece. The strains of the fair floated out from Three Acre Meadow. The peevish youth shuddered.

"They oughtn't to be allowed to have those things so near the village," he said querulously. "I hear they've got a sort of wild animal show there. Someone told me there was a lion."

"It's probably a tame one, if they have, Percival," said Miss Pettigrew's niece, stifling a yawn. "You needn't be frightened."

"Lions are never tame," said the youth. "Suppose it escaped . . . I shan't know a moment's peace of mind till the whole wretched affair's moved on somewhere else. I—"

Suddenly he caught sight of the lion's head through the laurel bush. His jaw dropped, his eyes started, his cheeks paled. A movement in the next bush caught his notice and his terrified gaze turned in its direction. Two ears and an enormous savage mouth. Another wild animal . . . A jackal . . . or was it a hyena? The whole Wild Animal Show must have escaped from the fair.

Jimmy, tickled by the inside of his head, gave a strangled sneeze. With a yell of terror the young man turned and fled. Jimmy stood upright from behind his bush.

"Good heavens!" said Miss Pettigrew's niece. She looked from him to Bobby, who was also rising from his foliage. "What on earth is all this?"

With some difficulty, the two removed their heads and told her what it was. She broke into a peal of laughter.

"Well, I'm very grateful to you," she said. "Percival has been pestering the life out of me and completely spoiling

WITH A YELL OF TERROR THE YOUNG MAN FLED.

my visit. Now he'll never dare to show his face here again. Thank you very much."

"It's quite all r-right," said Jimmy with mournful politeness, "but we aren't any nearer goin' to the f-fair."

"Don't you worry about that," said Miss Pettigrew's niece. "I think I can manage my aunt. Anyway, let's make sure of it and go to it now, shall we, the three of us? We'll take the heads and leave them at Jimmy's house on the way, then we'll go straight on to the fair and have the time of our lives."

"Th-thank you," said Jimmy fervently. He looked down at his donkey's head with an expression of regret. "I don't think it's a very g-good one. It didn't make any-one f-fall in love with me."

"Yes, it did, Jimmy," said Miss Pettigrew's niece. "I fell in love with you at first sight. You don't mind if I call you Bottom from now on, do you?"

"N-no," said Jimmy, "an' I'll call you . . ." he paused, searching his mind for an elusive name, then brought out triumphantly, "I'll call you T-t-t-titanic."

Chapter 26

The Criminal

Jimmy plodded down the road, his hands thrust into his pockets, his brows drawn into a scowl. Life was unusually gloomy for him. Bobby was away on holiday, and he was in disgrace at home. A well-meaning attempt to mend his father's lawnmower by incorporating into it some pieces from his mother's mincing machine had brought retribution from both his parents, and he was so deeply in disgrace that he felt the wisest course was to absent himself from his home till the memory of his offence had become less vivid in their minds.

I was only tryin' to help, he ruminated morosely, intensifying his scowl and digging his hands deeper into his pockets. They needn't 've treated me like a crim'nal jus' 'cause I was tryin' to *help*. All right – his brow cleared – I'll *be* a crim'nal. If people treat you like a crim'nal, you might as well *be* one. I'll be a real crim'nal an' see how they like *that*! He looked about him, considering the scope for criminal activities provided by his immediate surroundings . . .

He was passing Miss Pettigrew's cottage. Her hen-run was shut off by a door of wire netting from her bed of lettuces . . . He'd open the door of her hen-run and let the hens out into her bed of lettuces . . . He walked on down the road, something of his resentment assuaged by this imaginary exploit . . . He passed the post office and general shop, at the door of which was stacked a neat pile of tins – floor polish, furniture polish, boot polish, tile polish . . . All right! He'd knock the whole lot down and kick them about the road. In imagination, he watched himself doing this and felt yet further cheered and solaced . . . Next came Miss Tankerton's garden. In the middle of it stood a treasured fountain that she only turned on when she had guests. All right! He'd stop up the holes with putty, so that the next time she had a party and turned it on, it wouldn't work. He gave a sardonic laugh as he saw the picture in his imagination – a circle of Miss Tankerton's guests standing round and waiting for the shining cascade of water that never came . . . He walked slowly on to the end of the road.

In Mrs Bolton's garden her fat pug dog stood at the edge of the lily pond, sniffing the water. One touch of Jimmy's foot would precipitate him among the goldfish and water lilies. Good! Jimmy seemed to see him splashing about and snorting indignantly . . .

Then he turned to survey the road he had just traversed. He did not see the small stocky figure who had in reality trudged slowly and decorously along it. He saw the daredevil, the desperado, who had let Miss Pettigrew's hens into her lettuces, kicked over the tins at the door of the post office, sealed up Miss Tankerton's fountain, pushed Mrs Bolton's pug into her lily pond . . . He repeated his sardonic laugh and continued on his way. So deeply engrossed was he by his reflections that he almost ran into a boy with flaming red hair, wearing a striped jersey, who was coming from the opposite direction.

"Look where you're goin'," said the boy truculently.

"Look where you're g-goin' yourself," said Jimmy, with lingering traces of the desperado in his voice.

The boy seemed mollified by his aggressiveness.

"What's your name?"

"Jimmy Manning. What's yours?"

"Mind your own business. Where are you goin'?"

"Mind *your* own business."

There was no rancour in the exchange, but the conversation appeared to have reached an impasse. Jimmy, however, felt an overpowering desire to find an audience for his career of crime, and the red-haired boy was better than no one.

"Huh!" he continued with a swagger. "You'd be s'prised if you knew what *I've* been d-doin' this mornin'."

"What?" said the boy.

"I've let Miss Pettigrew's hens into her lettuces an' I've kicked over the t-tins outside the post office an' I've blocked up Miss Tankerton's f-fountain an' I've pushed Miss Bolton's d-dog into her pond."

The red-haired boy uttered a snort of amused contempt.

"Blimey! That's nothin'," he said. "D'you know what *I've* been a-doin'?"

There was a sinister relish in his voice that roused all Jimmy's curiosity.

"N-no," he said. "Go on. T-tell me."

"Well, listen," said the boy. "I found a caravan in a field, an' while the chap wot it belongs to was away I went in an' mucked up all 'is grub – put 'is currants in 'is salt an' so on – an I stuffed 'is shoes up the chimney an' threw all 'is tins of food into the ditch. An' 'e'd left 'is key in the door so I 'id it in 'is jar of sugar an' I bet it'll take 'im a month of Sundays a-findin' of it."

"G-gosh!" said Jimmy, breathless with admiration. He felt humbled in the presence of this superior artist. It was evident that the boy's imagination functioned on a far higher plane than his own. "*G-gosh!*" he said again.

"Well, s'long," said the boy. "Got no time to waste on kids."

With that he went on down the road.

Jimmy continued on his way slowly and thoughtfully.

"Blimey!" he said, twisting his small countenance into an imitation of the red-haired boy's contemptuous leer.

"Hello!"

It was a little girl this time, sitting on a stile by the roadside.

Jimmy stopped.

"Hello," he said.

She was an attractive little girl with blue eyes, amber-coloured curls and a vague look of Sally. Jimmy felt an overmastering desire to impress her.

"D'you want to know what I've been d-doin' this morning?" he said.

"No," said the little girl indifferently.

Her indifference increased his desire to impress her. But his own exploits seemed now tame and colourless. He came to a sudden decision. He would adopt those of the red-haired boy. Swaggering, legs planted firmly apart, hands in pockets, he began his recital.

"I found a caravan in a field an' while the chap it belonged to was away I went in an' m-mucked up his grub – put his currants in his salt an' so on – then I stuffed his shoes up the ch-chimney an' threw all his tins of f-food into the ditch. An' he'd left his key in the door so I hid it in his jar of s-sugar, an' it'll take him a m-month of Sundays to find it."

The little girl's reception of his story was flattering. Her eyes and mouth opened slowly during the recital till they reached their fullest extent . . . Then:

"Daddy!" she called.

A man whom Jimmy had not noticed rose from the other side of the hedge, where he had been sitting on a camp-stool with a sketching block on his knees.

"Yes?" he said.

"This is the boy," said the little girl, pointing at Jimmy. "The boy that did all those things to our caravan. He's just told me he did. He says he put the currants in the salt and your shoes up the chimney and the tins of food in the ditch and the key in the sugar jar. He *told* me."

"Oh," said the man. There was a gleam in his eye and a twist to his lips that made Jimmy's blood run cold. He came over the stile and laid his hand on Jimmy's collar. "So *you're* the little wretch who made hay in my caravan, are you?"

"N-no," said Jimmy. "I d-didn't really. I was only p-pretending I did. I was m-m-making it up."

"A curious thing," said the man, "that your flight of fancy should coincide so exactly with fact."

"He says that the tins are in the ditch," said the little girl, "and your shoes are up the chimney."

"Let's go and investigate," said the man, tightening his hold on Jimmy's collar and propelling him along the road. "No!" resisting an attempt from Jimmy to wriggle out of his grasp. "I'm going to have the greatest pleasure in dealing with you, you young villain!"

"But p-please," said Jimmy, "I d-didn't do it. The b-boy that did it told me about it. Th-that's how I know."

"That," said the man, "is an even more feeble explanation than your first one."

They had reached the field where the caravan was, and the little girl explored the ditch, while the man kept his hand relentlessly on Jimmy's collar.

"Yes, they *are* here, Daddy," she called. "All of them."

"Now go and see if my shoes are up the chimney and if the key's in the sugar jar."

The little girl went into the caravan.

"Yes, they are," she called a moment later.

"Well, that's pretty conclusive," said the man.

"But l-l-listen—" began Jimmy.

"Be quiet," said the man, giving him a shake. "Now you're going to put every single thing you've moved back into its right place again. Fetch those tins out of the ditch."

Jimmy fetched them.

"Now come into the caravan," said the man, pushing Jimmy up the wooden steps, "and take my shoes out of the chimney."

Jimmy took them.

"And now you can start on the currants," said the man. He took a bowl from a shelf and, pouring into it the mixture of salt and currants from a stone jar, set it down on the wooden table.

"You can pick out all those currants, wash them and put them back into the currant jar," he said, "and I'll be just outside the door, so it's no use trying to escape."

"All r-right," said Jimmy, resigning himself to the inevitable.

The man set up his camp-stool in the field near the door of the caravan, took out his sketching block and began to sketch a distant view of the village church.

Jimmy sat down at the table and began to sort out the currants. The little girl stood by, watching him. There was a look of sorrowful reproach on her face.

"Why did you do it?" she said.

"I d-didn't," said Jimmy.

"Don't keep saying that," said the little girl. "It only makes it worse. Why don't you try to be good?"

"I d-do sometimes," said Jimmy.

"I'll help you sort out the currants if you like," said the little girl, sitting down with him at the table and setting to work. "You'll prob'ly have to go to prison, you know."

"For how l-long?" said Jimmy.

"For years and years prob'ly. You're so bad that it'll take years and *years* to make you good." She looked at him with interest. "I've never met a really bad boy before."

"I'm not *r-really* bad," said Jimmy.

"Yes, you are," said the little girl firmly. "You're so bad that it'll be terribly hard to make you good, but you *will* try, won't you?"

"Yes," said Jimmy, who had now resigned himself philosophically to whatever course events might take.

"You'll try for *my* sake, won't you?" said the little girl.

"Yes," said Jimmy, putting a currant into his mouth, then quickly taking it out again. "They d-do taste of salt."

"That's your fault, isn't it?" said the little girl.

"N-no," said Jimmy.

They worked for some moments in silence, then Jimmy said:

"This is like the sort of thing p-people had to do in fairy tales, isn't it? And in the end they w-won princesses."

"Yes," said the little girl, "but they were good people."

Jimmy glanced at her.

"You're l-like a princess," he said, then, after a pause, "I s-say."

"Yes?"

"Will you c-come fishin' with me when we've d-done this? There are l-lots of tiddlers in the brook. I caught about fifty yesterday. It may've been m-more. It may've been sixty. I tried to count them but they k-kept movin' about. They nearly f-filled the jar, anyway. Will you c-come?"

The little girl shook her head.

"I'd like to but I couldn't. Not with anyone as bad as you. Besides, you'll be in prison."

"Oh, yes, I f-forgot that," said Jimmy, "but will you come fishin' with me when I c-come out of prison?"

"Perhaps," said the little girl, "but only if you'll try very hard to be good. You will, won't you? For *my* sake . . . You do like me, don't you?"

"Yes, I d-do," said Jimmy. "I like you very much. D-do you like me?"

The little girl sighed.

"I would if you weren't so bad," she said. "I'm going to try very hard to make you good."

"An' will you c-come fishin' with me then?" said Jimmy.

"Yes . . . perhaps," said the little girl.

They heard the sound of voices and, looking through the open door of the caravan, saw a man in gaiters – a farmer whom Jimmy knew – talking to the artist.

"He was a boy with red hair and a striped jersey," the farmer was saying. "I saw him muckin' about in your caravan and when I shouted at him, he ran off. He's drove my cows out of Top Meadow into the corn and thrown a stone through the post office window since then, the little varmint! Came from that London Children's Camp down in the valley, and they're a-packing of him off by the three-thirty this afternoon."

"But" – the artist turned to point at Jimmy – "I thought it was that boy."

The farmer laughed.

"Jimmy Manning?" he said. "No, Jimmy wouldn't do a thing like that . . . Well, I'll be gettin'."

The farmer took his departure and the artist returned to the caravan.

"I apologise, Jimmy," he said, holding out his hand. "I apologise most sincerely. And you can stop picking out those darn' currants."

"Th-thank you," said Jimmy.

He looked at the little girl and his spirits rose.

He was now cleared of all suspicion of crime and could claim the friendship from which his criminal record had debarred him.

"You can l-like me now," he said eagerly. "Will you come f-fishin' with me this afternoon?"

"Certainly not," said the little girl with a toss of her amber curls.

There was no mistaking the angry contempt in her voice.

"But you said you'd l-like to," said Jimmy.

"That was when I thought you were bad," said the little girl. "I didn't know then" – she elevated her small nose in disdain – "that you were just an ordin'ry good boy."

Chapter 27

The Stowaways

"Young people today have no initiative," said Mr Phillimore in his deep booming voice. "Can't stir a finger to help themselves. Just sit back and wait to have everything done for them."

"Well, you certainly didn't do that," smiled Mr Manning.

"I did *not*," said Mr Phillimore. "I wanted adventure, so I went out and got it."

Mr Phillimore was a tall, broad, thick-set man, with a weather-beaten face, piercing blue eyes, bushy eyebrows and a shaggy beard. He had been at school with Mr Manning and, happening to find himself in the neighbourhood, had dropped in on his old friend, and the two had settled down to a long spell of "reminiscing".

Jimmy was sitting on the hearthrug, absorbed by their conversation, keeping as quiet as he could, lest his father should remember his presence and send him away.

"Yes, your life's been one long adventure story," said Mr Manning. "You were only a schoolboy when you started it, weren't you?"

"Yes," said Mr Phillimore. "I ran away from school and went to South Africa as a stowaway and after that – gold-digger, cowboy, bushranger, stoker, engine-driver, store-keeper, even waiter and road-sweeper. There's hardly a country I haven't been in or a thing I haven't tried my hand at."

"Splendid!" said Mr Manning.

"I've made half a dozen fortunes and lost them all. I've got nothing to show for the whole thing but a parrot I brought back from Africa. Still – it's been worth it."

At this point Mr Manning suddenly noticed Jimmy, sitting there and listening, his eyes opened to their fullest extent.

"Run out and play, Jim," he said.

Jimmy went slowly across the road to Bobby's. Bobby was engaged in making a new cage for his piebald rat out of an old cardboard box.

"Look!" he said. "I'm cutting bits away to make bars. Some of the bits are bigger than I meant them to be, but I don't think he'll catch cold, do you?"

"Never mind about that now," said Jimmy. "We've g-got more important things to do than that."

"What have we got to do?" said Bobby.

"Listen," said Jimmy. "There's a man at home talkin' to my father an' he s-says we've got no – no—" He searched for the word and ended doubtfully, "initials."

"Well, that's a story," said Bobby indignantly. "We have. Mine's B.P. and yours is J.M."

"He didn't m-mean it that way," said Jimmy. "He meant runnin' away to sea an' bein' stowaways an' bushrangers an' that sort of thing. He ran away to sea when he was a s-schoolboy an' went to South Africa as a stowaway, an' we've got to do it, too, to show that we've got that thing he said."

"But we tried runnin' away to sea when we didn't want to go to Araminta's party," said Bobby, "an' we never got there."

"I know, but there was a f-fog," said Jimmy. "I bet we'd've got there if there hadn't been a f-fog."

"P'raps," said Bobby dubiously. "When do you want to start?"

"N-now," said Jimmy.

"Now?" echoed Bobby. "But it's nearly bedtime."

"That doesn't matter," said Jimmy. "I don't s'pose *he* bothered about bedtime. Stowaways d-don't . . . Oh, come on. We'll n-never get there if you waste all the time arguin'."

Still looking rather doubtful, Bobby put away his cardboard box and set off with his friend down the road.

"We'll go through the wood," said Jimmy. "I 'spect that's a sh-short cut to the sea. It's a short cut to m-mos' places."

"I think we'll get into a row," said Bobby morosely, as they climbed over the stile that led into the woods.

"No, we won't," said Jimmy, "'cause, when this m-man said he'd run away to sea an' been a stowaway, my father s-said 'Splendid!', so it mus' be all r-right. If you don't want to come, you can g-go back, an' I'll be a s-stowaway an' have – have initials by myself."

"No, I'll come, too," said Bobby resignedly. "It'd be a bit lonely at home without you."

"This man brought a parrot back from South Africa," said Jimmy.

"I don't think much of parrots," said Bobby. "Miss Pettigrew's got one an' all it can say is 'miaow'. You might as well have a cat an' be done with it."

"We might bring a m-monkey home," said Jimmy, "or—" excitedly: "*Tell* you what!"

"Yes?"

"What about a snake? A s-snake would be an int'restin' thing to have."

"Yes, it would," said Bobby, his spirits rising.

"A c-cobra," said Jimmy. "They're the m-mos' excitin' kind."

"They've got poisonous teeth," said Bobby.

"Well, we could have them t-taken out," said Jimmy. "We could g-give it gas an' then it wouldn't hurt. I 'spect our dentist wouldn't mind d-doin' it for us. He's a very k-kind man . . . It'll be fun, havin' a t-tame snake, won't it?"

"Could we teach it tricks, d'you think?" said Bobby.

"Dunno . . . Anyway, we could take it for walks on a lead."

"They walk jolly slowly, snakes," said Bobby.

"I s'pect we could t-teach it to run," said Jimmy.

They plodded on for some minutes in silence.

"I'm beginnin' to get tired," said Bobby. "Is it much further to the sea?"

"D-dunno," said Jimmy.

"I'm gettin' hungry, too," said Bobby. "I wish I'd had that other piece of bread an' jam at tea. I've got a feelin' I'm goin' to start bein' homesick soon, too."

"I 'spect they all felt a bit homesick at first," said Jimmy, "but they mus' have got over it or they wouldn't have g-gone on . . . Anyway, here's the road."

They emerged from the wood on to the main road and stood looking about them.

"Where are we?" said Bobby.

"Dunno," said Jimmy.

"Which way do we go?"

"D-dunno," said Jimmy, looking up and down the road.

Suddenly he noticed a car standing near a crossroads a

few yards away. He approached it. Except for a pile of rugs on the back seat, it was empty.

"*Tell* you what!" he said. "I don't see why we shouldn't g-get into it an' start bein' stowaways straight away."

"It might not be goin' to the sea," said Bobby.

Jimmy walked round to the back of the car and gave a gasp of excitement.

"Yes, it *is* going to the sea," he said. "Come an' l-look."

Bobby joined him, and the two stood gazing at the luggage grid. Strapped on to it was a trunk with the letters S.E.A.

"It is goin' to the s-sea."

"It mightn't be," said Bobby. "People don't have 'Sea' put on their boxes when they're goin' there."

"Yes, they d-do," said Jimmy. "My aunt was goin' to sea once an' I remember she had to p-put a special label on the boxes she wanted while she was at sea, so this mus' be the box they want while they're at sea, so they mus' be goin' to sea. Come on. Let's get in an' s-start bein' stowaways. We'll hide under the rugs . . . I bet someone'll be comin' s-soon to drive it to the sea."

They got into the car. Jimmy curled up on the back seat and Bobby on the floor and they drew the rugs over them.

"Where'll we keep the cobra?" whispered Bobby.

"We could k-keep it in the greenhouse," said Jimmy. "I don't think it'd d-do much damage there."

"What do they eat?"

"D-dunno," said Jimmy. "We'll have to f-find out. I 'spect it could share Sandy's d-dog biscuits. I 'spect Sandy'll like it. They can play together. He gets a bit t-tired of Henry."

"How'll we share it? Shall we have a day each or a week each?"

"A d-day, I think. I 'spect if we get fond of it, a week'd seem a l-long time to be without it . . . Sh! Someone's comin'."

There was the sound of quick footsteps on the road, then a man opened the car door and got into the driving seat. He threw a careless glance over his shoulder. Bobby was invisible, and all that could be seen of Jimmy was a tuft of fair hair emerging from the rug.

"Sorry to have kept you waiting, darling," said the man as he started the engine and slipped the lever into gear.

It was a long drive. Dusk fell as the car sped along through towns, villages, along high roads and country lanes. Bobby slept soundly, and Jimmy only occasionally awoke to see lights, houses, trees speeding past. Once the man turned and said: "You all right, darling?" and Jimmy, between waking and sleeping, gave a drowsy grunt.

Then the car drew up at a house. The man got out, stretched himself, opened the door of the car and drew back the rug. Jimmy and Bobby sat up, yawned and rubbed their eyes. The man turned pale and staggered backwards.

"Good heavens!" he said. "Who are you?"

"We're s-stowaways," said Jimmy.

"You're – what?"

"S-s-stowaways," repeated Jimmy.

The man clutched his head.

"But where's my wife?" he said.

"I d-don't know," said Jimmy. "There wasn't any w-wife in it when we got in."

At this point a policeman came up.

"Are you Mr Anderson?" he asked.

"Yes," said the man.

"GOOD HEAVENS!" SAID THE DRIVER. "WHO ARE YOU?"

"Sydney Ernest Anderson?"

"Yes," said the man.

"Well, we've just had a telephone message about your wife. When you stopped to make your telephone call she saw a pillar-box down a lane and got out to post a letter and when she came back you'd gone."

"Good Lord!" groaned Sydney Ernest Anderson. "What a ghastly thing to happen! I thought – I took for granted – But where *is* she?"

"One of our cars was coming along in this direction, anyway, so they're bringing her along. She should be here any minute."

"She'll be livid," said Mr Anderson. "She'll never forgive me. You see, we'd spent the weekend house-hunting – without any result at all, of course – and she was tired out, so she lay down on the back seat and covered herself with a rug and tried to get a little sleep and I thought she was still there. I didn't know she'd moved. When I saw these children, you could have knocked me down with a feather."

"Who are these children?" said the policeman.

"Search me!" said Mr Anderson.

Jimmy began to explain, but before he'd finished, a car drove up and a woman got out. She was small and slender, with blue eyes and short fair hair.

"Darling, I'm so sorry," said the man abjectly. "I shall never forgive myself. Never. What did you do when you found I'd gone?"

The woman laughed.

"I just went into the nearest house to ask if I could use their telephone. I thought I'd ring up the police and get them to try and stop you, and – oh, Sydney, it's our house. It's just what we've been looking for all these months. And they'd just decided to sell it, but hadn't done anything about it yet, and I've practically fixed everything up. We're going back there first thing tomorrow morning to do the doings about it. But, darling, *what* happened?"

"I don't know," said the man. "I only know that we seem to have picked up a couple of stowaways."

"Who *are* you?" said the woman to Jimmy and Bobby.

They tried to explain. It was a confused story of initials and cobras and bushranging and Mr Phillimore, but the woman seemed to understand.

"I think you'd better wait till you're older before you start," she said. "But I can't tell you how grateful I am to you. You've found me the house I've been wanting all my life. And now – how are we to get you home?"

"We'll see about that," said the policeman. "I expect their parents are crazy with anxiety by now."

Jimmy and Bobby were driving home through the dark. On the seat between them was a box of chocolates that the woman had given them just as they were starting.

"We'll get in an awful row," said Bobby.

"We m-might not," said Jimmy philosophically. "It's too late for them to do m-much tonight an' they gen'rally forget more or less by the m-morning."

"We never thought we'd be comin' home without that cobra," said Bobby regretfully.

"Well, we've got the chocolates," said Jimmy.

"Chocolates aren't the same as a cobra."

Jimmy bit through the smooth brown surface into a centre of luscious melting cream.

"No," he said indistinctly, "but they're n-nex' best."

Chapter 28

The Rain Tub

Jimmy stepped carefully from the middle of one paving stone to the middle of the next, touching the railings with his hand as he did so. If ever he stepped on the edge of a paving stone by mistake or missed one of the railings, he had to go back to the point where the railings started and do it all over again. At the end of the pavement came a low wall, and Jimmy climbed on to this and walked along it, stepping carefully on every third brick. The wall ended in a hedge growing closely against a fence, and Jimmy scrambled along, forcing a passage between fence and hedge. He had lately added to his programme a rain tub that stood by the road outside a cottage. It consisted of twenty wooden slats joined by two iron bands, and Jimmy walked slowly round it, touching each slat with the middle finger of his right hand.

He couldn't have told why it was necessary that he should do these things on his way to school. He only knew that it was. They formed his fetish and the savage that lives in every small boy paid homage to it blindly.

Roger and his friends watched these proceedings from the height of their eleven years with puzzled disapproval.

"Why does he *do* it?" said Bill irritably.

"Well, it's his thing," said Roger with a note of apology in his voice. "He's only a kid, you know."

This would have gone on happily and indefinitely, had not Archie Mould and Georgie Tallow suddenly noticed these proceedings and realised that they afforded an excellent opportunity of scoring off both Roger and Jimmy. For Roger, as Jimmy's elder brother, would be involved in any humiliation suffered by Jimmy . . . so they proceeded to inflict as much humiliation on Jimmy as they could. He found black paint daubed on his railings, wet cement laid on his wall, ingenious obstacles placed between hedge and fence. Doggedly, determinedly, in spite of all this, Jimmy continued to perform his ritual. The only concession he made to the situation was to perform it on his way home from school instead of on his way to school, as each day the obstacles became more difficult to circumvent, and his tardy and dishevelled appearance at school was leading to trouble that increased the jubilation of his foes.

"You know, I'd give it up, if I were you, Jimmy," said Roger one evening. "It isn't really worth it."

Jimmy considered the suggestion in silence.

"All right," he said at last, "but I mus' d-do it till the end of the month. It's only three more days."

For it was clear to Jimmy (if to no one else) that honour and his fetish would be satisfied if he did it till the end of the month.

Somehow or other the news leaked out, and Archie and Georgie intensified their efforts. It had become as vital to them that Jimmy's ritual should be stopped before the end of the next three days as it was to Jimmy that it should continue. Blackened, scratched and torn, he emerged triumphant from the first and second days' ordeal. Archie and Georgie began to look anxious and depressed. But on the third morning they appeared in school with sly, gloating smiles on their faces . . . and then Jimmy knew that Archie had a Plan and that the crucial test would come after school that afternoon.

Archie's plan was a cunning one. He had realised that nothing would stop Jimmy carrying out his ritual as long as the objects connected with it were there, and he had devised a scheme for breaking the magic chain by getting rid of the rain tub.

At Melford, five miles away, lived an aunt of his who had stayed with his mother last month and idly voiced a desire for a green-painted tub in which to grow geraniums. It was her birthday next week, and it occurred to Archie that to secure the rain tub and give it to her for a birthday present would serve the double purpose of out-manoevring Jimmy and winning his way back into his aunt's good graces. For relations between him and his aunt were just a little strained. During her visit, Archie had discovered her horror of mice and had played a series of tricks on her that had caused him and his friends great amusement – putting mice in her wardrobe, her hat-box, even her handkerchief drawer. She had in fact departed in a state of tense indignation after discovering the mouse in her handkerchief drawer.

Having formed the plan, Archie began to carry it out. He approached the owner of the rain tub – a thin, drooping man with a thin, drooping moustache, who gave away his position at the beginning of the interview by admitting that the rain tub was leaking through the wall of his cottage and that he'd be glad to be rid of it – and after a certain amount of bargaining arranged to buy it for four-and-six. Then, a crafty smile on his fox-like face, he went to interview the village carrier.

Jimmy set off from school on the afternoon of the third

day, wondering a little apprehensively what was in store for him, but determined to carry out his ritual to the last detail at all costs. He guessed that Archie and Georgie would make this afternoon the occasion of a great offensive and he trod cautiously, spying out the land at each step. Everything went with miraculous smoothness, however, till he came to the rain tub. There he had his first shock. For in front of the cottage stood the carrier's van, into which the rain tub was being lifted by the driver and his mate. Archie had meant the tub to be fetched earlier in the day, so that when Jimmy came along there should be no trace of it; but the carrier had been delayed and the tub was just vanishing through the door of the van as Jimmy turned the bend in the road.

The driver took his seat at the front of the van and started the engine. Jimmy ran up and, on the spur of the moment, without any clear idea of what he was going to do, opened the door and slipped into the van after his rain tub. There he crouched at the back, behind an antiquated gas stove, and took stock of his surroundings.

They were not reassuring. The rain tub had been put in front near the driver and between it and Jimmy was the driver's mate – a large man in overalls – comfortably ensconced in an armchair. Jimmy hoped that the man would go to sleep and so allow him to approach his rain tub and place his middle finger on each slat, in accordance with his ritual, after which he could have slipped off homeward at the first opportunity, but he proved to be both wakeful and chatty. He gave the driver a lengthy and pungent summary of the political situation, then discovered a mouse in the straw packing of a crate of china and proceeded to chase it all over the van, coming perilously near Jimmy's hiding-place several times.

At last the van drew up outside Archie's aunt's house. Archie and his aunt – a vague nervous untidy little woman – stood on the veranda. Archie had come over early to tell her about the present and was already well on his way back into her good graces.

"A very kind thought, dear boy," she said.

The man carried the rain tub up the path and put it on the veranda between them.

Quick as thought Jimmy slipped out of the van and crouched in the hedge by the gate, cautiously surveying the prospect.

"You see, Auntie dear," said Archie, "I'm going to cut it down and re-paint it for you and then plant it with geraniums."

Archie's aunt looked from the tub to Archie, from Archie to the tub, touched and pleased, thinking that Archie couldn't be such a bad boy, after all, to have planned this pleasant little surprise for her.

"Thank you, dear," she said. "Perhaps the man will take it round to the shed . . ."

But the man, after setting down the tub, had returned to the van and was already driving off.

"I'll call the gardener," said Archie's aunt. "He can take it to the shed and we'll keep it there till we can see about painting it and cutting it down."

At that Jimmy decided that he must act now or never. Once in the shed, the tub would be out of his reach, and he was resolved, come what may, to carry out his ritual to the last detail on this last occasion.

He stood up from the shadow of the hedge, opened the gate and walked up the garden path. Archie and his aunt stared at him in amazement. Without even looking at them, his face set in lines of firm determination, Jimmy

WITHOUT EVEN LOOKING AT THEM, HIS SMALL FACE SET AND
TENSE, JIMMY BEGAN TO PERFORM HIS ACCUSTOMED RITUAL.

approached the rain tub and began to walk round it,
touching the slats one by one with the middle finger of
his right hand. One, two, three . . . Suddenly a movement
inside the tub attracted his attention. He leant over it and
peeped inside, then put in his hand and drew out – the
mouse that had been chased unavailingly all over the
carrier's van.

Archie's aunt screamed, and turned on Archie.

"So this is another of your tricks!" she said. "I might
have known there was something like this behind it, you
cruel mischievous boy! . . . And who is this kind child?
One of your schoolfellows, I suppose, who heard of your
shameful joke and came to my assistance. Birthday

present indeed! Well, you'll get no birthday present from me this year. Or Christmas present either!"

Archie gaped and spluttered, so taken aback that he could think of nothing to say.

Jimmy took the mouse to the gate and put it down by the roadside; then returned to the rain tub and continued touching the slats with frowning concentration, ignoring the presence of the other two.

"But listen, Auntie," pleaded Archie. "I didn't know it was there. I—"

"Go away at once, you wretched child!" said his aunt, and Archie, who knew when he was beaten and never wasted time attempting the impossible, went away, muttering sulkily.

She turned to Jimmy.

"And what would you like me to give you, little boy," she said, "as a reward for coming to my rescue so kindly?"

Jimmy placed his finger in the centre of his twentieth slat, then, the all-important task completed, stood upright and gave her his attention.

"P-please," he said, "c-can I have my bus fare home?"

"Well, there you are," said Mr Manning helplessly to his wife later in the evening. "He stays out so long that you're nearly demented with anxiety, and when he finally comes home all he has to say is that he's been over to Melford in a lorry to touch a rain tub. We couldn't have heard wrong. He said it twice. He said he'd been over to Melford in a lorry to touch a rain tub. Can you beat it?"

"No," said Mrs Manning.

"I thought you said you understood children."

"I'll never say it again," said Mrs Manning.

Chapter 29

Toys for Sale

"I've got a French exercise *an'* a Latin exercise tonight," said Roger. "Gosh! Somethin' ought to be *done* about this homework!"

He was seated at the table, surrounded by his books, wearing an air of mingled exasperation and self-importance.

"Well, do it, dear, instead of talking about it," said Mrs Manning mildly.

Mrs Manning was in the armchair, surrounded by her household mending, busy on one of Jimmy's "specials", for the heels of Jimmy's socks seemed not just to come into holes, like other people's, but to vanish altogether.

"I've done my homework," said Jimmy, who was sitting on the hearthrug, reading *Uncle Remus*, with Sandy curled up beside him.

"Your homework!" said Roger with a short contemptuous laugh, as he chewed the end of his pen and glowered at the open page of his French exercise book. "C-A-T, cat. B-A-T, bat. One and one are two."

"Now, Roger, stop teasing Jimmy and get on with your own homework," said Mrs Manning, drawing a double strand of wool across the gaping chasm of Jimmy's heel. Then she glanced out of the window. "Oh, dear! Here's Miss Pettigrew."

Roger and Jimmy groaned and Sandy gave a sleepy growl.

Miss Pettigrew entered like a breath of cold, crisp air.

Sandy got up, smelt her shoes, obviously resisted a temptation to untie her shoelaces, and sat down again.

"Now I don't want to disturb you," said Miss Pettigrew, taking her seat on an upright chair and somehow managing to look as if she were already on her way somewhere else, "because I see that you're all busy, but I've come about toys."

"Toys?" said Mrs Manning.

"Yes. I'm getting up a little Sale of Work in aid of the fund for new hassocks for the Church, and I thought I'd have a stall of second-hand toys. They always sell well. So I'm calling on all the children I know and rounding up toys."

"Roger and Jimmy stopped playing with toys long ago," said Mrs Manning.

Roger gave his short sardonic laugh.

"I should think so!" he said.

"Yes, I should th-think so," said Jimmy with a not very successful imitation of the short sardonic laugh.

"Then you'll have some to give away, won't you?" said Miss Pettigrew.

"We've given them away ages ago," said Roger. "To hospitals and things."

"Surely you have one or two left," persisted Miss Pettigrew. "Haven't they, Mrs Manning?"

"Well," said Mrs Manning, considering, "I believe there's an old toy soldier left at the bottom of that cupboard where you keep your aeroplane kits, Roger. I was clearing it out the other day and I noticed it."

"A toy soldier?" said Roger.

His face wore a pained expression as if the very mention of the words were an affront to his dignity.

"Yes," said Mrs Manning. "That battered old creature you used to call General Mulligan. He's only got one arm and one leg left."

"Oh, that!" said Roger scornfully. "Yes, I do sort of remember."

"It's far too dilapidated for a Sale of Work, anyway," said Mrs Manning.

"Not at all," said Miss Pettigrew. "Nothing is too dilapidated. I'm going to sell the small and damaged articles in twopenny bundles, and I'm sure that some children will find pleasure in them. So if Roger doesn't want it any longer—"

"Me?" said Roger as if he hadn't heard aright. "*Me* want a toy soldier?"

"Of course not, dear," said Miss Pettigrew soothingly. "Well, he shall go to help with the hassocks. And what about Jimmy? Has he got any toys?"

"M-me?" said Jimmy.

"Yes, Jimmy," said Mrs Manning. "There's that old toy owl of yours."

"T-toy owl?" said Jimmy, imitating the pained expression with which Roger had tried to take his mind back to the days of toy soldiers.

"Yes, dear," smiled Mrs Manning. "You'd hardly recognise it as an owl now, but it was once an owl. Don't you remember? You used to call it Owly."

"Oh, that!" said Jimmy. "Yes, I do s-sort of remember."

"It's still knocking about somewhere," said Mrs Manning. "I believe I saw it in the bottom drawer of your chest of drawers."

"Splendid!" said Miss Pettigrew. "No matter how old

and battered a toy is, it will always find a purchaser."

"Well, run up and get them, then, children," said Mrs Manning.

Miss Pettigrew raised her hand.

"No, no," she said. "I want each child to bring his or her little offering on Saturday afternoon, and at the same time look round to see if there's anything they would like to buy in its place. And now" – she rose briskly to her feet – "I must fly. I'm going next door to see if Sally has any toys that she can let me have. I don't suppose that she plays with toys now. She's nine, you know."

As soon as Miss Pettigrew had gone, Jimmy went slowly upstairs to his bedroom and took Owly from the bottom of his chest of drawers. Owly was one of the skeletons in Jimmy's cupboard. No one knew that Owly still played almost as important a part in Jimmy's life as he had done when Jimmy first found him in his Christmas stocking four years ago. He was about four inches high, made of brown cloth, now rubbed and threadbare and shapeless. Only the two boot buttons that formed his eyes showed where his face had been. But to Jimmy, Owly was still a friend and companion – a fount of wisdom and kindliness and comfort. On the nights when he was unhappy or afraid he still took Owly to bed with him. On the days when anything important was going to happen he still carried Owly in his pocket. When he couldn't make up his mind about anything, he would bring Owly out of his drawer and ask his advice . . . and the twinkling boot-button eyes always seemed to tell him what to do. And now – he had taken his stand by Roger in the adult world of manliness in which Roger lived and he could not look back.

He tried to stiffen his resolution, but there was a

strange lost feeling at his heart as he replaced Owly in the bottom drawer of his chest of drawers, and the two boot-button eyes seemed to gaze at him sadly, reproachfully, as they vanished under the pile of pyjamas and shirts. Still, it was not in Jimmy's nature to remain depressed for long. Saturday was five whole days off. Anything might happen in five days . . .

But, slowly, relentlessly, Saturday afternoon arrived. Immediately after lunch Jimmy went upstairs and put Owly into his pocket, trying not to see the reproachful look in the two boot-button eyes, trying to face the bleak Owlyless existence that stretched ahead of him. Shame seemed to confront him whichever way he looked. On the one hand was the shame of betraying Owly and all that Owly had meant to him. On the other hand was the shame of falling short of Roger's high standard of manliness.

Slowly, very slowly, he went downstairs, his hand clasped affectionately round Owly in his pocket.

Mrs Manning was in the hall.

"Hurry up, dear," she said. "Roger started some time ago."

"All r-right," said Jimmy gruffly and went slowly, draggingly, down to the gate.

As he opened it, the gate of the next house opened, and Sally came out. She carried a toy rabbit, made of a material that had once been pink plush. It was no longer pink and no longer plush. It was as threadbare and shapeless as Owly. Even its eyes had disappeared.

"Hello," said Jimmy.

"Hello," said Sally.

There was an unusual note of friendliness in her voice.

"I'm taking this old toy rabbit to Miss Pettigrew's stall at the Village Hall," she went on.

Jimmy took Owly from his pocket.

"I'm takin' this old t-toy owl, too," he said.

"I don't play with baby toys any longer," said Sally.

"N-neither do I," said Jimmy.

They walked on in silence for some minutes, then Sally said: "His name's Pinky."

"Mine's c-called Owly," said Jimmy.

"I've had him since I was three," said Sally.

"I've had m-mine a long time, too," said Jimmy.

They had reached the stile that led across the fields to the Village Hall. By tacit consent they stopped.

"We don't want to get there too soon, do we?" said Sally forlornly.

"N-no," agreed Jimmy.

"He used to have pink eyes till they came off," said Sally.

"Owly's still got eyes," said Jimmy, "but they aren't the ones he had at first. They've been s-sewed on since."

Sally held the battered rabbit by the side of the shape-less Owly.

"He's not much bigger than Owly, is he?"

"N-no," said Jimmy and added with a sigh, "I hope someone'll buy them who'll be k-kind to them."

Suddenly Sally sat down on the lowest rung of the stile and began to cry.

"I don't want to sell him," she sobbed. "I love him terribly. He sleeps with me every night. Mummy under-stood about him, but she's away and – and – and I didn't want Roger to think I was a baby."

"Don't cry," pleaded Jimmy miserably. "Don't – oh, gosh! Here's Roger."

The sound of Roger's whistling cut through the air, and the form of Roger was seen, striding over the field on his way back from the Village Hall, with Sandy leaping around him.

Sally got up from the stile and turned aside, wiping away her tears with the back of her hand.

"Hello, you two," said Roger cheerfully and jumped lightly from the top of the stile.

As he did so, something fell from his pocket on to the grass. He bent to pick it up, his face crimson with embarrassment. But Jimmy and Sally had seen what it was. It was General Mulligan, one-legged, one-armed, almost bare of paint.

"Didn't you t-take it to the Sale?" said Jimmy, mystified.

"Oh, yes," said Roger, trying to carry off his confusion by an airy laugh, "but I bought him back. They put him in a twopenny bundle with some other things, so I bought it and left the other things there. You see—" He stopped for a moment, searching for a convincing explanation of his action. "You see, he's so messed about that it didn't seem fair to let anyone else buy him. There's practically nothing of him left. It isn't – it isn't really honest to let people spend money on something that's of no value even in a Sale of Work."

He sounded detached and judicial and a little cynical, but his moment of confusion had given him away. He loved General Mulligan – battered, legless, armless as he was. He couldn't bear to hand him over to someone who might laugh at him or ill-treat him, someone who hadn't known him in the pride of his youth, when, complete with all his limbs, waving his sword, gleaming with paint, he had led his army to victory across the nursery carpet, up the Alpine range of the armchair, through the rigours of the snow-covered rockery in the garden.

"Besides," he added, with a self-conscious laugh, "I'm – I'm quite fond of the old chap in a way."

Sally's tear-filled eyes brightened. She held out Pinky for Roger's inspection.

"Do you think it's honest to sell Pinky, Roger?" she said. "He's in an awful mess, too, and he hasn't any eyes."

"Well, no," said Roger, still preserving his judicial air. "No, I don't."

"Oh, Roger!" said Sally, her voice tremulous with relief.

"And Owly, Roger?" said Jimmy, holding out the shapeless object. "He doesn't *look* like an owl any l-longer. And he's been m-mended over and over again."

"Well, no," said Roger. "I don't really think it would be quite honest to sell him."

Jimmy heaved a long deep sigh and slipped Owly back into his pocket.

"Well, let's go home now," said Sally, hugging Pinky tightly to her breast.

They turned to retrace their steps along the road. For the time being the difference in their ages that ordinarily made them seem to belong to separate races was merged in a sense of comradeship. They were united by a bond of human weakness, human loyalty, human emotion.

Suddenly Roger put his hand in his pocket and brought out sixpence.

"Look!" he said. "I've got this left. Let's go to Mr Mince's an' get an ice-cream an' have licks in turn. All right, old chap!" as Sandy showed the wild excitement that the words "ice-cream" always roused in him. "You'll have your licks in your turn with the rest."

And then, whooping for joy, lighthearted with relief, clutching their toys tightly in their hands, the three raced down to Mr Mince's shop.

Richmal Crompton
Just Jimmy

"I'm not a kid," Jimmy said stoutly. "I'm seven and three-quarters and four d-days and a n-night."

Meet Jimmy Manning – a boy in a hurry to grow up, especially if it means he can join his brother Roger's gang, the Three Musketeers.

Whether he's waging war on arch-enemies the Mouldies, plotting to catch criminals with his best friend Bobby Peaslake, or fighting off the attentions of the dreaded Araminta, Jimmy's plans are always ingenious, hilarious – and destined for disaster!

First published in 1949 and lost for decades, *Just Jimmy* is a rediscovered classic from the creator of *Just William*.

The William Stories

Richmal Crompton
Just – William

There is only one William . . . His name is a byword for
irrepressible boyhood. His pranks are the scrapes of
every healthy youngster, recorded with keen observation
and an even keener sense of humour. He is – just
William!

'Probably the funniest, toughest children's books ever
written.' *Sunday Times*

Richmal Crompton

William – The Conqueror

"William," a voice said severely. "What on earth *have you been doing?"*

   William's eyes opened innocently.

   "Me?" he said, surprised and indignant. "Do you mean me?"

This time, it isn't William's fault. Not *really*. It was Ginger who showed him the book about Robin Hood. And it was Violet Elizabeth Bott's idea to steal from the rich to give to the poor.

William's latest plan to right the world's wrongs can only lead to chaos. Especially as Mr Bott, of Bott's Digestive Sauce, is very rich indeed . . .

A selected list of titles available from Macmillan

The prices shown below are correct at the time of going to press. However, Macmillan Publishers reserve the right to show new retail prices on covers which may differ from those previously advertised.

All Macmillan titles can be ordered at your local bookshop or are available by post from:

Book Service by Post
PO Box 29, Douglas, Isle of Man IM99 1BQ

Credit cards accepted. For details:
Telephone: 01624 675137
Fax: 01624 670923
E-mail: bookshop@enterprise.net

Free postage and packing in the UK.
Overseas customers: add £1 per book (paperback)
and £3 per book (hardback).